Swing Low
The Hangman Of The Woods

Brent Lindstrom

Blue House
Publishing

BLUE HOUSE
PUBLISHING
an imprint of
LightMinded Arts, LLC

791 N 100 E
Lehi, UT 84043

For information regarding bulk purchases, send a request to storyteller@LightMindedArts.com

ISBN-13: 978-1-943239-20-7

Library of Congress Control Number: 2025924908

For more books by Brent Lindstrom
Visit www.LightMindedArts.com

Acknowledgements:
Thank you dear reader for taking this journey with me.
Without you, I'd only be telling myself stories. They have
a place for people like that, but they rarely give them
anything sharp, like pencils.

Author's Note:

A few years back, I experienced a particularly sleepy period of my life, a time when I received very little actual sleep. I will simply call this time "First Child."

Up until then, I was a scheduled person. I would go to sleep every night at ten, and wake up every morning at six.

My daughter was an angel, and as I have learned, angels don't sleep! My mind started confusing reality with my dreams. This made for some interesting stories that my wife still tells at family gatherings today.

This book was one such dream, remembered in stark surrealism.

The only problem was that it didn't have a proper ending. I originally published this book under the name of B.C. Crow, and the ending plagued me fore years after.

Then one day, almost 8 years later, the ending finally resolved itself, and I had to rewrite it. This is the final, corrected version of that story, put to rest where it was always meant to go.

To me, writing is a craft which I am constantly trying to improve upon with each new novel. I hope you find them entertaining and unique. In this book, I've included much of what I dreamed, but expanded it a little, also. This story takes place in Southern Asia, but not in any real country. I've made up a territory that exists somewhere between Laos and Singapore.

The timing is meant to be in the very near future, sometime between now and the end of the century. While some references to religions and countries or races are mentioned, none are meant to be criticisms. They are just part of an imaginary world that existed one night in this head of mine.

I hope you enjoy it. If you do, please remember to leave a review, where ever you bought it. This helps authors like me, more than you can ever know!

Prologue

My name is Iddo. I am short and fat. If I'd been born in America, this might not be so bad, that is to say, the fat part of me. While most Americans seem fat, some even more so than myself, they're all much taller than an average person here. I, unfortunately, am short, even when compared to the people in my own region. Even so, there are many days when I wish I'd been born to that country of plenty. But if not the United States, then even Europe might have sufficed. Alas no, I live in one of many war-torn areas that sit between China and Australia.

This southern end of Asia, still suffering from the effects of the most recent wars, was governed by no less than four powers, as far as I can see things, though it seems incredibly jumbled. China was the closest and most obvious influence, even though they didn't escape fully unscathed by the war, about which tensions remain high, though that's no surprise. They've always been a tense nation. The second most prevalent influence on the region was the local government, which is ruled by none other than the sons of our own land. Criminals now, at least of bureaucracy. I don't know what they were like before.

Blessedly, in the last year, things have been improving. Considering recent events, it's no wonder.

The last two influences, at least at the time, were minor in the actual governing of affairs, but had a significant influence on day-to-day life. After all, the Europeans and Americans seldom encourage anything but the spread of their Western culture. This is accomplished primarily by language.

Everyone I know speaks at least four languages, while the Europeans speak two, maybe three. Americans seldom speak more than one. For this reason, English has slowly become the national language, that is, if we are to call ourselves a nation. While we have bodies acting as governing officials, we are basically without law and true country. Like the Mong, who sing the meow of the stray cat sonnet, we too are seeking blindly that sense of belonging where nobody can stand together.

This is a tale, a true tale that starts with me. My intention, however, is not to tell of my experience, nor that of our ragged region. This is about a strange man, more hideous in appearance than myself. But since I cannot tell of him without including something of my own part in the matter, I hope that you will patiently humor me.

A major portion of this happened a couple of years ago. Because of this, my memory may have faded somewhat. Still, these are my true feelings and the memories are as I do and wish to remember them. With any luck my story will be retold, lasting longer than the hapless prophet of old, whose name I bear. As I write this down, I would that my book not suffer the same fate as the lost scripture of that seer of antiquity. Of course, I'd have to publish it if I hoped to have any chance of it surviving. I don't know if anybody would even read this. I write it anyway, that I may bear witness, proving my efforts with the gifts He entrusted to me. After all, as the Believers say, the records we make here on Earth will be used to help judge us in heaven.

Thanks in part to Western influence, though we're still a disorganized people, the schooling system hasn't decayed like the rest of society. In fact, it has improved. If you ask me, this is how the Caucasians hope to eventually stabilize our land. Unfortunately, even the best schemes of man find ways to go astray. The meandering path which I originally found myself on, was the very path most encouraged by my father. To save you the doldrums of my whole life history, I'll begin when I was fifteen years old.

Chapter 1

School. What a circus of emotions and self-doubt. Where did the other boys find the confidence to stand out? I've spent my whole life trying to just fit in. Peer pressure has always pushed against my self-identity. I've come to learn that in this I might not have been alone, even if I was a complete loner. Friends would've been nice, but I didn't know the first thing about finding them. For a while I tried to shut out that chapter of my life. I resurrect it now, because it serves a need. Exposing my naked shame has become less burdensome. Sometimes a story is bigger than one's self. And one must bear that burden and its disgrace openly for the greater good. In truth, as I look back, my journey gave me a unique perspective. Sometimes I was just one of the crowd, other times I was the odd one. I had my own choices, but none were easy. Following the crowd meant betraying myself. Following my own will meant parting from socially accepted patterns. Perspective is something that should be treasured, so I am grateful for my humbling experiences.

I feel that my journey started just a few years ago. The particular day I think most of is so vivid in my mind, not just because it happened the day after I resolved to enjoy journalism, but because of an epiphany that I experienced. It was the start of much soul searching and questioning that has directed my thinking over the last few years.

"Hey buddy," a kid named Akamu yelled out. I turned, nervous and reserved. Now would be a bad time to trip on the war-torn cobble walkway. Akamu was in my class, but among the more popular of students. Having learned to be cautious, I opened my expression to one of accepting, but also not committing to the salutation. As Akamu ran up to me, my face remained passive. Inside though, little butterflies of hope tried to raise my hand in greeting. My emotional safety measure worked yet again. Instead of stopping to acknowledge me, Akamu rushed past as indifferent to my presence as I was to the many stray dogs that I too had ignorantly passed this morning.

I don't remember the other boy's name, but I do remember that he was new to the program. He'd transferred to grammar from computer science school last month. This transferring between programs is not uncommon, but after the first year of vocational preparatory schooling, the effort to catch up in the new field of study becomes much more difficult. What I do remember of this boy is that he was not the handsome kid that Akamu was and that I hated him. Okay, well, maybe hate is a little harsh, since I'm generally not inclined to harbor harsh feelings toward anyone, but I was jealous of him. Within only one month, the newbie was able to reach a level of esteem among the students that I'd been unable to accomplish in the whole year.

As many men know, fifteen is an awkward age for a boy. Maybe I'm overgeneralizing. Some, like Akamu, seem to trudge through this pubescent stage of life with enough confidence to betray their own misgivings.

Not me.

If the physical arrangements of this age weren't bad enough, the mental deficiencies are enough to vex the smartest of boys. I think everyone at this age is living in a muggy mental fog.

After Akamu passed, I fixed my eyes on his back. I wondered, if I did move to the pre-medical school of biology, would the fresh start be enough to propel me into the higher echelons of adolescent admiration? This fascination took root in my daydreaming as I continued my walk to school. All the while Akamu and his friend could be heard laughing in front of me, at least until we joined other students and were funneled into the school building. Good thing their faces were directed away from mine. Mine was blotching red with embarrassment. I don't know if their jokes were directed toward me. They probably weren't, but it sure felt like it. I hated being the timid loner.

Large green trees and shrubs had grown back, but still couldn't hide the drab after effects of the war. The school buildings were among the exceptions with colorful facades decorating the neighborhood. The exterior of each prep school radiated an atmosphere indicative of its study. The grammar school was bright and colorful: reds, yellows, oranges, all mixed with tie-dye patterns, cleverly insinuating the need for creativity. How else could a future journalist write such a convincingly vibrant lie for the powers that would soon pay their wages? The facades that displayed uniformed walls of reds and blues belonged to the two pre-med schools just two buildings down. Separating our field of study and theirs was the engineering school, a crisp gray-and-blue facade suggesting the need for strenuous mental focus. Along this whole street, various other schools were arranged, either connected to another building, sharing a building, or in some cases for the larger ones like business and manufacturing, standing alone.

Inside they all looked the same. If the colorful exteriors helped portray a high enthusiasm for academics, the dull beige interior was enough to transform any exuberance into melancholic submission. There were two main classes each day, the first of which I was walking into and finding my seat. The subject of both classes varied from day to day, with the first class usually dedicated to general topics that would be studied regardless of the school, leaving the second class for more-specialized training. Most days I would sit down a few minutes before Krystal. She was one of the few Caucasian kids I knew. I'm pretty sure she was from the United States, and it seemed odd to me that she'd end up here. While I don't know much about American culture, I had to guess that she was annoying there, as well.

Krystal, like most Americans, was a little on the heavy side. Her thick stumps for legs climbed into a milky sausage trunk before ascending into a perfectly rounded face. Taller and more developed than most girls her age, she boasted with every artificially fruit-scented pore of her body. Her hair was always done up so perfect and massive that the kids sitting behind her had to lean into the aisle to follow the instructor's lessons.

She wore more makeup in a day than my mother put on in a year. She must have had dry skin, too. This made little sense to me, since the climate here is so humid to begin with. Still, she almost always could be seen rubbing some fruity lotion onto some part of her body. Not even the expensive clothing she donned each day could compare with the one ornament she favored most. It wasn't something that could be seen, but definitely heard. Her prized possession was her voice.

Never before have I known anyone who loved to talk as much as she did. She always had an answer or question for the teacher, even if it was ridiculous. Her brimming self-confidence persuaded her to volunteer that voice of hers for any and every musical expression of talent, whenever the opportunity arose. Finally and most unfortunate for me, I was the one boy in the class she pitied enough to befriend.

"Hey Iddo," she often began. "How are you doing?"

Generally, before I could respond, she went into something more self-serving, like on this particular day when she mentioned, "Oh hey, did you know that I tried out for the multi-school play this quarter? They're doing The Wizard of Oz, that's an American musical, and I'm hoping to get the main part of Dorothy. Of course I already know every song in the show, so it would only make sense for me to get the part."

Not being completely oblivious to American cinema, I did know, and had seen the movie version once before. If I could have responded, I would've mentioned that

Dorothy wasn't the part I'd like to see her play, but the character of Glinda the Good Witch. The reason for the witch was because she had a much smaller talking role but was more elegantly adorned. Krystal and her natural pomp would never do as Dorothy because Krystal was the least humble-looking person the director could cast. I should know something of this, because, due to the poverty in this part of the world, humble-looking people were abundant. I was unable to convey my opinion to Krystal, as the instructor had scratched the outline of his lesson onto the chalkboard to begin the class.

The irony of comparing Krystal to a witch at the beginning of the day only compounded the experience I had during my lunch break. Like usual, I kept my head down and tried not to attract any attention. After having eaten my lonely meal, I endeavored to leave the cafeteria before Krystal finished hers and made a show of recognizing my singularity. I don't know if her intentions were usually meant to cheer me up, or if they were more an attempt to make herself look compassionate. In either case, the times she did catch me, it was usually to my social detriment.

Hiding from social interaction was depressing in its own way. But if I was going to feel like a loser, I might as well do it on my own terms. After making my way to the restroom, I locked myself in one of the stalls. I only had to urinate, but due to my self-consciousness, I wouldn't have been able to perform in the shared trough.

As I concluded my business, a group of five or six boys entered the room. From their voices, I knew them to be the sort that I shouldn't find myself alone with. Thus far I'd managed to avoid a situation with them, but I'd heard of others who weren't so lucky. So, pretending that my business wasn't complete, I stood on the toilet to wait for their departure. What I witnessed with my ears and to a small degree my eyes, for the cracks in the stalls did permit a little spying, I would never forget.

On the boys' agenda was an experiment in the black arts of witchcraft. I'd often heard of this practice, and my parents warned me of neighborhoods to avoid for that reason. But this was the first time I'd experienced with my own senses the abominable practice.

"I learned this from my cousin's dentist," Kelii bragged. Kelii, being the chief among the miscreants, went on to explain, "Yeah, he took me to this witch doc, and I brought my dad's phone with me to record what he said. The crazy quack must've been a hundred years old, but he said this chant with his hands on my head. Then with his bare fingers, man, he just pulled out my wisdom teeth—didn't even hurt."

"No way!" at least two of Kelii's friends said, not dis-believing, but rather in excitement.

Whether Kelii had transcribed the chant, or if it was by memorization, the boys began their ritual with Kelii acting the part of dark priest. After having all but one person link arms in a circle around a boy, Kelii placed his hands on the kid's head and repeated the spell that would bring strength to his fingers and numbness to the patient. Having made an end to speaking, he pierced his comrade's tongue with a cheap stud. With excited, albe-it distorted, praise, the newly adorned friend exclaimed, "Thweet, dood. Di'in eben hurt a-aull!"

Two others asked to have the task administered to

them, one of them chickening out when his turn came. The other had his tongue pierced with a similar result. During the entire ceremony, I couldn't help but feel what can only be described as a muddle of thought. My body felt as if it was being wrapped in a thick blanket of darkness. Not cold darkness, but hot clammy and numbing darkness. It made me shiver with claustrophobic discomfort. The Devil. It could only be the evil master of sorcery himself. In that darkness, I received my most disturbing epiphany ever.

If there was a Devil, and if he truly was capable of giving such powers to those who call on his nature, shouldn't this son of perdition have his opposite? Shouldn't there also be a God? Usually people are brought to believe in God by feeling good or guilty. For me the seeds were planted in my mind by that enemy of light. Everything I'd ever believed, or rather disbelieved, came into question.

Despite my experience, what followed later that afternoon would overshadow my morning epiphany. My questions about God would ebb over the next few days as I redirected my focus. Funny how inaction can dull the most powerful of epiphanies.

For the time, as I shifted in my hard wooden seat, my thoughts continued churning throughout the second-period class discussion. I just couldn't shake the memory of those piercings. I wasn't completely distracted from the lecture. How I paid any attention was a miracle. Master Haimi, the teacher of second period, was discussing political events. She mainly referenced the growing crime rate. Her lecture touched on the roving bands of marauders that plagued the region.

These mercenaries are like pirates of the land, pillaging and taking advantage of anyone they can plunder. Most of them, with exception of the youngest bands, are rarely punished. Even if they're caught, the sentence is only severe enough to give the appearance of justice. With few exceptions, the judges are as much invested in the marauding as the troublemakers, receiving bribes, gifts, and services from them.

Like a weapon without a cause, these remnants of the war contribute to the corrupt nature of our government. Since they're often employed by corrupt political figures and since we journalists-in-training would likely be helping with some of their propaganda, we needed to learn how to get on with them. Still, they weren't the most dangerous people we had to worry about. Usually they just rough you up and move you on your way. They don't care about politics. As long as they get paid and have their fun, the rest of the world could be swallowed into the earth.

According to Master Haimi, the real force to be reckoned with, when discussing politics, was the Believers. Those of us considered common pagans were the prime target for these religious enthusiasts. They wanted power. Rumor was, they had it too. At least they had it over nature. They still wanted political power, but their numbers were still too few. This also was something they were trying to correct. They wanted their celestial law to be common law. Master Haimi related how these Believers had once visited her.

"You'd better read up on these fellows, or you'll never be able to stand up to them. They come at you so meek and unassuming. But when they speak, their words stab at your bones. They leave scars that tear at you long after they leave. They aren't friendly toward the witches, but that's probably because the witches know all their tricks. Once you become a Believer, they have you for life. Only a few have ever escaped their spell. Those who do can never bring themselves to believe in anything, let alone God, ever again."

There it was again. God. I sat in my chair, chin resting on my desk. Master Haimi's voice droned on while I drifted into my own foggy world, trying to make sense of it all. There was a conflict happening. The Devil had never seemed so unassuming, but now I knew He had to be real. God had never seemed important, but shouldn't evil have its opposite? And if the god of the Believers was really the Devil . . .

"Iddo!"

I jumped in my chair, smacking my knees hard on the bottom of the desk. Laughter rippled around the classroom.

"Iddo, I asked you a question. Were you not paying attention?"

I pulled at my shirt. The back of my wooden chair had used my own sweat to plaster the shirt to my back. The breeze that often came through the open windows rarely cooled the un-conditioned air of the classroom. "Yes, Master Haimi, I just—"

The bell rang. My breath caught for an instant. I let it out with a sigh of relief. Master Haimi was waving her arms frantically, trying to settle the class down while she finished her interrogation. We'd all been sitting still for the last two hours without stretching. She lost the battle as kids ignored her and rushed to the door. I wove in and out between the other students, my book bag slapping against everyone's legs. Amid their annoyed protests, I was able to lose myself in the crowd before she could grab me by the ear and humiliate me even further. I had no doubt that she'd remember to pick on me first thing tomorrow, but by then I'd be in a better frame of mind to answer her.

There was one thing worse than being scolded by Master Haimi. That thing was waiting for me at my locker. I debated turning around and letting the master have her run at me, but I had little doubt that fate would be so kind. This threat at my locker would wait for me. It always did.

Chapter 2

We live in a unique time. Our pocket in this world seems like it is cluttered with lint. The only thing to be done is to pull that pocket inside out and shake it clean. Just like my dilemma of trying to fit in, shaking one's life clean would require a great deal of discomfort for most people. I don't think I could have always done it. But I've never been the boldest of my peers.

Like me, I think most teenagers use their peers as a measure of their self-worth. I don't know why I struggled so much then. No doubt confrontation, rejection, and self-doubt all contributed to my placid demeanor. Many of the other boys and girls had a sense of purpose or ambition that aided them. I didn't really understand them, or belong. I've often wondered, would I've had more friends if only my father had allowed me to follow the profession of my heart. I wanted to be a doctor, but they don't make any real money around here. They just get sick more often.

So I found myself at the mercy of the only friend I had in the whole school, but to be her friend came at the cost of my self-respect. I'd have rather had no friends. But now, looking back, I wonder if I couldn't have been better to her. Maybe I could've done something for her. Often, we look back on our past and see our experiences through the microscope of wisdom. In moments of re-flection, most people, despite regrets, feel they wouldn't change a thing. I know this as well as anybody. I feel the same way. However, if you did go back, isn't there at least something you'd want to change?

Krystal was leaning against my locker, pinning the flimsy yellow clanker shut. Her pink lips, too big and moist for human lips, reminded me of a peeled pomelo. I took a deep breath and dragged my feet across the hall to my locker. As I reached out to open the short metal cab-inet, Krystal's lips parted. Her tongue graced the top of her front teeth as if they needed wetting before her proud and relentless voice threatened to dry them out.

"How was your class?" she started, but, as usual, she didn't wait for my reply. "Same as usual, I bet. By the way, I checked to see if the theater director chose her cast yet, but she hasn't. I'll let you know as soon as I find out. So did Master Haimi give you much homework? I didn't get any from my teacher."

I had an above-average command of the English language, probably better than Krystal. Being born to it, she'd opted out of her language classes last year and was now ahead of me in the curriculum. Since Master Haimi had been her teacher last quarter, Krystal rarely failed to recap where she supposed I was in my lectures. This brought her some degree of pride. She had a great memory, but liked to flaunt it. I always felt belittled by her approach.

"I'm guessing she's started in on her whole political society lectures now, am I right?"

I could barely nod before she blurted, "Don't worry, the assignments will be easy enough. At least I had no problem. Of course, not everyone in the class aced them, but I found them to be so common sense. If you have any questions, you should ask me."

As quickly as possible, I replaced my textbook and grabbed a folder from my morning class. Even though I gently closed the locker door, when the latch caught, the whole thing rattled. *Please let Krystal have somewhere else to go*, I hoped.

"Good news—I can walk home with you today."

My shoulders sank. *Here we go again.*

There was one nice thing about walking home with her. Since she was a native English speaker, I could hone my own command of the language. Of course, that was if I ever got a word in.

Most everyone here spoke decent English. It was unusual to hear anything different anymore. Still, natives to the language, by which I mean Americans and Britons, had their unique sayings, like "pulling your leg" or "What's up?" These didn't make sense literally, and the more of them you knew how to use, the smarter you'd sound. Well, even if I couldn't get a word in, I suppose that was okay, too. If I didn't feel up to it, she could carry the entire conversation. She wouldn't even mind.

Maybe it was the way she brought up Master Haimi. Maybe it was just because I was flustered over being called out in class, but without realizing it, I was the one talking. I didn't dare share with Krystal the thing I'd witnessed in the restroom. I didn't even mention the thoughts I had about God and the Devil. I did tell her about my near humiliation in class. I shouldn't have. That just gave her the perfect opportunity to coach me through the next couple of weeks.

Krystal was quick to take the conversation back. "Since Haimi is starting into her politicking lectures . . . you're not a Believer, are you? Of course you're not. That's good. Here's the gist of it. If she ever calls on you again and you haven't been paying attention—because admit it, she's pretty hard to listen to—just make something up about how it's important to believe and not believe at the same time."

I looked at her a little confused and she backpedaled.

"Don't misunderstand me, I'm not talking about being a Believer-believer. What I mean is, you see, she's going to try and teach you how as a journalist you have to know how and when to believe in somebody and their story. You can't be a truly good journalist if you don't believe in what you're writing. But then you need to know when you can stop believing, and find the next truth to believe in. It's all relative to who you're talking to at the time and what the story is that you need to publish. One day you have to be a devout Buddhist, the next you must be a drunken brawler, or be convinced that you can find mercenaries a paying client. You might even need to sympathize with the witches and Believers if the situation requires it, only to be loyal to the municipal judges the next moment.

"Switching from supporting one political participant to their opponent in the same campaign is a trick that only the best journalists can pull off. You wait and see. I'm going to be such a journalist. My name will be famous. Everybody will know who I am and they'll all want me to represent them. I won't just be a reporter; I'll be a celebrity."

Krystal finished her lecture with a playful bump to my shoulder. It didn't hurt, but I rubbed it, anyway. If I rubbed it, maybe the memory would wear off and it'd be as if she hadn't touched me to begin with. Not that she had lice or germs or anything like that. Sometimes I'd almost get the courage to tell her that I'd rather walk alone, but every time I looked at her condescending face, I'd lose my resolve. There was just something behind those haughty eyes of hers.

I didn't say anything that day, nor would I ever, but I dreamed of it all the time. The truth is that I was afraid of confrontation. There were other times when I wasn't so annoyed by her, but it's hard to explain. I almost felt like she was wearing a mask, that below the layers of foundation, lipstick, and mascara there was another Krystal. Under that stylish blond mop was a smaller, more fragile Krystal who'd be hurt by my rejection of her. So, I bore my torment in silence.

We walked along the dilapidated lane together. The streets had been poorly maintained before the war. Now you had to look hard if you wanted to see that the road had once been paved at all. Tall trees hung over it, their large green leaves shaded us from the intense sun. A few rays of light spilled through the foliage, but we unconsciously skirted them.

Just like in class, my mind stopped paying attention to everything and recessed back into my own thoughts. Let Krystal talk. She wouldn't notice I wasn't listening. Even if she did ask me a question, she'd just answer it herself a second later. How could she ever hope to be a great journalist if she never learned to listen to others? Then again, she had apparently listened well enough to remember what Haimi had lectured on in the previous quarter. Who knows? From what she said, maybe listening wasn't the important part. Believing was the most important part.

I shuddered. Believing. That would just bring me one step closer to being a Believer, especially if I ever need to do any interviews around one of *those* fanatics. Everyone knew that was dangerous. But thinking beyond that group, how could I just sympathize with something or someone, then stop the moment my story was done? Being passionate about writing is one thing, but to believe is something that runs deeply. If I could choose to believe, then forget the next day, what kind of a person would I be? Would nothing be sacred?

An old bike tire bounced in front of us. We both stopped while three grubby children ran after it with sticks. The last one was too young to even need clothing. He was probably four years old or so. Another year or two and his parents would have to start buying him some pants. The kids' parents were nowhere to be seen. That was the way of it around here. The parents always had so much going on and the kids always returned home for supper and sleep. The little boy especially would not wander too far away. He'd still likely be nursing until he started school.

Krystal huffed, as if it was a big joke. She never could get used to it. Kids that old running around naked, breast-feeding till they were five or six. I looked at her as the kids darted out of sight. Her bewildered face still betrayed her foreign upbringing.

"You'll be quite the sympathizer." The words just slipped out of my mouth.

She looked at me, an eyebrow lifted. Had I really just said that? Her questioning glare turned back into a smile and she nudged me with her elbow. Again, I tried wiping her gesture off. Crazy girl. She probably assumed me to be telling the truth. Why not, though? Most people here hadn't quite picked up on sarcasm yet. I think the only reason I had, at least to a small degree, was because Krystal insisted on being around me so often. Americans are so rude. That's why they're one of the few cultures that fully embrace such demeaning chatter.

At last, about two kilometers from my home, she waved good-bye and headed up a side street. Her home was on one of the wealthier blocks. She'd told me once that when her mom had died, her dad moved here to be an on-site reporter.

I had a different idea of why he moved here. If he did much reporting at all, it was minor compared the other *personal* interviews he conducted around town. Fair skin and a thicker wallet could open many doors.

Once Krystal's street was out of sight, the lane took a meandering turn. I'd arrived at the corner of the city's market. The place was a bustle of activity. Everything you could buy was for sale here. Fish, vegetables, shoes, knives, snake oil. It may not all be quality merchandise, but what's a hammer that breaks when it pounds a nail? Nobody around here could afford a hammer made of good steel. Instead, you just learn how to hit the nail softer, so the hammer doesn't shatter. Since the nails were softer than, say, American nails, you also learned to hit them better, too, else they would quickly bend out of shape. That was the way of things around here. Times were hard, so you learned how to get by. We adapt to the circumstances before us. Such one-sided compromise is the only way to survive. It can also be unsettling at times, especially when it concerns the non-merchandised parts of our society.

Staring at the commotion of the market, I made a rash decision. I wanted to be alone with my thoughts. The market smelled like old meat and dried salt-fish. Then there was all the noise, which made thinking impossible. So I did something stupid. I stepped into the woods. More of a jungle, the locals don't refer to this tropical forest as such. That would suggest a sense of normality to the vast island of dense growth. No, the woods are different. Everyone here knows it. Not only was it foolish of me to brave the outskirts of these ominous canopies, but skirting the market would add an extra half hour to my walk home. I live every day in fear of people. Could a few trees really be any worse? Besides, I was in no hurry to get home.

I'd walked only a few hundred meters into the dense overgrowth when an unsettling circumstance presented itself. At first, I didn't think much of it. Just a rustling of shrubs and other vegetation. But as the sound drew closer, I caught sight of the movement. My heart quickened a few beats and my feet stopped moving. Maybe if I stood still I might go unnoticed. It could only be a witch or a Believer. I guess it could be an animal, but that would be too lucky. Animals are far from being the most dangerous things out here. Both witches and Believers were strange. Neither was the sort that you wanted to meet alone.

I slowly crouched, as low as I could, hoping the trees would make my fat frame invisible. What I would've given to be skinny right then. Whoever was coming was getting closer. I first heard them to my left, then my right. They were zigzagging, as if trying to find me. I held my breath and willed every hair on my chubby body to hold still. I closed my eyes and waited for the worst.

Suddenly he was right in front of me. His tangled hair and sweat-streaked shirt made him look wild. I didn't mean to scream. It just kind of happened. "Please don't hurt me, please," I squeaked.

The man, startled, tripped, landing only a meter away from me. I was sitting on my knees, his wild red eyes locked onto mine. They seemed to burn into my flesh as he scrutinized my presence. He pushed himself to his knees, then shot out a hand. The force of the fist was mild, but it knocked the air from my lungs as he grabbed the front of my shirt, pulling me off balance so that I nearly fell into him. "How long 'ave you been 'ere? Were 'ou following me? What'd 'ou see?"

"N-nothing, I s-s-saw n-n-nothing." I tried to turn my head from his flammable breath.

He said no more, but those red veined eyes bored so

deep into mine that I had to look down. I saw his hands. They were hard, callused hands. One of them was dripping blood. When he'd tripped, he'd broken a bottle of cheap booze, sending a shard of glass into the side of his hand. He didn't seem to notice. He was drunk. But this was a different drunk. He'd done something shameful. Witches prided themselves in their wicked ways. Believers would say that anything they did was justified by their faith. This man was trying to hide a powerful guilt in that bottle. I knew why he was here. I'd heard the rumors before. I'd never believed them and my parents denied the possibility, but I knew.

"I'm just going home from school. Please, I just heard you coming and got scared."

"You should be scared. Sneaking 'round 'ere like this, in the middle o' th' woods."

"I didn't mean to—th-th-the market is just right there." I pointed a shaky finger toward where I'd come from.

He released my shirt. I tried to move back. It's hard when your whole body feel like noodles. He seemed to waver a moment, but then he was back on his feet. He ran a few meters before tripping on a fallen log. He steadied himself, then disappeared in the trees. I could still hear him as he put more distance between us. Slowly I found the strength to stand again. I rested my hand against a tree, my arms and chest were still quaking. But the fright was over now. My body would realize that any minute.

I had a decision to make. Turn back and go through the market, or continue in the woods? I decided the market would be the safe play, but when my feet were firm enough to carry me there, I found them taking me deeper into the woods. I'm not an adventurous type. My decision to stay in the woods confounded even myself. I felt as if there was something deeper inside me, tugging me forward. It was a part of me I'd never felt before. Maybe I was under a spell, but that man was no witch and he was definitely no Believer.

Thick thorny brambles covered many of the open spaces beneath the canopy of tall ancient trees. Those places not forbidden by these noxious shrubs held the occasional banana tree or bamboo thicket. Directly below, in the shade of those impossibly high trees, of which were this place's primary inhabitants, hiking was made easier. Little grew beneath those branches except for the fungi that forever ate at the decomposing remnants of leaves and old fallen trees. So, I stuck close to these gravity defying behemoths, walking unencumbered as I searched for the better part of an hour.

Yes, I was searching. It took me the whole hour to realize that I was searching. My true motive was revealed to me. Nobody goes wandering in the woods alone. Not without good reason—and a compass. If you don't know the woods, and I didn't, you could get lost for a long time. At last I convinced myself that I wouldn't find what I'd unwittingly been searching for. I turned around and headed back in the direction I'd come from.

After two hours, I was still in the thick of it. I should've been back at the market by now. I stopped and listened. My throat whistled with every breath as I strained to hear any sounds from the city.

Silence.

My stomach knotted and I felt the forest closing in on me. I was too old to cry, but I wanted to. Nobody would notice out here. My eyes closed, squeezing just enough tears to blur my vision, until I heard a snap. I stood tall and rigid. Snap. There it was again.

Through the trees I caught a momentary glimpse, maybe even just a shadow of a man—no, a beast. It was huge. Too far away for me to see any detail, its hulking form appeared sporadically between open patches of trees. It walked like a man, but there's no way I could even fit my arms around its head. The thing seemed to be looking down into its massive arms. I couldn't see its face, but the way it hunched over, it seemed sad. But what do I know. My eyes were fuzzy. Even if they weren't, I had no idea what I'd just seen. Maybe I hadn't seen it at all. Maybe my fear was just playing tricks on me. My legs had no problem this time. They carried me away as fast as I'd ever run.

Like the drunken man I'd met earlier, I stumbled and pressed on. My chest ached. I was not the running sort. I didn't eat a lot. Maybe I had a bad thyroid. My belly just never seemed to take on any shape but round. Perhaps I just hadn't hit my growth spurt yet. After a while my body finally said, enough! Cramps in my side and mucus in my lungs forced me to take a break. I sat down, wheezing and coughing.

Will I ever get out of here?

A dog barked.

What other man or creature lurks in these woods, ready to kill me?

Another bark.

What am I going to eat?

The third time the dog barked, I stopped my self-pitying spiral. *Why would a dog be out here?* A faint smell of stew caught my nose.

I stood up, and life flowed back into my flesh. I'd done it. I'd found my way out!

Walking at a quick pace, I followed my nose and the barking of the dog. The trees thinned and I cleared the woods. I found myself only two blocks from home. The neighbor's dog had retreated, but I could smell dinner coming from several of the houses. Too tired to run, I walked as quickly as my feet would carry me until I got to the sagging slab of cheap weathered wood that was my door.

"Iddo! Where have you been?"

My mom was relieved and angry at the same time. Telling the truth would not be good for me. I tried to think of something that wouldn't involve me getting switched. Before I could come up with anything, I heard my voice mumble, "In the woods."

"What?" She let a pan drop two inches onto the table. It made loud clunk, and a few small splashes of thickened soup flew out. I think she let it fall on purpose, for effect. "You know better than to go wandering off in the woods! What were you thinking? Are you okay?"

"I'm fine," I breathed, not wanting her to know how shaken I'd really been.

She came over and wrapped her arms around me. That wasn't at all what I'd expected. "Please don't go in there. I've heard the most terrible rumors about those woods. If I lost you . . . promise me you'll stay out of there!"

I pulled back, not wanting to let myself crack under her embrace. "I'm sorry."

"Sorry is not good enough. I want you to promise that you won't go back in there."

I bowed my head. "Okay."

"Now get cleaned up. Your father will be home soon. Not a word about this to him."

"Okay."

That definitely had gone better than I'd thought it would and was she protecting me? Not a word about this to my father? My mother's name, Soportevy, translates to "angelic girl"—a fair assessment, especially considering the circumstance.

My father got home and we ate mostly in silence. At least I was silent. They tried to find things to talk about. My father asked me about my day and my mother diverted his attention.

"You're awfully quiet today, Iddo," he said. "Usually I can't get you to stop talking."

That was true. Even if I didn't say much at school, I usually found talking around my family much easier.

"I just have a lot on my mind today."

"Please, do tell," he pressed. "The air is getting a little

thick around the table with all this silence."

I looked at my mother, who had a worried look in her eyes. She knew that I couldn't lie, yet she didn't want me to tell him about getting lost on my way home.

"Come on, out with it," he demanded. His eyes took on a cold stare. "This is about being a doctor again, isn't it?"

My father, being a strict but poor man, wanted a life for me that was beyond his own reach. His shrewdness in public understanding moved him to place me in grammar school. This was preparatory to the vocational training in journalism that would soon follow.

To be a journalist in any other part of the world might be considered an honorable if not dying profession, but even in my muddled thinking, I knew what a journalist here meant. For me it stank of mildewed potatoes. But we'd argued this all before. I'd committed to following his plan.

Arguing with my father's logic was like telling a rock to dance. A journalist here could go far, so long as they printed the propaganda of the ambitious governing bodies. But an unbiased journalist would not only find their career at a short end, but sometimes their life, also.

The last time I'd raised the issue was a Sunday, on the first week of April. I'd complained to my mother in private, since all my direct appeals to my father had failed spectacularly. She always smelled of a fresh morning. Not the kind you might see on a soap commercial, but more of the morning that melded a clean smell of sweet-fruiting blossoms with the tangy scent of burning sticks. This from the endless meals she cooked by fire for our family. She was the essence of purity and hard work, and she seemed to absorb my sorrows and radiate comfort. I asked her to convince the dictator of our home to allow me to follow the course of my own heart. That was the first time I ever saw the sweet tears of my loving mother. In the pureness of those glimmering drops of polished glass, a thousand words of understanding were passed into my soul with the clarity that only the eye-dew of a mother can convey.

My ability to put into words what even the great Michelangelo might struggle to paint is obviously lacking. Still, she let me know that she loved me, that she fully supported my tender wishes to help others by studying medicine and that, despite her compassion, she could say nothing against her husband and master. My heart wrenched in disappointment, not only for the futile nature of my predicament, but also for her sorrow and the part I played in causing it. I decided then and there that I'd never trouble her heart over the matter again. I would follow the prescribed course set by my patriarch and bring them the monetary treasures that would, if not lighten my conscience, at least distract theirs somewhat.

My father knew I still disagreed with this course of study. So, I can easily see why he immediately jumped to the conclusion that this was the subject of the night's silence. "I've already told you that I'll stay in journalism," I said, trying to disarm him.

He eyed me suspiciously.

Nervous, I ran my hand through my hair. That was dumb. His face lit up and he reached toward me and plucked a leaf from out of my hair. He held it up and his stare dissected my silence. He knew. That leaf could have been from anywhere, but I knew that he knew.

If my skin was white like Krystal's, I'm sure my face would've been blushing bright red. Granted, it would have to first make its way through all her layers of make-up. Even though my skin is dark, a parent knows a blush from their own kid and my face was hot with it.

"I—I . . ." I sighed. "On my way home from school, I was on the edge of the marketplace when I saw a man run out of the woods. He saw me, and grabbed me. He accused me of following him, but I told him I hadn't, then he ran away. I've heard lots of weird things about those woods. I guess I'm just trying to make sense of them all."

There—I'd said something. I hadn't admitted that I'd been in the woods, but there was enough truth in it for me not to give myself away in a complete lie. Now, instead of releasing tension from the air, the opposite seemed to occur. "What kind of rumors have you heard?" Father asked.

His eyes were intense. Mother froze as if this new revelation was worse than my drifting into the woods.

"Silly things, really." I half laughed, not wanting to continue. But those penetrating eyes of his. "I hear rumors at school about men taking babies into the woods, only to return without them."

Mother stood up.

"I've also heard stories of witches, Believers, and a large man or creature, or something."

Mother walked quickly out of the room. My eyes followed her, then I looked back at my father with a question in my gaze.

His attention had also followed Mother out of the room. Looking back at me, his stare softened. "Did you see any of those other things, too?"

"No."

"I know you went into the woods. I can see the scratches on your arms."

I looked down. Sure enough, little pink pinstripes crosshatched both of my forearms. I looked up, ready to plead forgiveness. It wasn't necessary.

"You're old enough, you might as well know, but don't talk about this with your mother. Clearly it upsets her."

That night, I slept poorly. The things my father had told me confirmed many of the echoing rumors I'd already heard. I was right about that man leaving the woods. Father hadn't said much about the witches or Believers, but the large manlike creature, he did admit to having heard rumors about that. He said he didn't know what to think of the matter, but that there was danger there and it might be related to those men who go into the woods in the first place. He reiterated my mother's desire that I not go back into the woods.

I tried to sleep, but every time I closed my eyes, I saw that massive head. Giant arms would reach for me and I'd nearly fall out of bed.

Chapter 3

Do you ever have days when your inner conflict is so strong that every choice of thought becomes wrong? Circumstances even change to our liking, yet for liking them, we commit the greatest of sins. If we reverse the scenario and hate what has happened, we become enemies of our own conscience. Even though we tell our minds that we truly want the old ways to stay the same, we can't ever bury the deception that is told to us, by us.

As I once was, so now do I place you at the crossroads. The only way forward, as far as I can surmise, is to be true to yourself. The dead will always follow us. We can never shake their influence. To some, this will disturb, but for me, it lightens my burden. No matter how far we stray from our parents' best intentions at guiding us, their many other virtues will live through us, our future children, and theirs. This is immortality. With

any luck, every generation will grow in wisdom and strength, becoming better than the one before. I pity those who never knew their parents and who must start the chain anew. Even more, I pity those who feel complacent about their parents' progress, and fail to improve upon the generations of ancestors whose dreams were for us to pick up where they left off, and strive further than they could.

Weeks were inevitably followed by months. Every day the same. Go to school and try unsuccessfully to fit in. Not that there weren't any changes. The first was that I found myself walking through the woods more often. I knew I shouldn't. My mother would definitely not approve. I really felt uncomfortable disobeying her, but I still went almost every day now. Unless I had a reason to hurry home after school, I'd add an extra hour to my walk home as I moved deeper into the formidable jungle. My defiance to my mother's instructions was illogical. Something about my encounter with the drunken man made me push past my promises. I don't think even I understood this irrepressible urge to venture in. Still, it never stopped nagging at me. I had to know what was in there.

The place terrified me, but also seemed to sing to me. On more than one occasion, I'm sure that I'd heard the trees' serenade. This day, as if in the distance, that low sweet sound seemed to speak to me. *Sometimes I'm up, and sometimes I'm down / Coming for to carry me home / But still my soul feels heavenly bound / Coming for to carry me home.* My mind might have been playing tricks on me, but if I didn't hear the song plainly, I heard it in my heart. Usually as soon as I thought I heard it, I'd stop to listen, but it would be gone. The woods were a strange place, indeed, but I was a strange boy. I almost felt like I belonged there.

I paused at one point when I found a rare moonflower. The delicate blossom, native to these woods, was still folded in on itself. I knew that it would be the jewel of the forest when it eventually opened. The flower, so fragile, would remain closed until the sky was dark. Then, under the light of the moon, it would spread open in a wide graceful twist. Its silky white petals would almost glow with the moon's reflection. I wanted to stay here and witness it. This plant, so alone among all these trees, seemed perfectly at home. I wondered if I could ever be as comfortable in such formidable surroundings as this flower. Like the plant, I was at peace here. But I didn't live here. I lived somewhere, arguably more formidable.

By now I'd become somewhat familiar with at least the first kilometer that skirted the forest. When I reached a small valley, I followed a trickling stream. This same stream, only a few centimeters deep and a third of a meter at its widest, would trickle down to the edge our neighbor's garden. Every time they took advantage of the stream for watering their little track of vegetables, it would dry up completely for everyone else below them. Since most people relied on wells, this didn't bother anyone. At least not anyone I knew.

As I exited the last grove of trees, I dipped my hand into the water one more time. The coolness seemed to beckon me back into the trees. *Nothing at home for you. Only sadness. Only pain. Come back and stay.* These dangerous woods spoke peace to me. The stream was its voice. It truly was my imagination this time.

When I looked back up, I could see a lot of commotion at my house. We rarely had company. When we did it was seldom more than two or three people. This time there must've been close to thirty, milling in and out of our little shanty. Most of them were family and neighbors. My stomach fluttered near my throat. The way everyone was milling about, heads down, shoulders slumped, told me something was wrong. Very wrong.

Mother had been sick. For the last couple of weeks, she'd had a cough that wouldn't subside. Of all the days to waste wandering in the woods! I ran toward our home. Oh please, oh please—I tried forcing the fear to a back corner of my mind. If by chance everything was just fine, I wouldn't want anyone to see my eyes full of tears for no reason. But why else would everyone be here? And why did I even care what everyone thought of me? No one paid me any mind most of the time. Anyway, this was my mother!

But it wasn't my mother. I picked her out almost immediately. She was in the middle of the crowd, sitting— crying—alive. When she lifted her head, I could see how deep her sorrow truly ran. "Oh no," I whispered. "Father."

"I'm so sorry," and "Don't worry, we're here for you," wafted at me from family. The local Christian well-wishers bade me "God bless you" and "Peace be unto you." They always seemed to flock around tragedies, passing out their abundant supply of warm sentiments, not to mention a collection plate for donations to help support their prayers on behalf of the family. All this was happening as I made my way to mother. I paid little attention to who spoke. They were all hollow, anyway. At least I knew my relatives were sincere, but what, really, could any of them do?

Mother looked up at me as I approached, as if she sensed my coming. Her arms, held tightly to her chest, now opened and swallowed me into them. I know boys aren't supposed to cry. I tried hard to be the man that I now had to be, but as soon as Mother drew me in, my jaw felt ready to quiver away from me. My eyes melted into great overflowing pools of salt water. My perfectly clear nose, now blotchy red, bubbled with translucent mucus as it ran into my mouth, mixing with my saliva. In under half a second I'd gone from forced composure to sobbing volcano.

I'd let my mother down. I wasn't strong, not even for her. Lost in my shame, I didn't realize that she'd found some measure of composure. Someone always has to be stronger. She'd had more time to let this sink in than me, it was her turn to comfort me. Still, this was not acceptable. Why? I don't honestly know. I pulled away from her and ran. There'd be no place to hide in our two-room shanty and I needed to be alone. There was only one place to go. I ran back to the woods. I didn't go very deep into them. Just enough to avoid being seen by the mourners.

Back at the little stream I'd followed only ten minutes before, I found myself sniffling at my reflection. What a blubbering mess I was. Father would not be proud of my sulking. "Be the man you need to be," he'd tell me. Yes, the man that was needed, not the boy I wanted to be— but with him dead, I might be able to study medicine now. No sooner had the thought entered my head than I slammed my palm into the trickling water. It was a weak gesture and I felt more hollow for trying. How could I possibly look at my father's death as a blessing? He'd been a great man and he'd treated Mother well. This couldn't be said of all the men in our community.

Determined to rectify my disgrace, I pulled myself back to my feet. More slowly this time, I walked back to our little home. This time when somebody apologized for my misfortune, I acknowledged them.

"Thank you," to my aunt.

"If there is a God, I'm sure he'll watch out for us," to the Christians.

Finally, to my mother, "I'm sorry I ran. I won't leave you again."

"Iddo," she soothed. "I don't know how we'll get by, but at least we still have each other."

I hadn't thought about the future as it pertained to getting by. But now I wondered. Mother had no work. Her days were filled with cooking and cleaning our clothes by hand. Sure, she'd helped the neighbors with their chores, and this in exchange for a few eggs or an occasional chicken. That was meager compared to what Father had contributed. He went to work six days each week, and even then, we just scraped by.

If nothing else, at least all the mourners were good for one thing. They all pitched in a little money to help us until Mother or I could find a way to support ourselves. All except for the Christians. But they had their place, too. Those donations they gathered helped fund their part of the charity. They offered to bury Father in one of their above ground tombs. It was a free service they offered anyone who died.

After maybe five to ten years, when the body was just bones, it would be removed to make room for the next occupant of the concrete cubicles. They say that this was done in similitude of our Savior leaving his tomb, but everyone all knew it was because the cemetery had limited space. Besides, the Believers, who also claimed a belief in Christ, had soured a lot of people from the mainstream Christian faiths. Since very few people could actually afford a permanent resting place for the dead and in an attempt to garner sympathy toward mainstream Christianity, these normal Christians offered burial services to anyone who needed it. As a result, the cemetery was always overcrowded.

As children and teenagers, we used to make fun of the practice. We'd sometimes wander through the tall weeds of these cemeteries. The stacked tombs, sometimes six high, were each about half a meter tall, and just shy of a meter wide. Bodies would be inserted or removed through one end, then sealed up. Near the time that a body was ready to be removed, the weathered seal would break, revealing a perfect skeleton. As kids, we'd reach into the concrete boxes where the cheap ends had fallen away and scare one another with the white skulls inside. It seemed like an eternity since I'd been so brash or done anything for that matter with friends.

"Where is he now?" I asked.

"They've taken him to be cleaned." These words were hard for Mother to say and our next-door neighbor put a hand on her shoulder.

"How?" was all I could ask next.

This was obviously too hard for her to answer. She

tried but our neighbor with the comforting hand stepped in to help. Her sweet voice held none of the sympathies that the other mourners carried. Yet it was this firmness that made it so genuine. It was something real, from a real person. "It was an accident at work. My husband watched it happen." She paused.

Most of the men in our little community worked together. You could say that the Tusk White Concrete Company practically owned our neighborhood. I was just about to press her for more details, but held back as she inhaled deeply.

"Your father, may he never be forgotten, was on the shovel of a four-story building. They were setting the next lift when his scaffolding fell apart."

"Didn't he have a harness?" I asked. "They're always tethered."

Nodding, she continued, "The way my husband put it, their tethers are made with cheap stiff ropes. Most times, if somebody falls, curse those stingy Tuskies, the rope will swing them to a safe stop. This was one of those time, though, when your father was directly below the tether. There was no swing. It snapped his back. He died about an hour later."

There it was. One minute everything is great; the next, it's all ended by dangling at the end of a tight rope. Everyone knows the risks of working at the Tusk. Something like this happens most years. Usually it's somebody else. Everyone keeps working there because we're so poor that we take what we can get. But the Tusk owns us, and they know it. We'll likely get a month's wages from them, but they're not required to help us beyond that.

The next day after school, Mother and I walked to the company to collect Father's accident pay and to apply for a job. We would both work part time. The wife of a dead husband with a child to raise can work wonders on even the most hardened of business scum. By the time we left, we both had work. I would shovel aggregate after school for four hours on weekdays and ten on Saturdays. Mother would clean the tools and mixers, chipping hardened concrete off the surfaces if it had been left on for too long.

Neither of us was very good at the work, which earned us both a dock in pay that first week. I had a hard time because my muscles weren't up to the new task of lifting several tons of gravel each day, not yet at least. Mother's job, on the other hand, was especially hard for her. The job would normally give a person hard calluses, but then her laundry scrubbing would take them off again. Because of this, her hands were always red with blisters and cracked skin. At night, she wrapped them in old cotton cloths. I was always tired and I knew she was, too. Still, she managed to cook dinner every night and put on a pleasant smile. The time for mourning was gone. Now it was time for working.

School was like cleaning your foot off on the dirt. On the top clean side, all tuition for the year was required up front, meaning that I could finish that year of schooling without any additional costs. The bottom side, sinking as if it were in the new mud, meant that we'd have to save up for next year. Between Mother and myself, there was little extra to go around. Every week we set aside a little money for our basic needs, the rest would be saved for school. This caused me great consternation. Not that we were poor. We'd always been poor. A little more so now, but if

I had to work so hard for my own schooling, I wanted to go to school for something that I wanted to learn and do.

Weeks passed as I tried to muster the courage to talk it over with my mother. After all, hadn't I vowed not to bring this topic up again? I was supposed to be content with following my father's ambition and working in journalism, especially with his death sealing my honor to his will. Every quiet evening that passed, another brick was placed between me and my hope of ever breaching the topic.

One night, as we were sitting down for our late supper, Mother looked at me with those deep tired eyes. A mysterious smile threatened to overtake one side of her face as she held back one of her coughing fits. "I've been thinking," she started.

Naturally I was confused. Usually when she began a conversation with those words, there was no smile. She was taking her sweet time getting to the point, but I said nothing. I just listened with all the attention of a dog waiting for a scrap of gristle.

"I loved your father very much. But even though we loved each other, we still had our disagreements. He wanted the very best for you. A life in journalism here would provide a nice income for you. I never openly disagreed with him. Now that he's gone, I have to consider, do we keep you following his path, or do I let you follow your own? I know that you've been wanting to be a doctor for some time."

At this point, my eyes were wide with astonishment. Not only had she read my mind, but was she about to give me permission to change schools?

Her smile widened and she leaned forward. "Before this school year ends, I think you should choose. You can continue where you're at or move to medical."

I wanted to jump up and hug her, but I didn't. I wanted to shout for joy, but I didn't. I just continued staring at her with surprise. I even mostly suppressed a cheesy grin of excitement. "Thank you," I said as politely as possible, knowing that she expected more of a reaction from me. Maybe she could see beyond my display of restraint. "I've been thinking about this, too. I really, really would like to transfer. I feel bad to dishonor—"

"Don't you dare," she snapped. "Your father was a good man, but that doesn't mean he had perfect judgment. Life is full of disappointments, sorrows, and hard times. If you aren't careful, it will be too easy to get caught up in them. It happens all the time. If you can't find the joy in living, you might as well give it all up and don't you ever think of giving up.

"My joy is in seeing you happy. I know that your joy will be found in helping other people. Providing a financially stable home for us was your father's joy and that's why he wanted you to go into journalism, so that you could provide for your family better than he did. You have your father's strong will, but you inherited my compassion."

I didn't feel like I had anyone's strength of will. I didn't even know if compassion was the reason for me wanting to become a doctor, but now was not the time to argue that. My heart was pounding so fast now. I was afraid that my mother would see my excitement and for some reason I felt like I should be tempering my outward emotions. I know it wasn't important, but at my age, it felt necessary.

"Being a doctor might not be as lucrative, but it's still not a bad career. There's no school near here, though. You'd have to leave me at the beginning of the year and go stay in the dorms over near New Tum District."

At that comment, my racing heart tripped on itself. "But what about the pre-med building at my vocational school right now?"

She shook her head. "I've already looked into that. Vocational pre-med would start you in the right direction, but you could spend two years there, then go to college, or you could go straight to college, study real hard, and just take a couple of the college-level pre-med classes. You don't actually need to graduate from the vocational level. They're mostly a place for kids to grow up a little before getting into the real school.

"Besides, the next two years count as college credit regardless of which school you attend. You've already got the maturity to handle college and the brains to deal with a tough first year in a new curriculum. I've already called and cleared it with the college. With your grades now, they agree that you could probably manage the jump."

She was right. It would be hard, but I knew I could endure it. Besides, with our financial situation, paying for an extra two years of schooling versus combining those same classes in a real college or even testing out of them altogether, well, I would have to do it. Hard as I knew it would be, this was the path open to me. It's what I'd been wanting so badly. My body felt physically stronger and deep inside. I knew I had it in me to succeed.

There was one other implication. I knew it and undoubtedly my mother knew it, so it was hard to say it with a straight face. At this point, I figured it would just be a technicality, but I had to mention it anyway. "But that's on the other side of the woods, maybe a day or two if I walked straight through them." I know she didn't really expect me to hike through the woods. She knew what went on in there. Maybe she'd already thought of a way to pay for the trip around them.

Her smile faded and that minor change in her face caused my breath to pause. She nodded. "It's time you became a man. I can't protect you from the world forever. There are dangers and unforgivable things that happen in the woods. We can't afford to send you on a transport around them. Eventually you'll have to learn to master your fears. I already know that when your father was still here, you were disobeying us, spending more and more time in those woods. I think by now you must know a little of how to find your way in there."

My face grew hot with guilt. I slouched in shame. "I didn't know you knew."

"Remember, I wash your clothes every day. You expect me to believe that those sticks and leaves that broke off in your pockets came from the marketplace? Not to mention how you always came home at least an hour later than usual? I knew."

I looked back up at her. Her smile was fading, but not because I'd been disobedient.

"There is one small problem from what I can determine," she said. "School costs the same, but the dorms will be an added expense. We barely have enough as it is."

Chapter 4

You have a responsibility. I feel this deep in my bones. We all do. Despite my poverty, I never felt poor. Not until the year my father passed away. Growing up in a matter of weeks is never easy or fun. But life cannot wait. Neverland only exists if someone else can remain responsible. The pirate of childhood, the murderer of bliss, he's always lurking. To some he passes, they being too drunk to notice. Into others he hooks that stainless barb, and rips away their flight.

But the world still hurls itself through space, its denizens either living or dying. The world may suffer quakes and fires, but it never stops its course. All small things are witness to the structure of the grand. If a greater plan exists, beyond our mortal view, then eternal progression must be real. It must be necessary. Thus, all your actions are important.

We were all poor, so we didn't know any different. But there was poor and then there was destitute. Even

I found the pounds shedding off me little by little. I was still fat, but two months after my father's death, I noticed a thinning in my appearance. Not only was I eating less, an attempt to save more money to pay for next year's school and board, but I was physically more active. While some of that fat disappeared, some of it had to have been turned into muscle. I'm not saying that I looked strong, but I felt strong. In the mornings I'd go to school, then in the afternoons I'd shovel gravel. The work was getting easier, so I had to be gaining some strength.

Strength is a funny thing. The stronger I became physically, the more confident I felt mentally—sort of; I still had no friends. I still felt out of place in journalism. I still felt like people were talking about me behind my back. Most of all, I was still embarrassed to be doted on by Krystal. So, while I felt more confident, I hadn't quite overcome myself completely. Still, things were better. Instead of slouching in a corner, I kept my back straight. Instead of looking down at my desk when teachers asked me questions, I'd almost look them in the eye. But that's as far as I could progress socially.

The third quarter of school had started. I had all new teachers. While I continued to share the first-period class with Krystal, I'd advanced to the class she'd just completed for the second period. I suspected this meant that she'd have to coach me in the fine art she'd developed of surviving that particular teacher. I wasn't looking forward to it.

As usual, after our first class let out, she visited the restroom and I quickly walked ahead to find my place in the cafeteria before she had a chance to drag me to her usual table. How she managed to find anyone to sit with still astonished me. There were always several others who seemed to enjoy her company. I think it's because she's white and foreigners radiate a unique attraction among the natives, no matter which country they live in. Whether they liked her, or were just curious about her, I might never know.

Sitting alone, I unrolled my cloth package and took out a lump of rice and dried fish. The fish smelled sharply of brine and old oil. It could've been worse if not for Mother working it over. In its unprepared state, it would fill the whole school with a pungent odor, the kind you try to avoid when navigating the fish market. Even the poor people who shopped there would find their stomachs tightening. I had to eat quickly before anyone got too offended by its smell. Luckily, and unluckily, there wasn't much, so this was easy. Bad breath would be a serious consequence of the meager meal, but it was better than starving. Besides, I was already at the bottom of the social ladder. I couldn't get much lower.

As I was trying to carry the smell and flavor of it down with my rice, I committed the big mistake of withdrawing into my thoughts. Anyone of teenage years knows that you should act like a good soldier and not ignore your surroundings. You've always got to be aware, ready to act or react before a socially embarrassing situation creeps up on you. Sometimes when I found myself lost in thought, I was lucky to go unnoticed. This was not one of those times. When I came to myself, I looked up to see Krystal standing before me. She gave me one of her classic pity smiles before sitting next to me. She wasn't alone, either. Well, technically she was the only one who'd come over, but every eye in the cafeteria followed her.

"I've been noticing your lunches lately. I'm guessing

times are hard since your father . . . well, I brought you this."

She pulled from her plastic grocery bag an extra sandwich. "I made it for you this morning. I hope you like it. I can bring you one each day, if you'd like."

Did she have to say that so loud? Couldn't she see what she was doing to me? I didn't grab the sandwich from her. She set it down on the table in front of me. Somewhere behind me I heard a boy calling out, "Krystal--Iddo, such a lovely pair; kissy-kiss, smoochy-smooch, then cuddle like a bear."

Krystal didn't respond, but she had to have heard. My face went hot and panic took over. I bolted out of my seat, surely drawing every eye that wasn't already on me. I grabbed the sandwich and stalked over to the exit, dropping it in the waste bin before ducking out of the room.

I don't know what Krystal thought, but I could hear some laughter. I couldn't physically see her laughing with the other kids, but I was sure that she'd find a way to justify in her mind that all was well with herself. All the confidence that I thought I'd developed at work melted away, and I sought out a quiet corner where nobody would notice me. I pulled out my books and pretended to work on homework, just in case anyone did happen to look my way. I didn't want them to think I was hiding.

As I sat there on the floor, I ran through all the ways that I could have better handled my encounter. If I'd just thanked her for the sandwich, which I honestly would have liked to eat, everyone might have just given up watching. But no, I had to make a scene. Now everyone would be talking about it for days. My stomach grumbled. I held it, hoping it wouldn't keep voicing its hunger through the next class period. Maybe I'd be able to catch a break, and sneak back into the cafeteria and grab that sandwich after all the other students had finished their food and left. No, by then, the waste bin would be full, and if I were caught digging through it, there'd be no end to the ridicule.

That afternoon, despite every effort I placed into listening to my teacher, I couldn't take my mind off the lunchtime incident. I loathed the end of class, when I'd have to confront Krystal again. But when the time came, she wasn't waiting for me at my locker. I don't know what twist of fate allowed me this miracle, but I took full advantage of it. After making my exchanges, I nearly slammed the locker as I darted down the hall and out the school doors. I'd survived the day. Now I was on my way home, or, at least, to work. At work, I'd be able to sweat the day's humiliations away.

Something funny happened, though. The next day, I went to school, and Krystal chose to sit at the other end of the classroom in our morning period. I looked at her several times, wondering why she'd broken routine. She didn't once acknowledge me. At lunch, she continued to shun me. Could I be so lucky? I'd spent so much time trying to avoid her, now she was finally leaving me alone. Why, then, did my eyes keep going back to her? Was I missing her self-serving patronization? or was I just afraid it was too good to be true?

I really was a loner now. Nobody talked to me. I would from time to time get shoved out of the way, or have a wad of paper thrown at me, but that wasn't uncommon. I'd be gone next year and none of this would matter anymore. So why did my chest ache with loss, as if a deep sadness decided to root itself in my soul? Maybe I'd done wrong by her. Until now, I'd never even considered her to have feelings. This was Krystal after all. She was confident and pretty in her plump American sort of way. I felt that I maybe should mend the issue. Somehow, I might regret it if I didn't.

This impression made precious little sense to me, so I did the only thing I felt in my power: I ignored it. What a stupid roach I was. Some people believe in a divine hand or spirit that helps guide them throughout their lives. Whether it's your conscience, God, or some natural energy, if you ignore it long enough, it will leave you alone. Eventually my guilt subsided. My confidence disappeared with it. Somehow, even though I wasn't eating any more than before, my body started surrendering some of its newly gained muscle for fat again. Shoveling gravel at work wasn't getting any easier, it was getting harder.

At night, I would stare at a free Coca-Cola calendar, counting the days left until the school year was over. Even the perfectly beautiful peppy girl on the calendar, with her flowing black hair bouncing around a shower of bubbles and sparkles, failed to cheer me like it once had. She looked like the world was a party and nothing could ruin her joy. If anything, it only reminded me of my own miserable state.

Chapter 5

I've often looked at other people, believing them strange. As I've aged I've learned that I'm just as weird to them as they are to me. In our community, my father was the only man in my family who might have been considered normal by the metric of social conformity. As my school year ended, I learned that the right decision is often the hardest. A good lesson that would pay to remember. Nothing worth doing should ever be done lightly.

Finally, that blessed day came. The last week of the school year had arrived. At school the first order of business was to register for the next year. Since there were only a few optional classes, most of the program was highly structured in its progression. This meant that to re-register for classes in the coming quarter, there was little that needed to be formalized, mostly just a signature and a commitment to pay next year's tuition. When the form asked for my commitment, I penciled in "transferring."

Apparently once a person gets into the journalism

school, few ever transfer out. Not only does one expect to make good money in the profession, but there seems to be a sort of fraternal spirit abounding in the faculty and future alumni that prevents them from seeing any other professions with as high a prestige.

"Iddo has decided to transfer," the counselor suddenly announced to the whole class. For the first time in months, Krystal actually glanced my way. Everyone was staring at me. "Perhaps our star linguist can explain to us where he thinks his gift of speech will serve him better?"

I hadn't expected this rebuffing. In the last couple months I'd withdrawn from social encounters so much, that my face burned with embarrassment at having to explain myself. "I- I—"

"Stop stuttering," the counselor snapped. "And stand up. We've taught you enough here that you should be able to audibly convey your point."

The desk squealed as my belly pressed it forward a centimeter or two. When I was on my feet, I filled my lungs and held the breath for a second, then exhaled. There was no shame in my decision and I resolved to take pride in my new ambition. "I will be transferring to the medical college in the New Tum District."

I don't know what I expected, but what I heard was definitely not anywhere near the anticipated effect. Laughter bounced around the room. Not just from the students, but the counselor and my teacher were laughing at me, as well. "Skipping straight to college? You want to give up a career of comfort and luxury for a chance to get sick every day? How does cleaning bedpans and giving placebos compare to molding communities and the world through the spoken and written word? You'll become a slave to the rich and poor alike. Mostly poor."

My cheeks burned. This was exactly the attitude that disgusted me about journalists. I don't know where my courage to speak came from, but I felt so strongly about my calling to join the medical profession that I asked, "When you get sick or your child is born early, would you rather have an intelligent doctor helping you, or would you rather risk going to one of the local witches for help?"

A boy next to me immediately rebutted, "If I'm rich, I can get American doctors to help me. All our doctors can do here is prescribe placebos. They're basically witches pretending at being doctors. And if a baby has problems when it's born, big deal. We're only allowed one, anyway; better luck next go around."

Inside my gut, I felt a twist of anger and nausea. I remembered my first dangerous encounter in the woods, when the drunkard had nearly killed me. How had this disregard for young life become so ingrained in our culture that even the kids my age didn't see a baby's life as precious? I wanted to scream, but my shame outweighed my desire to be heard. Why should I cower? Wasn't I right? Wasn't all life sacred?

"Well," the counselor finally said, "Iddo can do as he pleases in this matter. But remember, boy, there is a transfer fee of three hundred yuan to leave this curriculum. Good luck to the rest of you. I look forward to seeing you all next season."

The counselor left the room. I slumped back into my chair, my heart drooping even lower. I was aware of the transfer costs to enter the college prematurely, but hadn't expected a transfer fee to leave this school. There was no way I could ever pay it. I was going to be stuck here. Not only would I be confined to this school and career, but now all my schoolmates knew of my dissension from the prevailing mind-set. Not having friends is one thing. To be openly abused for your belief is something entirely different. How could I go on?

As I was walking home, Krystal ran to catch up to me. I was surprised. We hadn't spoken in months. I looked up at her; she clearly wanted to talk, but she held her tongue for what must have been an eternity to her. When she brought her eyes to meet mine, I could see something there that I'd never seen before. I immediately turned my head back down. Sincere pity is a hard thing to accept, regardless of who offers it. Usually her pity felt more like a cartoon bandage on a pimple. This time she looked as earnest and honest as I could have ever imagined.

"You shouldn't be ashamed of wanting to be a doctor."

"Everyone thinks I'm crazy for it."

She put a hand on my shoulder. I flinched, and she withdrew it. "Listen, Iddo, back in America, becoming a doctor is a very respectable thing. I don't know why nobody here seems to think so, but I'm glad that you do."

"It probably doesn't matter. I can't pay the transfer fee. I'm going to be stuck here."

We walked in silence for a full minute. I half wondered if she might be able to help me with my financial problem, but quickly dismissed it. I knew enough about her father to know that he wouldn't part with any portion of his money. He might have been American, with more money coming to him monthly than I could ever save in a year, but he was well known for being stingy. With so many poor people around him, he felt that if he gave money to one person, then before long he'd be solicited to support the whole town. No, he wouldn't help. Even Krystal would find it difficult to gain access to his money.

In a way, I couldn't help but pity her in return. She might be a little pompous, but I suspected that she really did have a heart. In America, she could've become something bigger. Here, I feared that she'd adopt our culture. Her father, bum of an American that he was, would never be the source of opportunity that could've otherwise been hers.

"Krystal, I'm sorry."

She looked at me knowingly, but then feigned confusion. "You've got nothing to be sorry for."

I did, and she knew it. Why else would she have avoided me for so long? Silence hung in the air for another minute. This was the most balanced conversation I'd ever had with this girl. I didn't want to talk, but found my lips moving to fill the void. "I've wanted to be a doctor for a long time now. My father never approved of it. Like everyone else, he thought I'd be better off in journalism. The thing is, I don't agree with the school or the mentality of everyone in it."

Krystal really did look confused now. "What do you mean, you don't agree with it?"

"You heard the way the kids talked in class, didn't you? All they care about is money. They have no ethics. They even talked as if life didn't really matter that much."

"They were just being stupid. Nobody really thinks like that."

I shook my head. "Everything I've seen would suggest otherwise. No doubt you've heard the rumors. People taking their infants to the woods."

"Those are just stories," Krystal defended. "There's no truth in them. Nobody would murder their own children like that. I can't imagine you'd actually believe those tales. Just like witches, if you believe that fathers take their extra babies to the woods to slaughter them, just to avoid an extra-child penalty tax, I'm guessing you'd also believe in witches."

She said this as if I'd be crazy to believe in witches. I wanted to argue the point. I don't know if Americans have such things to worry about, but Krystal was just plain naive.

She apparently didn't want to talk about it. With easy effort, likely something she'd learned here at school, she steered the conversation back on track. "If you don't make it to medical school, do you think we could at least be friends again?"

"I'm not a very fun person to be around," I reminded.

"I like being around you," she said. She must've noticed my baffled expression. "You don't say much, I've noticed. But I can tell that you're a very gentle person." She immediately regretted saying that. Telling a boy that he's gentle is seldom a compliment. "What I mean is, while every other boy in our school is trying to be macho or suave, you're just, nice. You're a little shy sometimes, but that's not bad. I just get the feeling that you want to do the right things for the right reasons."

I didn't know what to say, so I just stammered a meager, "Thanks". We walked quietly until the smell of her aromatic body lotions was nearly overpowered by the smell of dried salt fish from the upcoming marketplace. It was time to part ways. "If I don't make it out of this school, I'll be your friend," I said. Making friends was not a priority to me this year. Why should it be? I didn't plan on staying. But now, changing schools was looking impossible. I'd have to make friends to survive. Krystal had friends. If I was to start, I might as well start with her.

She smiled, and this time when she put a hand on my arm, I didn't flinch. I was still awkward and didn't know what to do next. Luckily, I didn't have to do anything. She lifted the hand, patted my shoulder once more, then gave me a fake punch in the chest. "I'll see you around, big guy." She turned and walked up the gravel path that would eventually lead to her house. Mangy dogs yipped as she passed them by. She turned only once to wave at me.

Something was different about Krystal. I don't know what it was, but I realized that I was glad to have talked with her. Even so, that didn't stop me from brushing off my arm where she'd touched me. Force of habit, I suppose. I also realized that I was still standing in place, just watching her go.

Something was different about me, too. I felt lighter as I walked along. At work my duties didn't seem so burdening. I shoveled gravel for that first hour, not even tiring like I'd been doing for the last couple of months, but as the shift dragged on, my memory turned to that three-hundred yuan transfer fine. Again, my spirits sank and I wondered what to do. My mother and I had sacrificed so much to make this work, and in the end, I'd still be stuck here.

That night I was afraid to tell my mother about the bad news. I'd almost resolved to wait until tomorrow, but when she asked, "Iddo, something is troubling you?" She waited a moment. "Why not just have out with it?"

I lowered my head as a tear wet the corners of my eyes. I willed it to dry so that my mother wouldn't see. When I'd finished telling her, she just stared stoically at me. She was thinking hard, then a tight smile crossed her lips. She got up from the table and walked over to a small cedar box. From inside the musky container she pulled a beautiful pearl necklace, my grandmother's necklace. I hadn't seen her wear it more than twice in the last five years, the latter occasion being at my father's funeral.

"You can't sell Grandma's necklace!" I protested. It was the only real heirloom of worth we had. It meant the world to her.

She just rested it on the table, brushing a finger, then two, across the polished milky surface. Her eyes were full of tender memories. When she finished reminiscing, she smiled. Her eyes were moist with love. "When I think of the best way to honor our ancestor's memory," she said, "it's not by hoarding their old belongings. Even if some part of us lives on after we die, I don't think that money or possessions are what we'll relish. If we leave anything to our children or grandchildren, I think we'll be most happy by leaving them an opportunity. Your grandmother would haunt me if all I did with it was store it in a jewelry box. If this can help you live your dream, and you have a wonderful dream, I think that's what she'd want. It's what I want for you."

I couldn't hold my tears back anymore. It would seem that today I was ignoring most of my natural reservations. Without reservation, I leaped into my mother's arms and hugged her tightly. It was one of those rare moments of sacrifice that binds a mother and son. Yeah, mothers are always sacrificing for their children. That's just what they do. I know this, but this time I couldn't help but show my gratitude.

The next day I skipped my first class as I worked with the school counselor to arrange all the transfer documents. I went through the day, and didn't even see Krystal. I don't know where she was, but I had enough on my mind that I didn't really miss her. I did want to tell her the good news, but there were still two days left before the school year ended. There'd still be time.

The end of the week came and went. I'd just exited the computer lab, curious to find a map of the woods. All I found was an out of focus aerial image of the vast forested jungle. Going around this thing would be expensive. Did Mother really expect me to hike through them, or would she find some way of getting me to New Tum District? She'd already sacrificed Grandmother's heirloom. Did she have another piece of valuable jewelry to hock? The thought of cutting through the woods terrified and excited me. I could do it, I think. Maybe it was all just fantasy. If I ever got more than a kilometer into the dense growth, I'd usually turn back from fear. I was no adventurer. I was just hopeless Iddo.

The image of the woods from that computer screen were still fresh on my mind as I left the school building for my last time. I don't think I had a burning desire to see Krystal, but I still found myself wandering close to her house to see if I could catch a glimpse of her. I saw her father outside occasionally. He was usually drunk or throwing cat calls at passing women, but I never did see Krystal. I stayed at home for one month following the end of the school year, and eventually I stopped walking by Krystal's house. She was quickly becoming a memory of my past.

Since I couldn't stay at home while attending medical school and since I would need to find work in New Tum, my mother insisted that I leave now instead of later when school was about to start back up again. I wanted to stay at home with her, but she argued that finding a job before school started up would be better.

She was right, of course. I tried to get ready five or six different times, but the cement company kept offering some good overtime work. Finally, when there were only three weeks left until school started up, I couldn't put it off any longer.

With just enough money to get by, not even enough for a bus ride to the district, I packed what I could into my school bag. The rest of my clothing was bundled into a ball and tied to the end of a stick. Conversation was quiet as my mother accompanied me to the edge of the woods. I was suddenly aware of her quick breaths. I knew it had nothing to do with whatever illness she'd been unable to shake.

"Thanks, for everything." I gave her a hug.

"You will be careful, yes?" She asked.

"I'll be fine. Don't worry."

"Maybe we can find another way," she wavered.

"It's all right. I can do this. I love you. Good bye-" It was harder saying this than I'd imagined.

"Don't worry about coming back for any breaks. Just work hard and save your money. You can come back at the end of the school year."

"You're the best," I said. Again, I gave her one last hug.

She stood in place and watched me leave. My last image of her before the woods completely hid her from my view, was her looking helpless. Her one hand was over her chest, the other up high enough to bite at her knuckles. She would be lonely. I wanted to turn back, but I knew she'd beat herself up if I stayed on account of her fears. So I pressed on, deep into the thickest part of the woods.

Chapter 6

There are reasons people shy away from the woods. I had little choice. I had to brave them. It is true, death hangs below the branches of those age-old trees. Only a desperate fool braves the punishing shade. The desperate fool doesn't always come back out. The woods are full of life and death. It's the way of nature. But the abominations of man call upon the retribution of the woods.

There were no roads or paths cutting directly through the woods. Everyone knew that the woods sheltered the most dangerous of evils. Everyone except maybe Krystal. This was more than mere superstition; Stronger even than the religious believed in their own gods. It was just the way of it. If you had business on the other side, you found a way around. If you couldn't afford to go around, you didn't go at all. Sure, there were a couple of small trails that penetrated the very edge of this formidable place, but even they petered out quickly. They just serviced locals looking for firewood. Rarely did they venture deep enough that you couldn't see or hear civilization.

I followed one such trail, for the first hundred meters into the woods, before it ended. Trees and greenery crowded me, filling every void like water fills an ocean. I could still hear sounds of civilization. The blanket of bamboo, shrubs, and other plants were smothering the smells of the city. I noticed the stink of civilization again, but only upon exiting a particularly thick patch of undergrowth. Another hundred meters and even that was gone. Everything about the city was gone.

My chest tightened with fear. Ever since my first day at the concrete plant, I had little time to explore these woods. My nerves had nothing to do with it. There was just no time. Now I had no choice but to enter them. Unlike before, I couldn't just skirt the inside edge. I had to cut through the middle, hopefully emerging on the opposite side. I'd never been more than a kilometer inside here before. What awaited me in those mysterious depths, I would never have believed.

For an hour I walked. The eerie quiet that set me at unease before disappeared, replaced by the sounds of the forest itself. Maybe these sounds had been present before, but I hadn't noticed them. Trees creaked and groaned, straining under their own weight. Birds and insects sang to their own rhythms. Occasionally I paused as a loud crack issuing from some nearby thicket warned of larger, potentially dangerous creatures. Then, as if nothing had happened, all I would hear was the refreshing trickle of some stream, often no wider or deeper than my foot.

This was a kind of place I could lose myself in and

actually be happy, as odd as that might sound. The first banana tree I came to was empty, like it had recently been picked. I didn't know how I'd find food, especially if I had competition for it. I still felt at peace. No politics, no grind. Just nature—hopefully just nature. If one could learn to survive nature, one could easily thrive in nature.

Of course, there was still the folklore surrounding these woods. It would be nice if Krystal was right and it was all exaggeration. Just a bunch of tales meant to frighten and excite. My mind flashed back to every story I'd ever heard. Then like a cat slinking across the edge of my memory, waiting to pounce, the dangerous drunkard from my past assaulted my peace of mind. There had been someone or something more out here than even he. What was it that I'd seen back then?

The memory was a shadow. There was true bulk to the thing. It was larger than any man. It couldn't have been a man, maybe some form of gorilla. But no, there weren't any apes around here. The more my mind wrestled with the memory, the darker the woods felt. When at last, a nervous chill tingled through my core, I realized I was needlessly punishing myself. I'd taken something beautiful that I could sense and turned it into something horrifying.

I stopped and with a few calm breaths, collected my thoughts. I realized the feeling for what it was and it helped me relax. I'd just gained a small measure of wisdom and knowledge. If I looked for, or even thought too long about evil stories, I'd find darkness. Not only in the world out there, but inside myself. My mood would absorb the darkness. If I looked at nature or dwelled on the goodness of people, I'd discover the beauty all around me. I'd find peace.

This train of thought also led me to consider those sto-ries from another perspective. This time I wasn't thinking about the atrocities that were associated with them, I was more or less understanding how some people could work their way to doing dishonorable acts. Not that I could ever understand enough to see myself ever doing them, but I could see how enough talk could eventually morph a person into the very evil they were obsessing about. If one talks about a subject long enough, then they believe it. If they believe it long enough, they accept the reality of it. Eventually they surround themselves with like-mind-ed people and without realizing what has happened, they are part of a culture. Cultures are not all good. They serve to justify the behaviors of their members, even if those accepted behaviors are despicable.

While I knew that I shouldn't dwell on the stories I'd heard, I also knew that I should at least be mindful of them. I was making my way through the very woods that seeded these stories. If there was any truth to them, I should take every degree of caution that was practical to stay safe. As far as those stories went, I suspected that few people knew more about the folklore surrounding the woods than I.

From man-eating cat to raging bears, the scariest creatures were the men of the woods. The witches were said to have meetings out here somewhere. If you were unlucky enough to stumble into their ring, your body would be trapped in a stump, your soul feeding their dev-ilish spells until your body shriveled and turned to dust.

The Believers too would retreat to these parts, join

one another in singing and praying. While the witches summoned the dark powers, the Believers were said to draw powers of light from the sun. The heat of their fervor was said to blind a man to all sense. The Believers didn't just draw on your life to spread their spells like a witch, they brainwashed you into performing their spells with them. It's been said that a Believer is more powerful than a witch, because witches consume everything, whereas Believers just add to their numbers. It's rumored that they can even raise the dead to further their aims.

Then there was the hangman. Little was known about him, just whispered terrors that circulated among the groups of drunken men late at night. He was said to be more than a man, or, rather, less than a man; some creature of the forest itself. I'd heard more whispers of the hangman from the older men at the concrete plant. I didn't know what all to make of it.

I had serious doubts that I'd cross paths with any of those supposed dangers. The one thing that I feared most was the bones of the little ones. Deep in my heart, this was the reason I entered the woods in the first place. After my first encounter with the drunkard those eight months ago, I knew they'd be here. My secret hope was that I'd find the little ones still alive, maybe do something to help save them.

The problem stemmed from the birth control laws of the region. Afraid of overpopulation, poverty, and who knows what else, when the Chinese government tried to grab a piece of the territory after the indigenous countries crumbled, a law was enacted that each family could have no more than one child, even though for their own people, they no longer had such restrictions. Doctors were required to assist in all abortions to families with more than one child. Not everybody could afford doctors, though. Many children were born at home with the aid of midwives.

Despite a mother's hope, nobody could hide a second child forever. In one way or another, taxes will find you, no matter how poor you are. Once a baby was born, nobody would demand that it be executed, but when the authorities found out, a lifetime tax would be added to those families, most of whom were already in the dregs of poverty.

For some reason, regardless of how financially well off a family might be, many fathers would take their young seconds into the woods, only to return alone. Nobody ever asked any questions or pointed any fingers. It had become one of those cultural blind spots. So many were guilty that nobody dared accuse. Even I dared not ask my mother if she'd ever had a second child. I knew this was a painful topic for her, but that didn't mean that she or my father was actually guilty of it. I couldn't imagine it of them. If they were, I really didn't want to know.

It so happened that while I was pondering this, I heard another snap of a twig. This one was close. I froze, held my breath, and tried to hear beyond my own heartbeat and the slight whistle in my lungs. Every bird and insect seemed to mirror my stealth. But nothing happened. I exhaled and lifted my foot to take another step—but then another stick cracked. No, something was out there, and it was close.

My legs were aching, but I dared not shift to a more comfortable position. I was sure that I was about to encounter whatever or whoever was out here. Surrounding me was a thick curtain of trees. Somebody would have to be no more than four meters away to see me, but how close was the noise? Another snap, and I relaxed. The source of the noise was staying in one place, not terribly concerned with stealth.

I wanted to keep moving, but how could I? After having given myself a thorough self-evaluation, I knew that I'd be saddened beyond all measure if I ever found out that this noise was some helpless abandoned baby. Most likely it was just an animal and I was fretting about nothing. I'd walk over, scare up an unsuspecting creature, and be back on my way, laughing at myself.

Still, I lifted each foot, careful to place it back on the ground only if there was a rock or patch of wet leaves. Until I knew what lay before me, I'd be as silent as a ghost. As I neared the noise, I hugged a giant tree. It was almost as thick as myself. Using it for cover, I leaned my head around to get a better view. My breath caught. On the opposite side of the tree, just beyond a few smaller brush trees, I saw a man. He was slowly pacing around a small bundle on the ground. In his hand was a bottle of poor-man's wine, though he could obviously afford better. This wine, made from palm trees, had a nauseatingly sweet smell that I could detect from where I stood. It was strong stuff and he was sucking it down fast.

The man's hair was well trimmed in a longer cut that was popular with the thirty- and forty-year-old men of our region. From the neatness of his clothes, I could tell that he was a man of some means. He ate well enough, because his body was fit like only a balanced diet could provide. Instinctively I knew that he was not a Believer.

They never drank alcohol. A witch, maybe, but I doubted it. Then I saw a tiny innocent hand pop up from the bundle on the ground. It reached for its father. My heart sank. The man was here to dispose of a second. My blood boiled. Here was a man who could afford the tax but was choosing not to.

Seconds passed and a small cooing emanated from the bundle. This child, not even a year old, must've known something bad was happening. It was spreading on the sweetness as thick as frosting on a cake. It was that same skill every baby instinctively knows. It re-wires a woman's heart, turning her from a carefree woman into a mother. It morphs a selfish man into a providing guardian. Crying would not help it here. Crying would only make its father angry. It had to appeal to the man's heart. This appeal was probably why the man was still pacing around the child and hadn't already left it alone or killed it.

I watched intently. The man had come very deep into the woods to be rid of this infant. His resolve would not be easily deterred. Plus, every swig from his pungent wine bottle would allow a little more evil to fog his brain. The man was not simply going to leave the child alone. He planned to kill the baby, else why would he still be waiting around? He was trying to gain courage from the bottle to do that last terrible deed before he went back home.

I had to do something. The father never strayed far enough from the baby for me to run in and snatch it. I'd never been good at confrontation. He was a full-grown man, and despite the strength I'd gained in the last couple months, I couldn't hope to stand up to him if he got violent. Nor would I be able to outrun him. But would he let me leave and take the baby with me? He wanted to be rid of it. Maybe-

My body trembled. I had to act. I was to be a doctor because I valued life. How could I live with myself if I neglected my own conscience? My breath came in ragged gasps. I was going to do something. Sweat prickled all over my chest and I half wished I hadn't followed my curiosity to this spot. That kind of thinking was wrong. I gave my conscience a figurative prick. I needed to be here. Because I was here, I might save my first life. It was now or never.

With my back to the tree, hoping the man would not figure out where I spoke from, I shouted, "Hey!" Even though my voice sounded more like a loud squeak, I knew he'd heard me.

"Who's out there?" he threatened. "This is none of your business. Come out where I can see you!"

The tone of the man's voice alarmed not only me, but the baby, too. A startled cry rose from its blankets and I froze. Memories of another drunken man some eight months ago returned. I remembered how ferocious his temper had been when he'd run into me. This man's speech wasn't slurred, but it would be soon. Whatever compassion held him back was now replaced by guilty rage. This would not turn out good for the baby or for me. I had to make a run for it. I had to grab the baby and flee into the woods. Maybe I'd get lucky and he wouldn't catch us. But my feet would not move.

Though I wanted to peel away, my back seemed to press tighter to the tree trunk. All of a sudden, I found a muscular man with flammable breath standing in front of me. I had no route of escape. My eyes bulged. His hand was an iron vise that clamped around my neck. I could no longer hear the baby crying; all I could focus on was the protruding veins of his forearm as his muscles stretched his hairless brown skin tight. His unyielding hand was cutting off the air to my lungs.

I tried to kick, only to find my feet just flailing useless below me. He had me pinned to the tree, with my feet off the ground. My head went hot and dizzy, and my eyes felt like popping as I struggled to focus on the man's face. I don't know if my brain was oxygen deprived or what really happened, but at once, silence seemed to permeate the air, as if the absence of sound was a thick insulating mist. It's hard to notice how loud the noises of a forest are, until they stop. Despite my fuzzed vision, I could see his eyes widen. As if a spirit was entering the world, music could now be heard.

The melody grew like a wisp of wind, focusing like a vision. It amplified louder until it focused into a deep clear voice, soft and booming all at once. I'd heard this song before—eight months ago, just after I'd encountered the other man who'd entered the woods on the same mission as this man. As the man loosened his grip on my throat, we both listened. I hadn't seen many black men in my life, but that deep singing bass was the voice I would have associated with a very big black man.

"Swing low, sweet chariot / Coming for to carry me home . . ."

Chapter 7

In the woods, justice is swift. Judgment pronounced without a trial. The punishment can even precede the crime. But the crime would surely happen otherwise. The judge and executioner were one. No law, save a higher law, can guide such condemnation. Still, who could ever forgive a soul who waited till after the heinous crime was committed, especially when the murder was obviously imminent? There was one who wandered the woods, striking fear into all those who dare attempt the cowardice act. He couldn't catch all, but for those he did find, no mercy on earth is meted to them. They will never return home from the woods.

The man pinned me to the great tree. Bits of bark and twig wedged between my shirt and sweat slicked skin. He was frantic—I was frantic! He'd heard all the same stories that I had. Undoubtedly, he wouldn't navigate these woods, if not for the courage lent him by his bottle. In his distraction, he eased up his choke hold on me and I drew in short labored breaths. His clammy palms still prevented me from wiggling away, but my vision cleared enough to see again.

Sickeningly sweet palm wine assaulted my nose. Nasty alcohol laced saliva sprayed from his mouth. The stench assaulted me from every pour of his sweat tainted skin, mostly in great rivulets draining through his greasy hair as it beaded toward his darkened nose and chin. His body contorted as he struggled to hold me and look all around at the same time. The low voice of the singer bounced off every tree, as if its owner was everywhere and nowhere.

My captor's eyes swiveled, eventually returning to look at me. I could see a bloodshot panic around those dilated pupils. He knew something. A story that I didn't know. Enough to be terrified. If he was panicked, I was doubly so. With one free hand, he brought a finger to his lips, ordering me to be silent, as if that was a problem. I couldn't have made a sound if I tried. This whole thing was a nightmare. I expected to jump awake, get a drink of water, go pee, and go back to bed with hopes of a better dream. Somewhere in the back of my mind, I felt relieved that my bladder hadn't already emptied itself. I could still wake up from this. Only in dreams was I ever so frightened that running or speaking was impossible, but this was no dream.

I've often heard that the human mind can be brilliant, but slow. That's why we rely so heavily on computers. As this was happening, that axiom held little weight. My mind was racing faster than light, almost fast enough to give the illusion that these thoughts were all speaking at once. There was regret that I wouldn't make it to school; sadness, knowing my mother would never know what happened to me; the awful realization that I would die a coward; the curiosity of who or what was nearly upon us; the poor baby on the ground, swaddled in blankets, unlikely to live beyond the day; guilt for disappointing my father and wondering if this was his vengeance that he was directing from the grave; then, oddly enough, I thought about Krystal and wondered if she would cry when she heard of my disappearance. More than likely she'd just want to speak at my funeral.

"You brought'im ta me," the drunk whispered, snapping me out of my end-of-life daze.

Was it just me, or was his speech getting worse? "I didn't bring anyone here, I-I-I'm alone."

"I was'n born'esterday!" He hissed, spittle spraying from his lips, landing across my face. "No boy you'age has any reason a be out'ere alone. You're with'im, aren't you?"

"N-no, I d-d-on't know who—"

"Quiet!" He placed his free hand over my mouth. The taste of his salt, mingled with the sour sweetness of his alcohol-infused sweat, invaded my mouth. I nearly gagged, but knew better than to let that happen.

Only a moment ago, I was about to be strangled to death and would be by now if not for this new threat. Maybe it would've been a better death than suffering at this new monster's hands. Clearly my captor didn't expect me to help fend off the new threat. He thought I'd brought it to him. Then I realized why he hadn't killed me yet. If he thought I was connected to this singing beast, then he planned on using me.

No, not that, either. He was probably too drunk by now to think that clearly. He was just too distracted to finish me off.

Whoever was out there was no friend of mine. My captor had to know this. If anything, I would simply serve as a fat human shield, my captor holding off the threat long enough for me to die an ignominious death and for him to make a run for it. I doubted this man could escape, though. I'd just be a fleshy nuisance before the drunk was killed, too.

There must be a way to free myself. Planning under pressure was not my strong suit. All I could do was wiggle and squirm, try to break free. No sooner did I try, than I found a knee shoved hard into my lower gut. I'd never been outright assaulted before, but always thought that with my extra bulk, a blow like that might have been softened some. Yeah, right! If not for the hand holding me up by my neck, I would have collapsed in pain. All the fight in me was gone. How pathetic I was. Of the fights I'd witnessed in the past, few were ever resolved so quickly. Most men and almost as many boys, could take a punch and keep on fighting. Then there was me, pacified by a single blow. At least when I died today, nobody else would know.

"I am not going to swing today," the drunk whispered to me. "Do you hear me? If your friend puts that noose around my neck, I'll rip your throat out."

That confirmed it, I realized. The singing man was the one they called the hangman. Obviously, escape was possible. How else would any rumors about the hangman get started? If only I could—

No. It wouldn't work. I was not that agile. Very few people had escaped this hangman to tell about him. Someone like me wouldn't stand a chance. That's ignoring the fact that I first had to escape this drunk. With two seemingly impossible foes to escape from, I knew my death was inevitable. Still, I couldn't quite accept that. How does one accept one's fate? All I knew was that I was terrified. Fear of death, pain, brutality, and somewhere in the mix, I was worried about my mother. Compounding my discomfort, the bark and twigs that were matted to my back kept scratching and causing my back to itch.

My body trembled and a small whimper escaped my lips as my jaw quivered. The drunk whispered, "I'm going to move my hand. Don't you dare make a sound."

I resolved to obey, but I don't know why I cared what he told me. After all, regardless of what happened, he still planned on killing me. I watched his hand as it pulled away from my mouth. I choked back a sudden urge to cry. Instead I watched as the hand moved down. He lifted his leg and I saw him pull a large sheath knife from his boot. As he raised the sharpened steel, his eyes arched past me, then around in a circle. He was looking for the hangman. The hangman was nowhere to be seen, but his singing was everywhere to be heard. He sounded so very close.

Just as my captor's eyes found their way back to looking at me, a thick manila rope filled my vision. We both looked down at its sudden appearance. It was looped around his neck. His eyes went wide with delayed horror, then he was yanked backward. His knife fell from his hands and his feet flew high in the air. He landed about three meters away from where he'd been standing.

My body was heavy, and my feet failed to support me as the man was dragged away. This was my only chance to escape, but I couldn't muster the strength. I sank to my knees and watched in horror. In front of me, kicking and cursing, the man was being pulled by the neck with that thick fibrous rope. On the other end of the rope, about fifteen feet away, was the biggest creature I'd ever seen. At first, I couldn't believe he was actually a man. He was a veritable giant with features the likes of which I'd never seen on any man in my life.

Barely even straining, his muscular arms—almost as thick as my considerable belly—pulled the murderous father several feet with each tug. His body wasn't out of proportion, either. The trunk of his body was massive, covered in a tan homespun-style vest with brown cotton or wool trousers. But his head! The rest of his body could have passed for a normal, albeit stocky giant, but that head was enough to paralyze anyone from a single glance.

Most people's heads are taller than they are wide. This man's head was wider than it was tall. It looked almost lemon shaped, if the lemon were lying sideways and was as large as a watermelon. Stretching from one end of his face to the other was a gargantuan smile. Each tooth was at least twice as large as both of my thumbs put side by side. This bulking deformity of man could have easily bitten the head off the drunk who was now at his feet.

Great bushy eyebrows crowded close to each other above those dark slanted eyes. Maybe it was a shadow, but even the whites of his eyes seemed a darker shade of gray. The hangman looked down his flat nose at the now pitiful drunk. Anyone would be pitiful compared to this lumbering mass of muscle. With one hand, big enough to wrap halfway around the drunk's chest, he grabbed the man by the ribs and lifted him into the air. With the noose firmly snugged around the drunk's neck, the giant's other hand gripped the opposite end of the rope with a white-knuckled fist. As if it was no big deal, he single-handedly lobbed the man's body into the air, arching him over a high, stout branch of the nearest tree.

Arms and legs flailed wildly as the drunk flew into the air. Then his neck cracked as the full weight of his body was snapped straight. His limbs flinched, but he didn't have time to suffocate. He was spared mercifully by that broken neck. The giant let the body dangle for only a few seconds before lowering him. The whole while, through that massively toothy grin, the giant kept repeating, "Swing low, sweet chariot / Coming for to carry me home . . ."

The drunk never had a chance. Whatever stories he'd heard, he must have imagined them to contain some degree of exaggeration. If he'd known what he was really up against, he'd have run for all he was worth, not daring to wait around until the hangman showed himself.

The giant started into another verse as he unfastened the rope from the corpse's neck. "Sometimes I'm up, and sometimes I'm down / Coming for to carry me home / But still my soul feels heavenly bound . . ."

I'd escaped one death only to be confronted by another. Yet all I could do was stare at the casual brutality of the scene before me. I would be next, but running never crossed my mind. My jaw hung low in shock. I was hypnotized by this creature. I completely forgot about the baby, bundled several meters away, at least I forgot until the monster lumbered over to where it was crying.

Without thinking I yelled, "Not the baby! Don't hurt the baby!"

The giant looked back at me, pausing in his song for only a second or two. His smile remained, but he looked almost hurt. Then, more gently than I guessed a behemoth of his stature could manage, he cradled the child in the palm of one hand. He ended his song, "Tell all my friends I'm coming there too / Coming for to carry me home." As he intoned these last words, he looked at me again. With one huge hand, he waved for me to follow.

Chapter 8

I witnessed one such judgment with my own eyes. It hurt. But not as bad as if it hadn't happened. We all have dreams. Sometimes we rob ourselves of them; sometimes others rob us of them. Some men deserve what they get. The hangman has ended many men's dreams; I can only imagine they'd be nightmares if not otherwise. At the same time, he preserved and enriched the dreams of the innocent. I found a taste of those beautiful dreamers that day. That day, my dreams acquired a greater depth, not to mention, duration.

Each vine that slapped against my face and each cracking twig under my feet took me one step closer to a mystery that I couldn't have been prepared for. I don't fancy myself an adventure seeker and never have. If ever there was someone to hang back and play safe, I was that person. True, I had my moments when this philosophy was incongruent with my actions, but for the most part I've always been conservative.

While growing up I would position myself so that in a game with peers, I was safely out of the main flow. I did not want to be called on, or risk anything. In school, I never volunteered a comment or answer. If ever called upon, I would simply try to regurgitate exactly what I knew the teacher wanted to hear, even if I disagreed with the answer. Was I a coward? Yes. Definitely, but I was comfortable in my level of ambiguity.

Only in the last year had I deviated much from my typical behavior. I hadn't thought much about it until that day in the woods. I could find no reason for the change, but upon inspecting my life, I saw myself as two people. First there was Iddo the ever cautious and cowardly teen. Then there was Iddo the compassionate, or Iddo the bold, I wasn't sure which. That's the part of me that landed myself in this situation.

I couldn't kid myself. I was still afraid. More than afraid, really, I was terrified. Maybe shock was what compelled me to do the insane. The sounds of insects filled the air again and my cheap shoes glided over the spongy leaves of the ground like feathers. My feet felt so light, and my stomach was twisting so acutely, I barely realized I was walking. The hangman had bidden me follow, and despite my better judgment, I couldn't help but comply.

For a good ten minutes, I trailed behind this giant, oblivious to my own motives. Slowly my wits eased back into focus and I was able to clear the fog in my head enough to think beyond my automatic reactions. I looked hard at the hangman's back. If I'd never followed him, I would have always remembered him as a giant, twice the size of any normal man, thick with that bone-grinding mouth of his. Now that I could study him, I realized that he was likely just under two and a half meters tall. I knew that in some parts of the world this wouldn't be considered too terribly uncommon, but for us, being a good deal shorter than the rest of the world, he was a giant. Yes, he was still thick. Most of him was muscle, but his midsection hinted at a girdle of fat hugging his belly.

He didn't look fully Asian, either. I'd seen lots of people of mixed blood, usually an American or European white guy mixing his seed with some Asian woman. Their offspring were beautiful. They were the type you might find on TV. Never would they associate with someone of my class. This was the first time that, at least as I presumed, I'd seen a man whose foreign parent was black. He had the deep strong voice and darker skin that were unusual around here. While one of his parents must have been black, the other was obviously Asian. This was all too apparent in his face. In the couple times he looked back at me, I got to study his face a little more. Obviously, he was somehow deformed.

Yes, his face did look like a cross between an Asian and a black man, but it clearly wasn't right. Symmetry still ruled his features, but no race of man would have normally produced such a shape. I'd heard of Microcephaly, where a baby is born with an abnormally shrunken head. Could this be its opposite?

The farther I followed him, the more I learned about him. Sometimes you don't have to talk with a person to learn about them. His terrifying face was slowly taking a different shape in my mind. Instead of the spanning grin that at first held so much malice and intimidation, I now saw a physically and quite possibly mentally deformed man who was driven out here because nobody could accept him anywhere else.

I almost imagined him as a young boy, with parents who thought he might grow out of his face, only for them to discover that he would always be slow witted and deformed. Then, in desperation, they fell back on the only culturally acceptable practice they knew to follow. They abandoned him in these woods. This explanation made sense to me. If that had happened, and he survived, it would explain his resentment for all these fathers who came to forsake their children. He would wander the woods looking to dole out punishment for the inhumane treatment he'd received at the hand of his own parents.

But what of this infant he now carried in his hand? Take away that noose and coiled rope that wrapped around the man's shoulder and the hangman might actually look gentle. But how could I know? No way could he take care of the child. Then again, the baby was surprisingly happy. I could hear it coo and giggle.

The more I watched the hangman, the more I felt my heart calming to a normal beat. Finally, I found myself in possession of my own wits enough to address him.

"Sir?"

He didn't respond.

"Excuse me, sir—"

He turned around.

For a moment those giant teeth that stretched around his face seemed to stare right at me. His eyes were almost completely covered by his dark bushy eyebrows. I had to look down at his feet. "W-where are we going? What's going to happen to the baby?"

He just let out a deep hearty chuckle, then started back into his song. "... Coming for to carry me home ..."

If he didn't want to answer me, then fine, but I was still going to follow until I knew the baby would be safe. Not that I could do anything if the hangman suddenly turned violent. Still, I had to know. If he wouldn't answer me straight, I'd have to see for myself. Maybe I'd be able to grab the baby while this hangman slept. I could sneak away at night. Then again, he did seem gentle enough with the child. But what was he going to do with it?

After half an hour of hiking, my legs throbbed with the pace this much larger man set. I also wanted to scream out and demand that if he didn't know any other songs, to either quit singing or to talk like a normal person. He seemed to never run out of verses, but often repeated others for no apparent reason. But he was no normal person and I knew I'd never find the courage to voice my annoyance.

As we continued he must have read my mind. He went from singing his repetitive song to humming it. For the next couple of kilometers, the woods seemed to thicken and I had a hard time keeping up. Stumbling along, I wiped little droplets of blood from the itching scratches that spidered up both my arms. Maybe this man was purposefully trying to torture me, leading me along the most wretched parts of the woods to test my resolve. If he wanted to see me crack, he wouldn't have much farther to go. I was ready to sit down and give up. We were traveling deeper into the forest, and more or less in the direction I needed to go, but his hiking was too fast for me. I'm certain that I could have found an easier way around this stretching thicket. My backpack kept snagging and holding me back and my pack stick was always in the way.

With infuriating exhaustion, I stopped, leaned up against a tree, and wheezed. A dull ache was growing in my side and if I didn't stop to rest, it would have become unbearable. The hangman just kept trudging along. Part of me wanted to shout for him to wait. Another part of me thought good riddance. It didn't matter. Within a minute he could no longer be seen or heard. I was alone again.

I looked up into the sky. Streaks of sun blazed down through the canopy. The smell of sap from the broken branches left in my wake was not exactly pleasant. Maybe it was because of the abuse they reaped on my bare skin, or maybe they just stank naturally. I never would've guessed that so much time had passed since I first took to the woods, but from the angle of the rays, I could presume that noon had arrived, and maybe even passed. My stomach chose this time to growl its confirmation of the lunch hour.

The side ache that hindered me was fading and I debated pulling out my meager packed lunch. My options were eat, try to catch up to the hangman, or continue on my way to New Tum District. Several kilometers of forest still separated me from the town. In fact, because of my delay, if I abandoned all thoughts of pursuing the hangman, I might still have to spend two nights instead of just one in these woods. I hadn't brought enough food for a third day.

I struggled with indecision. My thoughts kept getting

distracted by the humming of an insect or the alarmed chirping of birds. Then I heard something else, totally out of place. It was distant, but audible enough not to be mistaken. It was the muted sound of cheers and laughter. The sounds bounced off the trees, hiding the direction of the sound, but there could be no denying, I was hearing people. The only place I could imagine the voices coming from would be from wherever the hangman had hiked to.

I pushed off the tree, forgot about my lunch, and walked with every degree of caution I could muster. If there was really a group of people this deep in the woods and if the hangman had been leading me to them, they might be just as weird and dangerous as he. I couldn't turn away. Carefully I avoided snapping even the smallest twig as I moved. Too many questions needed to be answered and I couldn't live with the unsolved mystery of this day lingering forever in my mind.

As I crept along, the sounds both diminished and grew louder. The stinking sap that invaded my nostrils was replaced by a savory aroma that made my stomach growl louder. I only noticed this because my stomach was making more noise than my feet.

The closer I got, the fewer voices were heralding the hangman's return. Still, those that were making noise had become clearer. I was moving in the right direction. Then the dense undergrowth of the woods cleared and I found myself in a relatively open section of forest. I studied the ground at my feet. Many other feet had compacted the earth where I stood. Slowly I raised my head up. I had to blink a couple of times to be sure. What I saw was impossible to believe.

Chapter 9

Truth. Life is easy to organize in our heads. We do it every minute, even our subconscious performs the task while in our sleep. But you've met the people who've organized everything wrong. Maybe you're one of them. For those of us fortunate enough to have organized things appropriately, we pity them. They don't notice their error, because they already have a firm grasp on their own reality. Funny how they look at us the same way as we look at them. Who knows, maybe they are right and we are the mistaken lot.

Well, in my case, I was lost, but found my way. Like most everyone else I knew, I'd been raised on rumors that turned out to be false. I knew they were false the second my eyes beheld the truth. Truth may be interpreted differently by all. Usually truth is confirmation of our own opinion, but when it's not, then it's much harder to accept. In my case, while truth went against the grain of everything I thought I knew, in fact it was a source of great relief.

I had to stop myself from approaching too quickly. My feet had a mind of their own. Only a couple steps ago, I'd been shoving my way through some of the densest undergrowth I'd ever had the displeasure of scratching against my skin. Now I was in a clearing. Giant trees still cast a greenish shadow, but not a single shrub threatened my flesh with thorny spikes.

Up ahead was a pristine lake. Distant ripples suggested an abundance of jumping fish. I could smell it. The body of water carried a unique scent. Unlike the sappy herbal smell of the forest, or the savory aroma from cook fires, this was a humid, refreshing sensation. The lake alone might have beckoned me on, but that wasn't the biggest reason why I was compelled to advance. The voices I'd barely heard on the other side of the bramble were not only clear, but now had faces attached to them.

There must've been close to a hundred, at least that I could see right now. Not an adult among them. None that is, save the hangman himself. Children of all ages flocked around this monstrosity of a man, oblivious or unconcerned with his scary appearance. All were eager to see the newest addition to their—family? I was fifteen years old myself, almost sixteen. Not a single kid here was older than me. Their ages ranged from just a few months old to about fifteen years, or so I guessed. With no adult guardians, the older kids were taking care of the younger ones.

I stood, taking in this community of what I could only assume were the seconds that the hangman had saved over the years. Suddenly I found myself to be the focus of curiosity for one boy, about eight years old. He approached me with eyes full of interest and caution. There was something odd about him—a sense of maturity generally not found in children his age. I studied him and he studied me. For such a large and isolated gathering of children, I was surprised that they were self-sufficient. Most of the kids over five years old had clothing, even if many of their outfits resembled this eight-year-old's garb.

His clothing was limited to a large flag of woven plant fiber, but was draped over his shoulders falling in front and in back, nearly to his knees. A thin piece of cordage, probably made here, tied around his waist, securing the sheets in a half robe half dress sort of fashion. Though for him, fashion wasn't the right term. My guess is that his only goal was to keep the flaps from flying open and exposing his more tender regions.

"Hello there," a girl's voice called out.

I looked up from this little boy and saw her. She was one of the older kids, close to my age. She wore a slightly more complex garment, but not by much. Her face was smooth and her long, gnarled black hair hung nearly to her waist. I guessed that a comb was a scarce commodity around here. Still, she had kept her hair from turning into a large dreadlock, which was commendable.

"Hello," I replied. Normally I wasn't much for formality, always too shy to meet many new people. Still, I was quite possibly the first person raised outside this community to pay a visit. So, I hesitantly stuck out my hand to shake hers. She just looked at it, curious. Self-consciously I drew it back. For lack of anything better, I said, "My name is Iddo, what's yours?"

"And aren't you a handsome one, Iddo? Yes you are," she said with mock flattery. "You look like a little Daddy

Smiling, yes you do."

How was I supposed to respond to that? "Uh—"

"I'm Midnight. Yes I am. Midnight," she continued in that same condescending tone, tapping her chest as she spoke.

Of course, I realized. She and most of the children here would only know a primitive amount of language. Most of them had been brought here at such a young age that few would have learned how to speak very well. I'd already learned that the hangman wasn't much of a conversationalist, so they would've learned from one another. Likely the most any of them knew would have come from the simple baby talk their parents once used on them.

She smiled. It was a pretty smile. "This is Grub. Yes he is." She pointed to the eight-year-old boy who was still staring up at me. "He's my baby. Such a good boy."

Now it was my turn to be a little confused. Did she seriously want me to accept this eight-year-old boy as her son? How could she possibly claim him as her baby? As I tried to understand, she stepped closer, and put an arm around the boy. He said, with his eyes still fixed on me, "Mommy, this new daddy has big round tummy. Squishy-squishy."

He reached out and poked my stomach. I pulled back as he giggled. "Big round belly, yes it is." And to think that just a minute ago I'd thought this boy looked more mature for his age. He probably was just building up the courage to stab his finger into my gut.

The girl laughed a little, too. My face burned with embarrassment. I wasn't used to pretty girls laughing at me. I didn't like it. Even if she meant no harm by it. I was clearly no father to this boy.

"I'm not your daddy," I said.

There was a silence as they stared at me quizzically. The boy broke the moment by stating, "You're not my daddy. You're Daddy Iddo. My daddy is Daddy Chirp-chirp."

"Does this Chirp-chirp take care of you?"

"Mommies watch babies," Midnight explained. "I watch Baby Grub. Grub is my baby, yes he is. Daddies find food. Daddy Chirp-chirp finds food for Baby Grub and Mommy Midnight. Mommies cook food and mommies stay here. Daddies do not stay here. Daddies work."

It was making sense in a crude way. As I looked around the camp, I could see that most of the older girls had young children close by them. There weren't many boys older than Grub, so I could only guess that the older boys were out hunting or gathering food.

"Daddy Smiling brings new babies. When baby girls are big girls, big girls get babies and are mommies. Baby Grub is such a big boy, yes he is. Soon Baby Grub be daddy. I want new baby next time."

"So Daddy Smiling brings new babies?" I repeated.

"Yes. Smiling is big grand-daddy." She pointed at the hangman.

This all seemed so simple, and in this case, simple

was a hard thing to come to terms with. The hangman, or Daddy Smiling as Midnight called him, was saving new babies, bringing them here, and giving charge of them to the older girls. Midnight couldn't have been much older than Grub when she'd first been given charge of him. No wonder these kids radiated a higher degree of maturity, even if they all talked like a parent cooing over a newborn. They had a large degree of responsibility thrust on them at a very young age. And I thought I was being forced to grow up early.

"You hungry?" Midnight asked with a playful poke at my belly. She giggled.

Instinctively I placed my palm over my stomach to prevent any more probing fingers. Eat? Lunch? "I am hungry," and then for no reason whatsoever, I added, "Yes I am."

She waved me to follow. "Come on, it's okay, let's fill big bellies."

I shook my head, a dumb smile playing across my face. I could tell she was smart. Something about her eyes. I figured she'd be a quick learner if I tried to teach her to speak like a normal person.

She smiled back at me with the most genuine smile I'd ever seen in a girl my own age. I remembered Krystal and her haughty grin. When she curved her lips, I always felt small. But Midnight's smile buoyed me up. I took in a breath of fresh air. The air tasted fresher because it was in the presence of her radiant face. Yes, I wanted to teach her how to speak better. Not so much to give my charity to her, but because she deserved it. Maybe it was just my imagination, but I felt like she hungered for knowledge beyond what she could get here. I couldn't explain.

Crude huts made of sticks and thatch dotted the area, growing more numerous as we walked deeper into the little community. These doorless shelters were little more than lean-tos and offered little to no privacy. They were simply a place to sleep and find refuge during a rainstorm. In the middle of everything, I found several small fires burning. Many young girls were tending them. The area was like a community kitchen. Hanging from trees were dead birds, snakes, rodents, and various sorts of forest vegetation like bananas, fruits, roots, and herbs. The older girls were helping the younger girls learn as they prepared a late lunch.

Walking into the camp, I followed closely behind Midnight. She kept turning back, making sure I was following. I would've stepped up to her side, but I had to keep dodging Grub, as he hadn't yet lost his fascination with my unusually round body.

"Wait here, okay, I'll be right back. Just you wait."

I savored the wood smoked smells of cooked meats, nearly drooling with hunger. I shifted my attention back to Grub. He sat down on the ground and I followed his example. Midnight went to what could have only been a homemade clay pot. She tip-toed back, each step taken with care as she carried our lunch. She'd apparently been cooking before she'd met me. Then she scooped thick stew onto a single large banana leaf.

"Four piles?" I asked, looking at the steaming food. I knew that I was huskier than anyone else here, but did she really think I needed two servings? I studied the stew as its heat darkened and softened the wilting banana leaf.

I sat myself in front of one of the servings. I looked first at the various forest creatures that hung dead around this outdoor kitchen, then back to this slowly wilting serving leaf. I promised myself not to ask what was in this particular gruel.

Midnight didn't have to answer my question about the fourth pile of food. The commotion that grew from across the kitchen was all I needed. Several boys from about eight years old to my age were arriving in groups of three to five. Almost all of them were carrying some form of bounty. The smaller groups brought bundles of bananas, mushrooms, or other plant life. The larger groups carried dead animals of every forest variety, even little fishes from the lake. One boy dropped his load and rushed over to us. His eyes were a little suspicious of me when he asked my hostess, "Who's your daddy?"

My skin prickled with alarmed. That wasn't the right thing to say to a girl. I was pacified when Midnight responded, "Daddy Chirp-chirp, you're such a good boy, yes you are. Isn't he such a good boy?" She pinched his cheek.

Grub chimed in, "Daddy Chirp-chirp, this is Daddy Iddo."

"Hello Daddy Iddo," he said casually as he pinched Grub's cheek, then followed up by pinching mine. "You have no mommy to cook for you?"

"Uh . . . no. I'm new here. Midnight was kind enough to offer me lunch. I hope you don't mind."

"You talk funny, yes you do." He laughed. "You like Mommy Midnight's food. It's yummy-yummy, yes it is."

Well, so much for any possible territorial hostilities. This guy seemed pleased to share a banana leaf of food with me. At least now I understood why Midnight had prepared the fourth serving. Without any silverware, I followed their lead, and picked at the stew with my fingers, using my middle and index finger to scoop some of the more liquid portions into my mouth.

As soon as we were done, Chirp-chirp patted Midnight's back three times. Midnight released a belch that any teenage boy would've been proud to claim. She showed no signs of embarrassment. Rather, in turn, she patted his back three times. He responded with a burp of his own. "You're such a good girl, yes you are." He stood up and raced over to his friends.

Midnight repeated the patting on Grub. Grub had to really strain to burp, but he managed a small "Urp," to which Midnight responded, "Good release." Grub blushed slightly then ran after Chirp-chirp.

Midnight was about to come pat me on the back, but I had no burps in me, and little chance of forcing one. This strange custom had to have come from the practice of burping young infants. If I stayed for another meal, I'd have to keep this in mind. I stood, hoping to discourage her from the formality and asked, "Could you show me around the place?"

She drew near. "You want to see all. You're a smart one, aren't you? Yes you are."

I walked slow so she could take the lead. When she was next to me, she said, "Come, I'll show you all."

She didn't pass me. Instead, she walked next to me

and motioned for me to leave the cooking area. I took one more step when I felt three distinct thumps on my back. I was surprised to hear a gurgling burp rumble up my own throat.

Chapter 10

I'd found happiness. When I discovered it, I wanted to keep it. Why would anyone deny such a good thing? I guess I never was all that great at understanding the human psyche, not in anyone else and definitely not in myself. One thing I did learn, was that the hangman, the man the children called Daddy Smiling, is a good man. No, I wouldn't consider him a good member of society. Obviously society rejected him, else he wouldn't live like a recluse. Nor would his actions be condoned. Every month he killed men, sometimes more frequently. Almost every day he hiked through the woods, always searching for another man to dangle at the end of his noose. Every day he sang that same familiar tune, "Swing Low."

I could never dole out the punishment that he gave to the murderous fathers. For at least fifteen years, he's been a shadow. A mythical creature of the dark forest. Truly a humble vigilante who saved the most innocent

of lives. For this I both pity and admire him. He is physically deformed and mentally challenged. I don't know what goes through his mind, but the burden to punish and the drive to save those innocents—it consumes him. For anyone else, that burden would destroy them. In the eyes of his newly adopted children, he is larger than life. He is a hero.

That first afternoon with Midnight was memorable. The frenzy of teenage girls who wanted to accept care of the new infant was staggering. Bumping, pushing, and prodding. Every girl from ten years old to fifteen was clamoring to gain custody of the newest addition to the community. Everyone that is, except Midnight. Apparently, I was distraction enough to keep her attentions occupied.

"So . . ." I hesitated, not that I was attracted to her or anything, but I couldn't help but wonder: "Daddy Chirp-chirp, are you and he a thing?"

"He's a big boy. I'm big girl. Trees are things."

"Not what I meant." This would take some getting used to. Like me, she spoke English, but clearly communication would take some work. "Do you love him?"

"Yes. I love all. But not Flore." She hesitated, then added, "And not Burr and not Trula. Daddy Smiling loves all, so we love all, almost."

How was I to make her understand?

She must have noticed my consternation, because she placed a hand on my back and gave me a sympathetic smile. "Are you sad? Is my Iddo not happy?"

"I'm okay. I just—things are different here. I don't understand any of this. I mean, obviously you were all saved by Daddy Smiling and as you get older, the oldest take care of the youngest. And somehow you've broken into little family units, with a mother and a father. But is that because you and the father are—well, I'm sure you're not married, but you obviously are together. I've never heard you refer to each other as husband and wife or boyfriend and girlfriend, but I don't know if those words are even in your vocabulary. I hope I'm not offending you, this is just a lot for me to take in."

When I looked back in her eyes, I felt stupid. I could have been talking Russian for all she understood. Her eyebrows were stretched high on her forehead, as if by opening her eyes wider, she might understand better what I was saying. She nodded her head, but even while smiling, her mouth was hanging open just a bit. It betrayed her inability to follow what I'd just said.

"Hey," I sighed. "I'm sorry."

"You talk funny, yes you do."

We walked around the community. She took me down to the lake where some of the kids were swimming and spearing fish. Chirp-chirp was among them, Grub at his side. I couldn't tell if Chirp-chirp was playing with the younger boy, or if he was trying to teach something. Grub just seemed to be playing, though.

After walking around the camp several times, I realized we'd been talking, or rather, trying to talk, for the whole afternoon. With a shiver, I wrapped my arms around my chest. The temperature had dropped a few degrees. The sun was still up, but the clear blue sky was slowly giving way to slightly orange fingers of cloud that streaked in from the west.

"I need to make dinner, yes I do. It's almost night-time. You have no mommy, so I make food for you."

"Thanks," I said, not sure I could explain that I did have a mother. Undoubtedly, she wouldn't understand. As we walked back to the community kitchen, I could see that the frenzy of girls were still trying to get the new baby from the hangman. While Midnight worked on the dinner, I sat and watched the hangman as he sorted through the crowd of overzealous girls, each one striving to prove her own ability to care for the infant.

The hangman patiently held the baby. At his feet was a basket filled with bottles, no doubt a collection from all the babies he'd rescued over the years. The girls would each grab a bottle and race out to find a boy. Many of the boys retreated whenever a girl approached them. But they continued to go from boy to boy until they found one willing to help. The willing boy retreated to the woods, coming back several minutes later with a plant. I'm not sure what kind it was, but he'd break the stalk into several pieces, then squeeze each piece until a few drops of thick slime dripped into a pot. The girl then added water and cooked the milky colored sap until it resembled a dirty-cream-colored beverage. The girl and the boy then poured the liquid into a bottle and together presented it to the hangman.

The hangman felt the temperature of the drink, then tasted it. He then looked deep into the faces of the boy and girl, gauging how suitable they were for the responsibility. Then he fed the baby, seeing if it would drink and burp afterward. The couple was then obligated to remain at the hangman's feet until his decision was made. Occasionally one of the boys got up and left. This was apparently a sign that he wasn't committed to raising the child, because the girl inevitably walked away, her face a painting of dejection. One or two of those girls tried to find another boy and repeat the ceremony, but most of the willing boys were gone by that point.

I'd just started smelling the stew from Midnight's pot, at least I think it was hers, when the hangman stood. A deep inviting laugh summoned all eyes. Even several of the teenagers who weren't trying to adopt the baby gathered around to hear the verdict.

The smile that seemed to split his head in two, somehow it grew even wider. Holding the baby high, he bellowed, "Daddy!" and brought the baby down, placing it in one of the boys' arms. Sighs of relief and disappointment filled the air. Someone hollered a congratulation. Then the hangman lifted the baby out of the boy's arms and placed it in the arms of the girl he'd been waiting with. "Mommy!" boomed from his throat. Just like that, the newly formed couple accepted responsibility for the infant. If I was to guess, I'd say that the girl was no older than ten and the boy couldn't have been any older than Grub.

I looked over at Midnight. How old had she been when given Grub to take care of? If Grub had been as young as that infant tonight, she would've been only seven or eight. So young for such a large responsibility. This little ritual, somehow, helped the hangman find enough maturity in these children to care for a baby. At least, after witnessing the ceremony, I could see how Midnight and Chirp-chirp might've been paired. She was a willing mother at the time and he was a willing father. Was that as far as their relationship extended?

Dinner was much like lunch had been. Chirp-chirp brought Grub over and smiles were exchanged all around. Chirp-chirp didn't seem to mind that I was sitting between him and Midnight. It wasn't by design, at least not mine. After the meal, he thanked Midnight with a pat on the back and a belch to go with it. Not more than half an hour had passed from the time dinner started and I was left alone again with Midnight. I finished my last bite and thanked her.

She gave me a pat on the back, but this time I had to fake a burp. It was a horrible attempt and she laughed heartily. I laughed, too. I was feeling a little giddy. Not just because we were smiling and laughing together, but because she still had her hand resting on my back. Maybe it was because of another custom that I was unaware of, but I didn't want her to remove it. The night was chill. I wanted to scoot closer to her, put my arm around her, or to place a hand on hers. Not that I was really interested in her. After all, it could never work out between us. Still, there was a part of me that knew she'd be dancing around in my dreams tonight.

Of course, nothing happened. Well, she did withdraw her hand after what must have been two or three minutes, but those minutes had happened. I would never forget how her touch on my back made my toes tingle.

After talking for half an hour, our conversation flattened out. I didn't mean to say it, but with little more to discuss, it just happened to come out. "I'm going to have to leave tomorrow."

She looked down at the ground for a minute, then lifted her eyes to mine. "You go bye-bye?"

"Yes, tomorrow morning."

"I want you to stay."

For a second I wasn't sure if her eyes got a little pink. If they did, it was just for a second. I'm sure my face flushed at her admission. "I have to go to school and get a job. I like it here, but I don't belong here."

"Why school, you say you finish school already? And what is job?" She paused, then added, "All can live here."

"Yes, I finished some school, but I have much more to do. It will teach me to help people. And a job is work. I need to go to work to pay for school."

"Pay?"

"Yes, with money—right, you don't have to worry about money here."

"Stay. We help and you help here. You not need school to help."

I sighed, "You're right, I can help people without school, but if I go to school I can help people in a different way. I'll be able to save people's lives."

"Daddy Smiling saves lives. He not have school."

Midnight tugged at her fingers as if she was deep in thought. She looked over at where Grub was playing, then at the kitchen, then back down at the ground. "I want come with you," she said softly.

My breath caught. "But what about Chirp-chirp and Grub?"

"Grub almost daddy." She started to justify, but exhaled, her protest deflated before she could even convince herself. "I want come with you, but I stay."

I didn't know what to say. Obviously, she thirsted for more than this. She really did want to learn, but she'd outgrown this place. I felt for her.

Part of me imagined another reason why she might want to come with me, but that was ridiculous. We'd only known each other for half a day. If she ever got to know the real me, she wouldn't even want to be my friend. Even if she did have feelings for me, I was the new guy in town and it would've just been some new-guy charm for a community where the only new people were babies or toddlers.

Besides, I wasn't sure what I thought about her yet. When I'd first seen her, she wasn't much to look at, though I'll admit, that might've had something to do with the lack of a good hair stylist and modern clothing. As I'd come to notice, she truly was beautiful, if even in a very humble way. As fun as the idea might have been, I was in no position to be chasing any girls. Especially not one like her. She was so primitive and simple—and sweet and caring—but no! It could never work out.

That night I tossed and turned. Midnight was sleeping with some of the other girls and I was sprawled out under the stars within arm's length of Chirp-chirp and Grub. Grub still poked fun at my belly. Chirp-chirp tried to be amiable, but we had little to talk about. Surely he could see what Midnight was unable to see yet, that I was just some boring kid who could easily be forgotten.

I didn't dream about Midnight like I thought I would. In fact, I didn't dream at all. I don't know if the hard ground was my problem. I'd often slept on a hard floor at home, but I couldn't fall asleep here. The whole night I rolled and fidgeted, trying to get comfortable, but couldn't quite manage it. If I had dreamed, she would've been in it, because the whole while that I tried to sleep, I kept imagining her smiling face. I kept wondering what might happen if I did stay. It was all in vain and I suspect that was part of my restlessness. Several times I tried to push thoughts of her out of my head so that I could sleep, but she kept crawling back into my mind.

When the endless night was nearing completion, the muddle of my brain finally settled just enough for me to drift into sleep. Unfortunately, this is exactly when Chirp-chirp sat up and shook me and Grub. "Good morning, sunshine," he said with a smile.

There was no sunshine, just a slightly lighter sky that threatened to hide all the stars in another hour. All around, like roosters crowing at the dawn, little babies woke each other with hungry cries. Grub moaned a little and I just lay staring up.

"We go work now," Chirp-chirp said.

I sat up. All around us, the boys were stirring and getting up. Somewhere in the distance I could hear the hangman humming his usual song. The girls stayed down or tended to their babies while all the boys made their way to the kitchen. Two baskets were in easy view, each brimming with stone-grilled bread that had been made the day before. With their breakfast in hand and a basket or spear of their own, the boys split off in different directions.

"You work with us?" Chirp-chirp asked me.

As curious as I was, I shook my head. "I need to go now. Thank you so much for everything."

Chirp-chirp gave me a hug. "You're a good boy, yes you are. Stay good, okay."

"Okay, you too."

Next it was Grub's turn to say good-bye. He did so with a punch in my stomach and a giggle as he ran around to hide behind Chirp-chirp.

I shook my fist in front of a laugh of my own. I couldn't help but like that kid.

As they hiked away for their hunting or gathering, I found my own pack and got ready to leave. I wanted to say good-bye to Midnight, but thinking better of it, I made up my mind to just walk out.

It didn't matter. She found me before I could leave.

At some point last night, she'd tied her hair into a rope-like ponytail. She must have slept on it like that, because I could still see the imprint of it across her cheek.

"You come back?" she asked.

No. "Yes."

She smiled and I felt guilty. I'd only said what I knew

she wanted to hear. We stared at each other for a min-ute. I twitched, signaling that I was ready to leave. She responded by stepping closer and giving me a hug.

"You're a good-good boy, yes you are. You stay good, okay." It was the same sort of good-bye that Chirp-chirp had given, but with a lot more sadness in it.

If that was the customary good-bye, then I felt obliged to return it. "And you're a good girl, yes you are. You stay good, too, okay?"

She smiled, then stepped back. "Your talk gets better, yes it does."

I gave her a small wave and awkwardly turned around. My eyes were still heavy and my feet dragged as I put dis-tance between us. If I'd allowed myself to keep sleeping, it would be lunchtime before I was ready to go. Even still, just one more hour of sleep would've been nice. I won-dered if I should stop in an hour and try for a short nap.

I turned around to see her one last time before duck-ing into the woods. She gave a final wave and I turned around only to be smacked by a protruding tree branch. I heard her laugh as I disappeared into the early morn-ing shadow. My cheek smarted from the branch, but my mind stung more with the confusion I felt. Why did I find it so difficult to leave?

Maybe when the school year was over, I might try and get some time off from work. That is, if I could find a job. I would visit my mother and would it be so wrong if I happened to find my way here again? It would just be a friendly visit along the way, but really, who was I kid-ding? There was no way I'd be able to find my way back here again.

Chapter 11

Utopian society is often envisioned as a hub of wealth and prosperity. It's a place where neighbors come together in the best interests of one another. It's a place unburdened by crime, social injustice, and disease. After my brief stay with the children of the woods, I'm compelled to amend my vision of utopia. They had no monetary wealth, but they were wealthy in friendship. Mothers and fathers were the only stations held that offered any degree of respect. They all looked out for one another. The better traits of childlike innocence never seemed to leave them and the hangman was at their head, inspiring them to follow the higher path. They were of one heart and one mind.

I never saw disease, though I'm sure they experienced it. I have a feeling that even when hard times hit, this band of children would only come together in unity to help one another even more. Their culture was one of kindness and caring. Every single one of them had

**been abandoned as either an infant or a toddler, reject-
ed by those who should've loved them unconditional-
ly. Yet they developed a culture of their own, separate
from the whole world. A culture we should be so lucky
to find.**

Streaks of morning sun curtained through the misty
trees at angles that revealed the sun's rising position. I
trudged on, setting course by this natural compass before
the day burned it away. Northeast for only a few hundred
yards and already the incredible community of orphans
was hidden from both sight and sound. If the sun was up
higher, or if I looked very closely, I might have been able
to spot an old footprint in the ground. I suspected that by
the time the sun was blazing overhead, I'd be far enough
away that even those impressions would be rare.

I was glad to be on my way, but even the tune of the
early-rising songbirds did little to lift my soul. I knew I
was doing the right thing. I couldn't afford to delay my
journey. I needed a real job, so that I could stay in school.

Lack of sleep wasn't the only reason my feet dragged.
In the last sixteen hours or so, I'd found a sense of happiness that I'd never known. There were people my own
age who didn't judge me by my appearance or social
skills. Then there was Midnight. My first impression of
her hadn't been all that remarkable, but as I remembered
her last good-bye, I saw the most beautiful girl I'd ever
known. That beautiful image with the long black ponytail
and genuine smile replaced all other impressions from
the day before.

She was kind, gentle, and perfect. I would be a fool to
take her with me, but I'd also be a fool to stay. As I walked

my feet kept pausing. Part because I was tired, part, I might as well admit, was because of Midnight. Why was it so difficult to resist the urge to turn around, sweep her into my arms, and carry her off with me? I'd never do it, of course. That was just a foolish imagination of a daydreaming boy. I can't even image what she really thought of me. I was pretty sure I didn't want to know. Instead, I just kept pushing my way through the woods.

Even if my head wasn't just caught up in the clouds, I was never one to be so bold, and nothing I knew could change that in me. Besides, deep down, I knew that I wasn't in love with her. I'd only known her for a matter of hours. True love is something of fairy tales, not practical in the real world. Then again, she didn't live in the real world. Maybe she'd see nothing wrong with it, or with me. I would. I did live in the real world. A few hours in Neverland could never change that for me.

The farther I hiked under the canopy of trees, the more I knew that I'd never see her or the others again. I didn't know how the hangman could do it; there were no landmarks to find one's way. You'd have to know every single tree, shrub, and rock of these woods to navigate. Oh, to have a GPS device that I could mark their location with! Something to help me find my way back someday. As it was, I didn't even know where I would pop out of the woods. I knew that if I kept walking to the northeast, I'd eventually find my way out. If I came out where I hoped, I'd only be about twenty kilometers from the city where my schooling would take place. But that was only if I exited the woods at the perfect spot. Before I'd left, I would have considered myself lucky if I came out within forty kilometers of my destination.

I clawed at my memory, trying to remember the aerial image I'd seen of this place on my last day of school. I couldn't recall ever seeing the small lake that the hangman camped by. But it had been over a month since I'd seen that fuzzy layout of the land from who knows how many kilometers above the sky. When I was following him yesterday, I was only aware that I was going deeper into the woods. In my stupor, I didn't pay enough attention to the direction we'd gone. It had felt like the right direction, but for all I knew, I was so far off course that I'd have to walk an extra hundred kilometers once I emerged.

So much green. It even hid most of the brown trunks of trees, either by moss, vine, or simply by overwhelming it with so many shades of the one color. The foliage above and in front hid everything in my path. Occasionally I'd crest a hill, but it was never tall enough to survey the land beyond. I pressed on anyway. With no real trails to follow and only the rare clearing to illuminate the position of the sun for reference, I wondered if I might just be going in circles. I'd heard of this happening before. Nighttime was only a few hours away. Maybe I'd find myself back in the orphans' camp after all.

Two more hours of hiking put the sun clearly at my back. I'd been successful in keeping a steady direction, but I thought I should be nearing the edge of the woods by now. Then again, how would I know until I actually emerged. As dense as this jungle was, I could be less than a hundred meters from civilization and not even realize it.

Stopping, I listened hard, hoping to hear any signs of a city just beyond the looming trees. I could hear a faint whistle coming from my throat and some invisible rodents as they scurried through the underbrush around me. A large colorful bird ruffled its feathers above my head, oblivious to my presence. There were no sounds of cars or people, though.

After one more hour of blistered walking, I gave up and set up camp. I wanted to start a fire, but I'd pushed myself too far for the day. Once I'd slumped down onto my butt, I couldn't bring myself to stand again. I reached into my backpack and pulled out a water bottle and a bag of what was now stale Spanish rolls. The bread was dry but satisfying. I rationed the last of my food. I could have easily devoured everything I'd brought. This hike had famished me, but I wanted to put something in my belly when morning came, before I continued my walk. Hopefully this would be my last night out here. I wasn't like Chirp-chirp. Even Grub might know how to find food in the forest, but I'd likely poison myself with the first berry or fruit I came across.

Without a blanket or a tent, I fell asleep with my head on my bundle of clothing. I woke once with a shiver. I'd only slept for an hour or two. I was cold, something I rarely felt in this perpetually hot and humid climate, and I had to pee. Relieved, I unpacked my clothing and layered it on myself to keep warm.

I lay down again, but sleep came slower this time. After having slept so little the night before, followed by my muscle-draining hike today, I knew I should sleep soundly. But there was something about being alone, unsure of exactly where I was. The noises were disturbing. The silences were more so. The extra layers of clothing didn't help much against the cold, either. Uncomfortably I curled into the fetal position and tried not to let my fears wring me out.

I was afraid. Afraid that I might never find my way out of these woods. Afraid that I would starve to death only a hundred feet from the edge of the town. Yes, I did think it would be nice to snuggle up to Midnight for warmth, but that was a foolish and fleeting thought. Fear was the caffeine that kept my mind alert this night. Every snap of twig or rustle of leaves, even the nighttime insects, cast an eerie mood on my waxing paranoia. Few stars were visible under the broad-leaved canopy above my head, but where I hadn't noticed any shadows during the day, now I was surrounded by what seemed like dancing phantoms of black; evil fairies playing back and forth all around me.

Sometime before sunrise I fell asleep. The green shade of morning light woke me up. I just curled into myself tighter like a pill bug in a toddler's grip. Two horrible nights of sleep, and I wanted to rest all day. High in the sky overhead, though I couldn't see it, I heard the familiar thunder of a commercial jet ripping across the sky. It could have thousands of kilometers to go before landing, but it reminded me that I should find civilization sometime today.

I finished the last of my bread and washed it down with some water. I would need to keep an eye out for more water to refill my bottle this morning. Food I could likely do without for a meal or more, but I would need water. About two hours into my hike, I was rewarded with water. Granted, it was a bittersweet bounty. While I did need the wet stuff, what I found was more of a curse.

After resting for half an hour, funneling the torrent of

rainwater through a leaf into my water bottle, I realized that the deluge would not be letting up anytime soon and neither should I. Water was already pooling at my feet as I stepped out from under the shelter of a fallen tree. I don't know how, but even though the sun failed to penetrate the treetops before, the rain was unhindered by the umbrella of foliage. Within seconds I couldn't have been wetter than if I'd jumped into a lake.

The rain pounded more steadily against the ground than did my feet. By midday, amid the drowning white noise, the first hints of civilization tickled my nose. The blanket of water drowned all sound and almost all smell, baptizing the polluted atmosphere, washing it nearly clean. That faintest of smells that stubbornly clung below the treetops, defying all nature could cast against it, was the scent of a lingering wood-burning cook fire.

My mind took too long to register what my nose was begging me to notice. I was on the outskirts of civilization. I was nearing New Tum, or at least I hope that's where I was emerging. I'd finally reached the other side. I quickened my pace. Through the pouring veil, as if from heaven, I saw the fuzzy shapes of homes. Please don't let them be my own hometown I thought. I'd go crazy if I'd just walked in a complete circle. Almost falling over myself, I raced closer, hoping to find a compassionate family, one willing to accept a dripping sponge under their roof.

"What town is this?" Were my first words as a rickety old man greeted me at the door of his equally rickety old house.

"Id youw jous come from da woods?" He asked with a toothless accent, slowly, as if his old lips struggled to form the words. Or maybe it was because he was so old that English wasn't his first language.

"Please, just tell me what town this is?"

"Why dis int no town a'all. Dis's New Tum Disdirk. A'youw okay? Youw loo'like youw been hikin in da wrain fur a ho'week. Cum in, fore youw cach'a coughin."

I just nodded my head. "Thank you."

Chapter 12

Like a dog returns to its vomit, so too did I return to mine. Funny how progressing toward our goals can take us right back to where we started. I knew sacrifice was required to reach my dreams. I suppose that I can thank my father for giving me the experience I'd need. Ironically, had I not fallen back to journalism, I might not be able to write this supplication. If you believe in divine destiny, or even the gentle prodding's of a higher power, then maybe you can accept my supplication to be of credible value as I plea for Daddy Smiling's case.

Finding my school was easy. That first day after the rains, where I emerged from the woods, I found myself to be only five kilometers away from the school. On-campus dormitories were available but not free. The real struggle was finding a job that could support me.

While my hometown did have many schools, this new city dwarfed anything I had to compare it with. Not that the city was big, because it was anything but. It's just that, the school was much more dominant. My hometown was filled with the usual go-to-work, try-to-survive families. Schooling was a part of that, but more of an afterthought for most people. Here, the non-school-attending locals were obsessed with the academic environment. They attended everything from special lectures to sporting events. The schools in my town didn't even have a sports team. Here, casual talk on the street or in the shops revolved around the schools. One day of job hunting was enough to show me that the college dominated the city's culture.

That night, still alone in my dormitory, while sucking clean a bowl of instant noodles, I reflected on my day. Like me, most people who attended were not from around here. In my first day of job seeking, I'd developed a pessimistic outlook on my prospects. Against the entire new class of students, I was competing for only a handful of jobs.

After dropping my bowl in the sink, I got ready for bed. At least I had two things going for me. First, I'd arrived on campus before the majority of the other new students. Second was—well I, didn't want to think about my second advantage. I bent over, resting my head in my palms. No use denying it though. I couldn't think of any alternatives. I would make use of my second advantage. At least I would try. After all, I couldn't just ignore all my previous schooling. Nobody here was studying journalism. Careful not to smack my tailbone on the hard plywood that supported the bottom of my futon mattress, I eased under a single sheet, exhaled loudly and tried to justify my dirty resolve.

Early the next morning, I half-heartedly pulled on a shirt and pants. Apparently, even near the dorms, there were enough chickens to make an early riser out of even the most drowsy. Next, I counted my money. The weight of the coins felt good. I rolled them into my pocket with the rest of my money. It wasn't much and it would disappear far too quickly. But I had to make the sacrifice. Still early morning, before the humid air got muggy and hot, I left my room and walked onto the campus. Few people were milling about and I was totally lost. Not wanting to waste my whole morning exploring, I walked up to a man with dull black eyebrows, bushy against his round pock-marked face. Wearing the traditional blue coverall uniform of a custodian, he was emptying trash bins from the day before. The smell of garbage mingled with his cheap aftershave. Amazing how every smell is so distinct in the morning. "I need to find the school store," I said to him.

"And I need to find a wife, a better house, and a job that doesn't smell like rotten bananas," he replied in a slow and groggy drawl.

Whoops, I'd found a grump on my first try. I looked around, not sure how to respond. Then I heard him chuckle.

"You new guys are all the same. I'm just giving you a hard time."

I choked a laugh.

"Just head down two more buildings over there." He pointed, then hacked several times before spitting into the open garbage sack that he was about to heft. Wiping his lips on his sleeve, he added, "It's just on the main floor, right smack in the middle of the students' center."

Then as if to punctuate, he smacked his lips with a satisfied grin before returning to his duties.

I was about ten feet away when he called out, "You're a bit early. They won't be open yet."

"Okay," was all I could think to say as I dipped my head in acknowledgment. In the back of my mind, I could almost see myself through his eyes. If I was to get the job today, I would have to try my best not to look like my usual insecure self, afraid of my own shadow.

I was in a new place. Nobody knew me. I could have a fresh start.

When I arrived at the school store, the shop was closed, true to the janitor's word. Not only was it closed, but it wouldn't open for another three hours. If I waited for the shop to open, my morning would be nearly spent before I applied for a single job. This had better work.

To kill the next few hours, I wandered the campus. The buildings were old but well maintained. The institutional tan paint on cinder and concrete walls of the old classrooms radiated an established dignity. There were also new buildings, ones that had replaced the rubble from the war. They were sleek with black glass walls with modern interior finishes.

Granted, the wars hadn't been a disaster for the whole world. But for some reason, the big players in the global struggle all wanted to stage their attacks on our soil instead of their own. We hadn't been part of the war until both sides of the conflict found us to be a strategic staging ground. After seeing the destruction that came about because of the engagements, I don't blame the enemies or the victors for wanting to let someone else live with the aftermath. To us, both sides ended up being our enemies.

Maybe I'm a little harsh. Some money did flow back into our countries from both the English allies and the Chinese. Whatever this school had once been, because of the sympathies of those once warring nations, the college was now something that I figured could rival any Western university.

I've heard that in America, students don't start college until they are eighteen or nineteen years old. My birthday was in a week, and I would be sixteen years old when my classes actually started. If I'd stayed home, my next two years of journalism school would have counted as college credit.

Here I was starting pre-med. Without any medical background, this would be a busy year or two of playing catch up. Then of course, I'd have two more years of heavy medical instruction. At the end of that, I could find a job as a paid intern. Still there'd be courses above that, but the goal was to survive until I could gain that paid internship.

I've wondered if Americans start college on a higher plane than we do, or if we just learn more quickly than them, thereby excusing us from the two extra years of pre-college education. Or when I graduate, will I have an inferior education? No, we were still on par with them. At least I hoped we were. If not, there was nothing I could do about it except keep moving forward, doing the best my circumstances would allow.

Finally, the school store opened and I went in. My precious, carefully budgeted expenditure went toward the crisp, new red-and-blue T-shirt, blazoned across the front with "T.U.M." Obviously, this was a play on New Tum's name. Not only was it the name of the district, but it was the abbreviation for the school, Tum University Mandrills. Mandrills don't live around here, but someone must have thought that the baboon made for an intimidating mascot.

Wasting no time, I pulled off my old soft shirt and tugged this stiff new shirt over my head as I ambled off campus. It made my back itch, even after I ripped off the sharp tag.

Clothed in my new flag, I was prepared to show off my patriotic fervor for the only topic that seemed to matter to the majority of townsfolk here. I stopped only briefly at the front doors of my final destination. At least I hoped it would be my final destination. If I couldn't find a job here, I didn't know what I might do.

The old newspaper publisher, like so many others, had long since added electronic distribution to its platform. From the outside, though, the building still looked like a distressed newspaper printer. Granted, they did continue to have print material in circulation. My guess was that their print was still more read than their electronic journal. Anyone who had an electronic mobile device would be using that for their news now. But I didn't have one, nor did many of the people I knew.

The building displayed several layers of red paint, generations of coatings, now nearly all peeled off. At only one story tall, the structure was fairly wide, and very deep. I imagined hearing the whirring gray paper as it raced through rollers of ink and knives. I could imagine the folding and stamping of bands where the daily stories would be bundled and plopped on a pallet for delivery. If journalism was as simple and innocent as this, I might not mind it so much. Decent work, informative articles, nothing wrong with that. Yes, I could have probably continued in this field if not for all the bias and corruption that influenced those finger-staining pages.

As I caught my breath and tried to dry my sweaty palms, I brushed my hand against another sales tag from my new shirt. How'd I miss that one? I tried to tug it out but the plastic punch threatened to tear my shirt. So I changed my style. Tucking the shirt, tag and all, into my pants, I inspected myself in the reflective glass of the front door. Not bad. Maybe even an improvement. I might have to tuck in my shirts more often. One more lungful and I pushed my way through the door. The rusty hinges made a terrible shriek, announcing my arrival.

After returning to my dorm, I skipped dinner and went directly to my room and plopped myself onto my futon. I smacked my tailbone hard and bit my lip to hold back a curse. After rubbing my poor backside, I stared up at the ceiling. The dirty white plaster suggested that this room had once been flipped. The ceiling gave the worn impression that it had been walked on for years before being elevated off the floor. As my eyes lost focus on the world around me, my mind drifted to replay my interview at the publishing office. I had been successful. The job was mine. It didn't pay as well as I'd like, but this was a college town and I was told that no other job would even come close to the commissions that I could make.

I was now the newest liaison for the New District Times. My articles would focus entirely on campus life. I would write for the paper's print and electronic circulars about everything from ball games to campus politics. Every year this job was given to an ambitious student and my previous schooling in journalism had set me apart from most other applicants the publisher was used to getting. It didn't hurt either, that I was the first person this school year to apply.

For the next week, I had the dorm all to myself. On Saturday, my sixteenth birthday, I was filled with anticipation. Not because I would get any special treatment or gifts, but I was getting something. Five of them actually. Three of which would significantly influence my life. On this weekend before school started, my five roommates arrived. Two of them came together. They'd obviously been friends for some time. They didn't give me their real names, they just called themselves Thing One and Thing Two, inspired I suppose after the popular Dr. Seuss book, The Cat in The Hat. They strolled in as if they'd always lived here. I felt somewhat threatened by these two things, and couldn't tell if they would be nice or rude.

Thing One was my complete opposite. Tall, skinny, he had all the good looks. His friend, Thing Two, was a little more on the heavy side, with acne and a thick curly mess of hair that might never be tamed.

"Hi, I'm Iddo," I said, hoping that I displayed a sense of confidence. It was hard since I was at least two years younger.

They both studied me as if I were a lab rat. Truth be told, they almost looked surprised to see me. Thing Two stepped forward, then grabbed my face. "Fresh meat!" He turned to Thing One, "This is going to be so great! I won't chase them off this time, I promise."

Thing One sighed, "Just don't corrupt anyone this year. He looks like a nice guy. I'd hate to see him or anyone else follow your self-destructive lifestyle."

"You're such a party pooper. Why do I keep rooming with you?" Thing Two let go of my face. He made me so uncomfortable. I wanted to squirm.

Then Thing one approached, "Iddo, it's nice to meet you. Please forgive Thing Two. We've been friends for ever. You could almost say he's my pet project."

Thing Two's stifled laugh sounded like a snort.

"Okay," I said, very unsure about what had just happened. Maybe they weren't both rude. Perhaps neither of them were. Maybe my social immaturity was responsible for my unease and I simply didn't know how to respond to the situation properly. It did seem like it would be nice to feel that comfortable with a friend as these two were with each other, even if they acted polar opposite from each other. They had a sort of laid back way of bantering that I immediately envied. Still when they decided to room together, I was relieved. I was pretty sure that I could not keep up with either of them if they decided to split up and bunk with me.

That left one and a half rooms to be filled. Would they be as strange as these two?

The next two boys to come in were from well-to-do families. Their parents brought them in their own personal cars. I'd never known anybody who owned a car. Well, not really; Krystal's dad owned an old Mercedes, but these looked like nice new cars. The white and blue paint glistened so pristinely that I wouldn't be surprised if the owners polished the things every day. Even the tires shone as if coated with high-gloss clear paint. I understood that these two guys probably had more in common with each other than they might with me. And yes, they did seem nice enough, but I still felt rejected when they chose to bunk together in the second free bedroom. They introduced themselves as Charles and Jhon.

The last guy to arrive came with humble belongings. This was to be my roommate. His clothing was faded and patched. His boots had obviously been re-soled, probably more than once. I could tell, because they'd lost their shape. Just like mine, the leather was soft and too rounded. It looked like it was only a month or so away from wearing a hole in any number or spots. Still, his hair was trimmed neatly and with his charming smile and perfect skin, he'd be catching a lot of looks from the girls. That is, if he had a winning personality to go with it. Then again, he might not even need the social skills with a face like that. The only ornament he wore was a small ring with what looked like a green coat of arms. I knew I'd seen its match elsewhere, but I couldn't remember where.

"I'm Duy, from the Ubon Province."

"Sorry, I've never heard of it. My name is Iddo. I'm from just the other side of the woods down there." I pointed in the direction of my home.

"Wow, you came through the woods?"

I nodded.

"That's not something I'd dare hike. Our town is just

about fifty kilometers northwest of here. It nestles right up against those same woods, but you won't find me taking a stroll too deep into them."

"You like it there?" I asked.

"Yeah. It's not a bad place. A little poor, but we're generally happy. By the way, are you a Believer?"

Chapter 13

When I started school here in New Tum, my circumstances made an ignominious life impossible. Completely by chance I was facing an apartment full of other boys near my age. They were as different from me as stone is from air. There was no getting around it; I would have to learn to interact with others.

These new roommates changed my life. I will forever be grateful to them, or at least to the circumstances that put us together. While I will always be Iddo, the clumsy fat boy who's scared of his own nose, I now have the seeds of a backbone. Through these boys I learned to be an agent for myself, thus becoming truly independent. I earnestly plead my case to the public. If I can shrug off my former handicaps and opinions, then anyone can. The case of the hangman is wrong, and if you open your hearts, you too will see unethical evil in it. How can we punish someone who is saving the most innocent of lives and raising them in a community of

love and family care?

"Am I a Believer?" I scoffed at my new roommate. We seemed to be the only two in the apartment with anything in common. Even then, he accused me of being one of those weird religious fanatics. "Are you kidding? Do I look like one of those freaks?"

Duy cast his eyes down. "I didn't mean it like that. I just thought that—"

"You thought what?" My temper was hot, but as usual, it was simmering back down. I felt ridiculous for my forwardness. I didn't know how to back down completely, though. If I did back down, then he'd know how big of a pushover I truly was. But even as I stood my ground, my knees shook and threatened to buckle. What a sap I was. One word from him and I'd melt into a pitiful lump of flesh.

"I just thought," he said meekly, "that we might have something more in common."

This time shock did buckle my knees. I almost fell, but aimed my rear to plop onto the futon nearest me. My tailbone smacked hard again. Just what I needed. Another thing to make me look ridiculous. "Y-you're a Believer?" I stammered, trying hard not to let my pain miscommunicate some other message via my contorted face. I was suddenly afraid that, if he chose, one word really could magically melt my flesh.

"Forget I mentioned it."

Yeah, right! "Uh . . ." My eyes darted from side to side. I needed to escape. But I had nowhere to go. Maybe I could sleep in the hall. No, that might offend him. Then I'd really be in trouble.

He sighed. "I take it you've never actually met one of us before?"

I shook my head.

"I'm not going to cast some ridiculous spell on you, I promise. We don't actually do that sort of thing. Whatever stories you've heard, they're all wrong. I used to believe those same stories until proselytizers came to my town, too."

My mind flashed back to the hangman. He too had rumors circulating about him. They all painted him as some grim killer, reaping the souls of anyone who ventured into the woods. And yes, there was some truth to the myth about the giant, but there was much more to him than the stories depicted.

"Would you care to hear me out? I'll set the stories straight."

"N-no. I'm pretty b-busy right now." That was a lie. Well, it was a half lie. I was about to find something to make me very busy.

"Another time, then?"

No! "Sure." Stupid me. If Believers could brainwash people, then all my new roommate needed was a little time to talk with me. After all, if the hangman stories had some truth to them, there was likely some truth in the stories about Believers. What was I to do?

"All right. I'll look forward to getting to know you

better, later," Duy said with a little hint of meekness.

I just nodded and followed my one foot that had already sneaked its way out the door. I nearly tripped on Jhon's suitcase. As I caught my balance, I pulled my head up, slamming it into Thing Two's nose. A torrent of profanities filled the hall and I slid past him as he checked for blood. Once outside I squatted by the side of the building. My heart was thumping as loud as my heavy breathing. My face was red and my mind was drowning in a thick fog of regret. I closed my eyes and tried to calm myself. When I finally opened my eyes, I saw Thing One squatting next to me. His eyes were calmly trying to read mine.

"Gee," he said to me nonchalantly. "For a fat kid, you don't sweat much."

I snorted a laugh. "Some good impression I made in there."

"Don't sweat it. Thing Two had it coming. He's fine, actually. He picks his nose so much, anyway, that he's afraid any little bump will start it bleeding again. You probably bruised his finger more than his nose."

"Would you guess that my roommate is a Believer?"

"I guess he's got that look to him," Thing One replied in his easygoing manner. "Why? Does that bother you?"

"Wouldn't it bother you?"

"Engh—I've known enough Believers. Would you believe that they don't really grow horns on their heads?"

I laughed. "Of course they wouldn't. Sure, I've heard that before, but even that sounded silly." But even as I said this, I was remapping my vision of them. I actually had believed it just before now.

Thing One reached down and grabbed my arm. For such a tall skinny guy, he was remarkably strong. He nearly lifted me off my feet before I had a chance to push myself up.

Once I was back on my own two feet, he gave me a hard but reassuring slap on the back. It reminded me of the burping pat that Midnight had given me back in the woods. "Give your roommate a chance. You'll see. I doubt he's half as scary as you imagine." He gave me a wink, like he knew more than he was letting on about.

Then, just like that, Thing One was gone again. The walking bamboo pole of a roommate had really lifted my spirits. But I couldn't go back inside the apartment just yet. My wounded pride was still too damaged to return and face the mess I'd created. Instead I paced aimlessly, trying to digest everything that happened. I had one roommate who, despite looking just like anyone else, was a Believer; two rich guys; and two clowns, one that I'd mildly wounded and the other who seemed wiser and friendlier than his years.

This all gave me a wonderful idea for my first story to write. What better way to ring in the new school year than with a news article about different people coming together and learning to live with one another? I would interview new students as they were settling into their apartments and get their takes on coping with new roommates. The only problem was, I'd left my pen and notepad in my apartment.

Since going back inside was out of the question, I

cautiously approached the large main waste bin in the parking lot. The bin had been emptied prior to everyone arriving. The stained asphalt below still reeked of waste from weeks past. In a haste to clear out space, the last occupants must have overfilled the square container. I found a used notepad that had either been hastily thrown or fallen from the pile, landing on the ground next to the dumpster. Its cover was smeared with something gooey, but it still had three good unused pages, and I ripped them out. Then I tipped the used portion of the notepad into the small but growing pile of waste. All I needed now was something to write with.

In the main lobby of the apartment complex, I borrowed a pen that was used for signing contracts or writing maintenance notes. I then made a mental note to carry a pad and pen with me at all times. If I was to be the campus journalist, I must be prepared for any possible articles to write about when the opportunity arose.

Walking to the side of the complex, opposite my living space, I passed up on several potential interviewees until I found someone less intimidating than the majority of the people. By *unintimidating* I mean that he was alone, not busy doing anything, unattractive, and reeking of insecurity. Not much different from me, I realized.

I tried to make his acquaintance. He acquiesced to a degree, but when I pressed him for any details on his roommates, he squirmed. His face darkened with anxiety and his eyes seemed to look at everything but me. After stammering for a minute, he hinted at being very busy and had to go. Strike one. Nothing from him.

I was a miffed. Was that how I came across to others, also? If I was to get any quality commentary, I would need to interview students with better people skills. I would need to develop those people skills. How else was I to interview someone who intimidated me? What kind of job had I gotten myself into?

For the next three hours, I met with students. Boys and girls. Rich and poor. The first hour was difficult, but as I got my questions better organized in my head, the task became easier. Around ten in the evening, I returned to my apartment. What had earlier started out as a fear-filled project had morphed into an exciting study of people. Duy and the two rich boys were getting ready for bed. The two Things were out for the moment.

I had little desire to sleep. My mind was spinning with the excitement of the article I was to write. My studies in journalism had taught me that the best stories were written while the fervor of the moment was still fresh and exciting. By midnight I'd finished. I called it "A Kitchen of Souls."

The morning had started out fine. I did oversleep a little. My foot caught in my bed sheet as I stumbled to the door. My roommates were already up and getting ready for the day. All of them, that is, except for Thing Two. Which was fine with me; I wasn't ready to confront him yet. A quick brush of my teeth, a look in the mirror to remind myself that I still was fat and in need of a haircut, followed by a visit to the toilet. One toilet, six of us to a dorm and one of the boys had a spray nozzle instead of a jet stream. I would have to remember to either wear shoes to the toilet each time, or come prepared with a mop.

On my way out the door, I scraped the burned crust of rice from last night's rice pot, and sprinkled a little sugar on it before bounding out the door. Not a healthy breakfast, but no diet I knew of could transform my body into the pinnacle of fitness. So, big deal. Besides, I had to drop off my "A Kitchen of Souls" article to the paper before I went to school.

My editor hated it—a response I later learned was typical from him. Though, in this case, it might have been true. If I'd stuck it out another couple years in journalism school, I might have learned what this job later taught me. Every article is rubbish. The single biggest difference between a bad article and a good one is the commission I'm able to negotiate with my publisher. So by that standard, this first article of mine was lacking considerably.

The reduced commission my articles garnered went into a fund that would be paid out every two weeks. I would have to contribute at least one article per day if I was to make enough money just to survive. Even if I contributed two articles per day, my budget would be lean. Besides, I didn't think my publisher would be happy if their newest student reporter contributed little to their periodicals. Not only that, but no more morning drops. I'd have to submit all my articles by ten the evening before if I hoped to get paid for the next day's printing.

I had just enough time to look at the school's events board so I could line up a list of possible articles for the coming month. "Don't forget," my publisher had reminded me. "You need to predict the future. People don't want to read so much about what happened yesterday, they want to know what's happening today." I scribbled down the activities that were posted and made a mental note to check the computer lab later to see if anything more was posted online.

My first classes of the morning were discouraging. Most every student had already been prepped for years in biology and pre-medical classes. I was starting at the dummy end and the depth of the topics already threatened to drown me. I'd be required to spend many hours above the normal workload just to catch up to the beginning.

I did have an hour for lunch before my next round of classes. I used the time to eat two bananas and write a rough draft of an article about the first day of classes. Yes, this would be an article about yesterday by the time it got published, but I hadn't gotten into the swing of things yet. The events board had mentioned some welcoming activities that would be starting tomorrow. Following my afternoon classes, I'd need to find and interview somebody about them. I would then prepare a second article to deliver later tonight. Somewhere between or after that, I needed to find time to study and do homework. This was not going to be easy.

By ten thirty that night, I'd returned from the publishing house and was nodding over a textbook in the corner of my room. In the background, I heard a toilet flush and the sink run for a minute. The next bob of my head revealed Duy, still drying his hands on his pants. He was looking down, first at my textbook then at me, as if trying to decide something.

"You're new to the medical field, aren't you?" he ventured with some hesitancy.

My heavy eyelids hid my weary discomfort at talking

to the Believer. I nodded but figured that the gesture looked little different from the sleepy nod I'd been doing for the last fifteen minutes. "How'd you know?"

"Thing One Told me."

How'd he know? "You could say I've got some catching up to do."

"What did you study before this?" Duy asked.

"Creative writing." I placed the textbook down, spine up, using the floor as a bookmark. I looked back down at the massive hardback and realized I couldn't remember a thing I'd just read. With dreamy frustration, I placed my pudgy fingers on the spine and lifted the book off the floor. Its pages clapped together. No sense in saving my place if I just had to read it all over again.

"I know this must be hard for you, and maybe I'm not the right person for it." He hesitated.

I lifted my nose out of my own misty thoughts and studied my roommate. What could he be getting at?

"I know you aren't too keen on associating with Believers. Frankly, I don't blame you, with all the stupid rumors that go around about us." His shoulders shrugged up, and his eyebrows lifted. "But if you'd like a tutor, I'd be more than willing to help you get caught up."

Thing One's counsel echoed in the back of my head. "Why would you do that for me?"

"It's part of what I believe. I want to be able to serve my neighbors. As a roommate, you're kinda the closest neighbor I have. Besides, if we're going to be living together, I'd rather do so on friendly terms."

I thought for a moment. I might be able to get by without a tutor, but I was so busy. It might help, or might prove to be another distraction, further setting me behind? I'd never studied with anyone else before. How would that even work out? "Okay, just one thing—"

Duy tilted his head as if to emphasize his attention.

"I don't have any desire to be converted as a Believer. No proselytizing strings attached, if you get my meaning."

Duy smiled. "It's a deal. I'll help tutor you, and you won't run away each time I come into the room."

I blushed. "I didn't run away."

Duy smiled and softly punched my arm. "You know what I mean."

The next several weeks found me busier than I'd ever been in my life. I was cranking out two stories per day for the paper, going full time to school, studying and doing homework, then spending an hour with Duy each day as he helped me understand all the things that were still foreign to me. Maybe it was these tutor sessions that did it, or maybe it was my job exerting its ever more powerful influence. I was getting so used to asking questions, especially of him, that when my curiosity got the better of me, I didn't realize what I was doing until I'd done it.

"Do you guys really do magic?"

I half expected him to give me a spat of feigned contempt for being an indolent stereotyper. Instead he just cast his eyes down in a contemplative look, neither confirming nor denying. Gently resting his hands on his knees, he brought his gaze up to meet mine. He was just about to answer when Jhon burst through the door.

"Party tonight. You two coming?"

I had too much studying to do. But could I afford not to go? After all, I was the campus life representative for the paper. My job almost demanded that I be involved.

"There'll be girls," he added with mock seduction in his voice.

I didn't have time for flirting. Not that I'd be any good at it, anyway. But, "Sure, I'll go. When?"

"Half an hour. What about you, Duy?"

Duy was not going to go. What little I'd learned of him so far was that he was a teetotaler. His beliefs demanded it of him. I had little experience, but a college party seemed no place for avoiding vices. As for women, I doubted that he'd ever think of kissing a girl until after he'd been married for five years.

The more I learned of Believers, the more I realized that they had strict moral and health rules to follow. There was almost something enviable in the degree of self-control they possessed. Maybe that's why my eyes flew wide open with surprise when he blurted, "Yeah, that sounds like fun!"

I decided not to let him know, but I wanted to study this Believer in a real social setting. Up until then I'd learned that Believers professed to acknowledge the same Christ as most Christians, but they held stricter tenets than the other denominations.

I still hadn't figured out what their special ceremonies were all about. To be honest, I'd learned less about them than I'd hoped. True, I'd grown more comfortable being in the same room with Duy. Maybe that's how they started working on you.

"Way to go," said Jhon. "Hey Charles, we're bringing our own Believer!"

From another room, I heard Charles reply, "Just don't let him curse me when I'm talking to the pretties."

Jhon laughed, "You couldn't pay a pretty nearly enough to talk to you!" He then slapped the hollow-core door in amusement, his head shaking as he left our room.

"Could you really put a curse on somebody?" I asked.

"I don't know, maybe."

"So you guys do practice magic?"

"Well, not so much magic." Duy hesitated, almost afraid that I too would scorn him. "It's more like God's power, delegated to us. We have to be worthy and have really good faith. We use it to perform ceremonies and to heal the sick. I've heard of cursings but never really known anything about them. It's not something we generally do."

"So do you have this power?"

"Yeah, I guess so."

I slid forward. Weird. I probably should have scooted back from him. But my curiosity was piqued. "Could you show me? Something small, you know, nothing crazy, just—could you make this book float in the air?" I held out my textbook.

He shook his head. "I'm sure some could, but it doesn't really work like that. The power isn't meant to be used for show. You know, I'm not too comfortable talking about this. I'm going to get ready for the party."

"I didn't think you'd actually go."

"Just because I'm a Believer doesn't mean I'm dead!"

I slunk back. "Sorry, I didn't mean that you were, well, I just sort of thought-"

"Ah, you're fine Iddo. You're strung up too tight. You need to learn to relax a little."

"Yeah, well, no better time than now, right?" I half laughed. "Let's go."

The party was everything I'd imagined it to be, meaning that it wasn't meant for someone like me. Duy and Thing Two paired up and navigated the crowd like they'd done this before. They were instantly popular. Funny, but they were the last two I thought would pair up or be popular. This mostly because Thing Two was not an attractive sort, even if he loved the riotous lifestyle. Alcohol, drugs, sex seemed to all fit into his brand of a *good time*, though I hadn't ever seen him participating in any of those. If this truly was his nature, how did Duy's chaste and abstinent nature complement the party hawk? Maybe Thing Two was using Duy. Even with his good looks, Duy would be little competition among the ladies. Maybe he'd make Thing Two look good by giving the appearance of having already made friends. Like they say, you've got to have money to make money—or, in this case, friends.

I noticed that though Thing One hadn't come, there were some remarkable differences between the two roommates. Thing One was still peppy and active, but he seemed smarter or wiser than Thing Two. He wasn't the type that would be taken by the vices that Thing Two hoped to find. I almost wondered how they got along so well. Maybe one day I'd ask him. I felt like I could talk to him. Thing Two always radiated a macho attitude and I didn't think I could have asked him about anything deeper than a raindrop.

At least Jhon and Charles didn't abandon me at the party. We stayed huddled together at the entrance, watching Thing Two make his rounds.

"That guy's got some balls," Charles stated. We just shook our heads as we watched him put his arm around an insanely attractive girl with silky smooth hair and movie star looks that complimented her movie star motions. All three of us caught ourselves leaning to watch. We righted ourselves without saying a word. But wow! Beautiful would have been too sweet to describe her. I couldn't help but compare her to Midnight. Midnight was beautiful in a common sort of way, a more down to Earth beauty.

This girl on the other hand was really working the field. She was dressed to make men drool. I knew she was only a year or two older than me, but her makeup added at least five more years, not to mention five hundred feet of razor-wire fashion fence between us. Thing Two obviously had no problem scaling those defenses and getting her to smile. To his credit, he didn't linger, he just winked at her and moved on to the next.

"It looks like he's going to get every hot girl pining over him before the night is over," Jhon commented.

"I'm going to check out the food table," I said. That seemed like a safe place in this shuffle of bodies. I expected Charles and Jhon to follow, but they didn't. I wanted to turn around and stay with them, but I'd already committed myself.

Loud music drowned out the hum of voices all around. The mingling crowd was like a thick cloud composed of human flesh and I had to squeeze through, rather than around, them. How could anyone even think in a room like this, let alone hold a conversation? At the table I found the condiments already picked clean. Apparently, food was not to be the main draw for this party. I filled a cup with some blue punch, only to find it burning my throat all the way down. I'd never tasted spiked anything. My mother wouldn't allow alcohol at home. She hadn't even let my father drink at home. When he did drink, he'd come home tipsy and sometimes angry. I didn't want to see what I'd turn into if I got drunk. It would probably be newsworthy.

I put the cup down and looked around. Charles and Jhon had made their way into a crowd of their own. They'd waited for a good chance to break away from me and I'd given them a prime opportunity without even knowing. At least that's the way I saw it. In a room that would've been overcrowded with under twenty people, I was alone competing for space with at least fifty and adding.

Though there were several fluid groups of people,

most had only one or two main participants with the others flinging in their approvals. None of these active participants had anything interesting to say. Some of them held their group's attention by expressive gestures, others by the mere beauty of their bodies. Every group I tried to enter, I felt that people were judging me, wondering who I was and why I thought I should even be there.

Before I realized what I'd done, I found myself shimming between two people and out the front door. The warm night air felt cool and refreshing compared to the stuffy hive I'd just emerged from. I lingered for a few minutes, attempted to start a conversation with a girl, but quickly lost her and found myself in the company of another guy who felt just as uncomfortable as I did. Since I'd rather spend the night alone than with somebody like me, I fibbed a little; told him I was only here for a minute and that I had other engagements to go to. I then walked back to my apartment.

In my empty room, I tried to do homework or write an article recounting my observations at the party, but my social failure scraped bitterly against my chest. I couldn't feel included there and I couldn't keep my mind off it here. Part of me wanted to go back and give it another try, but I'd already told one person that I had another engagement. Would the others know that I'd ditched out, only to crawl back as a pathetic loser? I didn't know. All I did know was that I was not going back. I'd have to do better next time. I should have observed Thing Two more closely to learn how he mingled. But I was no Thing Two. Even if I emulated his actions, I doubted I could pull it off.

I lay down on my bed and tried to sleep. Hours crept

by. I must've fallen asleep because one instant I was alone, then, after I blinked, Duy was pulling off his clothes and flopping into his bed.

"How was the party?" I asked him.

"Ungh," he grunted.

I was surprised to notice that he smelled badly of rum. Did he not realize the punch was spiked? "I thought you didn't drink?"

"Doen judje me. Ye're aways judjin me, Gaud's judjin me, eveyone's judjin me," he slurred before getting up and tripping to the bathroom. I listened to his pitiful heaving in the other room. He must not have completely emptied his sour stomach, because he didn't come back into the bedroom. I fell asleep.

In the morning, I went to the bathroom to shower. Showering was a luxury I looked forward to. Back home, we just used a bucket of water to clean ourselves with. But these campus apartments had real showers with warm water. Stepping into the bathroom I flicked on the light. I was immediately assaulted by the smell of bile. There was Duy, resting in a crusty pool of vomit that glued his hair to the floor. With a groan of agony, he curled his legs up into a ball at the base of the toilet. He must've passed out there last night. I held my breath, afraid the putrid stench would ruin my appetite for breakfast, then I turned the light off. I could wait till evening to shower.

In the kitchen Thing One was eating warm rice with a saccharine salt-pickled cabbage. With it was a red, sticky sweet-and-spicy sausage. That happened to be my favorite breakfast food. Being the typically perceptive guy he was, Thing One offered me a full serving of the meal and added, "Poor Duy." He wasn't so much sympathizing with Duy as he was with me. "You know it can't be easy for him."

"What do you mean?"

"The Believers aren't only ridiculed by everyone not of their religion, but they're finding it increasingly difficult to believe in their own teachings themselves. They're so devoted, that if they fall away from their beliefs, they often feel guilty and or duped. They tend to fall hard, and it looks like he's on the brink of falling away. I'm just saying, be easy on him. I hate to see him stumble from his beliefs. He really is a good guy. We just need to be there for him if he needs us. One of these days, he'll see his folly, and he might need a friend to help him back up."

I hadn't noticed it in myself, but Thing One had seen the disappointment in my face. I actually felt disappointed that Duy hadn't been true to the commitments his faith demanded. "How do you know so much about these Believers?"

But in typical Thing One fashion, he just tossed the last piece of meat into his mouth and slapped me once hard on the back. "You're a good man, Iddo." Then, grabbing his books, he left the house.

Again, that slap on the back brought back memories of Midnight. I pushed the thought away, along with the urge to burp. Nobody had ever called me a man before, let alone a good man. I felt inadequate for the title, but I wanted to be that man. Of everyone I'd met so far in my life, I wanted to be like Thing One. Then it hit me. One of these days, I should learn his real name.

Chapter 14

The woods hold strange people. People who can't live in normal society. Maybe they were unwanted children, or perhaps they are the deformed and simply seeking a life free of persecution. In nearly every case, these people were rejected by our society. They are the strange and detested; then there are the dark ones. Some venture in looking for this brand of evil talent. Some find it. Clearly though, not all who reside in the woods are bad.

Our last week together was fun. I still didn't understand Thing Two very well and Duy seemed to be struggling more and more with his resolve to live up to the Believers' covenants. For some reason, those two were always together. Somehow, I'd grown comfortable with all of them, even Jhon and Charles. We may not have played much together, but we all got along just fine. Our mutual satisfaction was good enough that we all decided to room together again the next semester. For the next three months, before school was out, we were all anxious to go home and visit our families.

Jhon and Charles were the first to leave. Not by any choice of theirs; it's just that their parents arrived early on a Saturday morning in their shiny cars. Their good-byes were stiff and awkward. Duy was next to have his belongings packed. He'd gotten up earlier than me to start. As a Believer, he wasn't allowed to drink alcohol. I don't think he wanted me to see him cleaning out the dozens of empty beer and rum bottles from under his bed. Even if I had been able to sleep in, the thin glass of his new forbidden vice made a gentle clink that was just sharp enough to shatter any hopes of early morning dreams. Really, it's not like I didn't know about his drinking. It was often on his breath. Even worse was the smell his body made after sleeping the night while sweating it out, but if he felt shamed by it, I'd play ignorant. I wasn't a Believer, but even I saw the evil in alcohol. Mostly I felt sorry for him.

When I finally did get up, I took a quick shower. Showers are always quick when they're cold. I suppose the apartment managers didn't feel like paying for warm water for one more day than they absolutely had to. Not a big deal. It's not like I grew up with warm water. The air was generally hot enough that cold water usually felt good.

"Well, I guess I'll see you when school starts back up," Duy said to me.

I was just toweling off. The stiff fibers were quick to scratch, but slow to dry. I made sure to tuck the towel firmly around my waist. With one hand firmly on the towel, in case it decided to slip, I reached with my other to shake his outstretched palm. He was my roommate and I was forced to dress in front of him occasionally. But that didn't mean I was comfortable being naked around him. I gripped his hand in mine. "Three months, Duy. I look forward to it." There wasn't much more to say. We'd already stayed up late last night talking about our plans for the summer.

"But hey, when school starts up again, Iddo, you and I will need to play some more. You're almost to the point where you don't need me to tutor you every free minute you get. You're way too busy besides that."

It was true. I was making good progress in my schooling. Toward the end I was almost able to keep up, only requiring about an hour each week of help from Duy. I said, "You can count on it" but I didn't really mean it. I knew deep down that, even though I was catching up to the other students, I'd be too busy to play much with Duy. Maybe because experience told me that I wouldn't be given any breaks. More likely though, I didn't want to spend that kind of time with Duy.

His idea of play was drifting toward a lifestyle I didn't admire. I don't think the Duy of nine months ago would've approved, either. Hopefully being back with his family for a few months would strengthen his integrity. I don't know why I worried so much for him. If he wanted to rebel from his faith, that was his choice. Still, it's sad.

All of this passed through my head in half a second while he gripped my hand. With my sympathies running high and my other hand holding my towel, I realized I was rendered defenseless when his free hand swung around. Too late. I prepared for a totally awkward hug, but instead received a hard jovial slap on my bare wet back.

I wrenched my hand away from his as his face contorted into a maniacal grin. "That'll leave a mark," he laughed.

"Go home," I jested back. "Nobody likes you here, anyway. Go torment your family for a change." The hand-shaped welt on my back felt like a gigantic bee sting. I suspected that in a few hours I could look in a mirror and still see every fingerprint of Duy's hand, etched into the full handprint that was now there. Of course there'd be no mirrors where I'd be sleeping tonight.

Thing Two looked curiously sad as Duy left the apartment. I got dressed and was next to go. Thing Two went in for a slap just like Duy's, but I dodged it. I'd come to understand that those two were remarkably similar in personality, though Thing Two was a little more extreme in his mood swings.

Thing One just gave me a wink and waved good-bye with a finger. "Take care of yourself. I know you will," was all he said before retreating into his room.

Of all my roommates, I'd miss him the most. He was the most mysterious of them all, and yet I felt a connection with him. I almost hoped that next year the sleeping arrangements would stay the same. I'd hate to room with him only to learn that he had darker secrets that made me lose some degree of respect for him. Somehow I knew that was silly. He was a good man.

After two hours of walking in the woods, I wondered if, for my return trip, a compass might be a good investment. I had no intention of visiting the hangman, nor his lost children. I remembered the general direction of where they'd been holed up. Since it was out of my way, there was no reason to extend my hike there. It would just delay my trip back home. The woods held less mystery to me now that I'd crossed them once and learned one their biggest and best-kept secrets. This illusion of comfort was stupid on my part.

I'd been walking for about eight hours when I stopped to rest and eat my evening meal. I planned to hike for another couple hours before bedding down, but my stomach ached with hunger. I hadn't even sat down yet when I felt a small prickle running up my back. Stupid Duy, he didn't have to hit me that hard. But the prickle was followed by a chill, as if his handprint was warning me of something I should've noticed by now. The first telltale sign was a small flicking point just under a shrub of undergrowth. No, there were several small flicking points all around me. The sun hadn't set yet, but everything seemed darker.

I froze as I focused on the shiny yellow-and-black-striped bodies attached to the flickering tongues. The cylindrical bodies of the kraits were now distinctly visible. These nocturnal snakes, though extremely venomous, were often shy and rarely bit humans. But at least twenty, each between one and two meters long, were surrounding me in an ever-tightening circle.

That shouldn't have been happening. Snakes don't coordinate, especially this cannibal variety. They were more likely to fight and eat each other than to attack a person. But coherent thought had been replaced by panic. I spun around once, twice, my frantic eyes desperately seeking out any avenue of escape. But I couldn't run between any of them without getting bitten. Somewhere deep down in my instincts—it had to be instinct—I knew that I was going to die. *Thanks a lot, instincts.* Not very helpful.

Unlike the last time I panicked in a life-threatening situation, this time instead of freezing up, my legs moved without my realizing it. I knew it was useless, but I raced toward one of the smaller snakes, anyway. As I reached it, I leaped as high and far as I could. I don't think I'd ever jumped so powerfully in my life. I felt suspended in the air as I floated over the earth and across the snakes. I suddenly thought that I'd been very foolish to panic. All I had to do was jump over them. I knew that as soon as I hit the ground and put a few meters between us, I'd feel silly for having nearly lost my head.

I was feeling good when something twisted around my ankle. I felt the sharp fangs of the deadly snake puncturing the back of my calf. I tumbled to the ground, rolling and kicking. The snake held on for the longest three seconds of my life. Finally, it let go and slapped to the ground beside me. For a moment, we both stared motionless into each other's eyes. Those glassy black beads were cold and pitiless. A black forked tongue flitted out of its mouth, tasting the victory. Then it turned around and slithered away. There were no other snakes in sight. It was as if they had all gathered to see which one could bite me first. Satisfied that one of them had poisoned me, the rest to lost interest.

I lifted my pant leg and stared at the two aching holes in my skin. Thin red trickles oozed from the bite. It hurt a little but didn't fester. Maybe the snake hadn't released its venom. I stood up, trembling. A quick survey told me that I was definitely alone again. I walked with a slight limp, not so much from the pain in my leg, but from fear that if I used my leg too much, the poison might circulate more quickly throughout my body. A foolish notion, I know. I didn't need to study medicine to know better. But I was too far away from any medical help. My chances of dying tonight were high. Treated, I'd likely have a fifty percent chance of survival. Untreated, that chance was more like ten or twenty percent.

I was a wounded animal. My only desire was to put as much distance between myself and the place of attack, in case the demon snakes came back for more fun. The farther I moved, the more my stomach muscles constricted and cramped. Walking upright was increasingly difficult. I staggered first to one side, then the other. Still, I lumbered on, bumping into trees as I went. My eyes struggled to focus when I smelled something burning. No, my eyes weren't fuzzy; my eyelids were drooping uncontrollably. I was entering the early stages of ptosis.

My nostrils caught the burning smell that had to mean somebody else was out here. That or I was experiencing another symptom I hadn't learned about yet. The scent had a disgustingly sweet bite to it, like somebody was cooking a slab of meat, but with the hair still on it. I tripped on an exposed root and fell into a small clearing. A disorderly camp, well used from longer-term dwelling, lay before me. A pile of stones stood about a meter high with smoke billowing up. It made me think of an old-fashioned altar for burnt offerings. The cooking smell had been from some unfortunate animal that was lying on top of it. It looked to be either a goat or dog. All that was left was the skin blackened with fire and that sharp smell of burned hair. The heat-stretched face of the animal gave no clues as to its identity, because all its teeth were missing.

My muscles spasmed and I curled into the fetal position. Then I became aware of somebody over me, speaking in a language I hadn't heard in a long time. It was one of the old languages from before the war, before English had come to dominate our tongue. I only understood part of it. Even the words I should've recognized were of a different dialect and were difficult to put together. Then the voice addressed me, as only a longtime smoker could. With raspy accusation, and still somehow amused, she said, "You's spek Engish? You's bited by dark kin eater. I is waited for you long time. Come, I fixin you up."

I tried to lift my head; I could scarcely make out the woman. She had feathers growing on her. No that wasn't right—she was wearing a shawl made of feathers.

"Come on!" she demanded. "You want die like dis?"

Somehow I forced myself into a crouching stand and half ran after her. I felt myself falling forward as I entered her hut, but could do nothing to stop my fall. When she leaned over me and looked into my face, I could see that she wasn't nearly as old as she sounded, not much older than forty. And then there was her shawl. I had to crane my head up to see from under my drooping eyelids. It didn't just have feathers sewn into it. It was a shawl made from the hide of a large bird, unnaturally dyed black. A small cord pierced its lifeless eye sockets and tied where the beak should have been, holding the feathered cloak around her neck.

Everything I saw from there seemed to spin in a dizzy blur. She was a witch. The world around me darkened with each motionless twist of my vision. As I slipped into blackness, I hoped that she'd save me. I hoped it, almost as much as I feared what would happen to me if she did save me.

Chapter 15

I've seen the good and the evil. Most of us never see the full depth of either, because we live in our gray shelters with our own artificial fluorescent lights. There's danger in ignorance, yet most of us prefer to live with our eyes only half open. I don't know if we're afraid of being wrong, or afraid of having more accountability. Either way, I know that evil has real power. Because of this, God must be real, too, with real power. Evil cannot exist without righteousness. And if this is the case, do we really have to wonder who will eventually triumph? Why, then, do most of us sit on the fence, trying not to offend either force?

In the darkness, I could see an enormous yellow-and-black-striped snake. Its jaws unhinged and a gaping mouth with dripping fangs scooped up my feet. My legs were wet with warm reptilian saliva as my waist moved closer and closer to its hollow eyes. I tried to scream my protest, but the only sound was the wet suction of my body entering its mouth. Its neck bulged and my chest scraped past its scaly lips, into that balmy neck.

Its mouth clamped shut around my neck, and my head, the only part of me not yet swallowed, stared past its disjointed jaw and into its eternal eyes. I could see fire in those glassy balls. The monster seemed to smile before opening its mouth one last time. I felt the snake's muscles contract as its squeeze pushed me further into its stomach. Its mouth closed, plunging me into darkness.

I was slipping and sliding down the inside of the snake when I awoke with a jump and a yelp. My arms and legs spasmed up wildly before I came to my senses. I was lying down on a wooden plank bed. My clothes were missing and I was covered in a stinking paste of mud, blood, animal guts, and who knows what else. I looked around and, for a second, I thought I saw the snake's fire-lit eye again. I drew a sharp, painful gasp. The eye was just a round metal teakettle, reflecting the fire that burned below it in a small rock hearth. With a chilled shake, I exhaled.

Nobody was in the room with me. I couldn't remember how I'd come to be like this. I certainly hadn't smothered myself in this tarlike substance. At least the witch had the decency to leave my undergarment on. Remarkably, I felt much better. I don't know how long I'd slept. Some of my muscles were still a little stiff, but even that may have just come from lying on the hard, flat plank of wood. If it weren't for the fact that I looked like the Creature from the Black Lagoon, I might get up and continue my way home.

My stomach grumbled, and I realized I was famished. No, I wouldn't get very far at all. I needed to get cleaned up and get a good meal. Lifting myself off the wooden bed, I stood. My head spun with unexpected dizziness. I had to sit again and focus on my breathing. I was alive, though weak.

A sheet of canvas ruffled to the side of the doorway and the witch entered the room. Around her neck she wore a necklace of teeth. Bracelets of bird beaks made a dull clicking noise as she raised a hand to grab my jaw. Staring deep into my eyes, she first turned my head left, then right. "You owe me. I save you life, you lucky I here. Dat bite nough to keell el'phant."

"Who are you?"

"I is you savior, dat's who I is." She walked over to the kettle of hot water and poured it into a large bowl. Dipping an old torn rag into the steaming bowl, she wiped my skin clean of the black goo. Each time the scalding rag touched me, I flinched. How could she keep dipping her own fingers in that bowl and not recoil from the heat?

As she cleaned, she pulled off an occasional black rock, inspected it, then dropped it to the bottom of the water bowl. The rocks weren't the only thing besides black paste that were stuck on me. Giant leeches, the size of my fingers, were also attached all over my body. She delicately cleaned around these bloodsucking creatures, then pulled out a sharp knife.

She noticed my wide, horrified eyes. "Hush. I is not tryin' hurt you." She laid the edge of the blade flat on my chest and shaved the first leech right off. A small bead of blood lifted from my skin as she continued to scrape off more of the black slugs.

My face and legs were next to be cleaned. The water wasn't as hot by this time, but that made the stinking tar-like grime harder to remove. When she got to my belly, she tisked in disapproval a few times. The whole process took about half an hour. All of it was done in near silence. Not complete silence. I may have whimpered a little. She kept giving satisfied grunts, especially whenever she'd remove an especially fat leech.

When finished, she left the room for a minute. I used the time to pull on my clothes. I'd just woken up, but I felt so tired and weak, I could scarcely stand and put on my pants at the same time. I hoped she'd removed all those nasty leeches as I pulled my shirt over my head. That was when I noticed: My head was bald. She'd shaved my head while I was asleep. This was too weird. When she came back in, she gave me a plate of eggs, overcooked strips of goat meat, and milk.

"Eat. Get you strong. I serve you now, but you is soon to serve me. You be workin' hard to please me."

I ate the eggs and meat with my fingers. The food was nothing special, but such was my hunger that I would've inhaled it in a single bite. Only guilt slowed my pace. Guilt at letting myself be so vulnerable that I'd eat from a witch's plate. For all I knew she had some other cruel poison or potion that would help enslave me to her will.

After drinking the whole glass of milk, I felt remarkably better. I stood and didn't feel like tumbling to the ground. Slowly I made my way to the canvas flap. Parting it I looked outside to where a fire was burning. The lady was there, quietly chanting something I could not understand. In one hand she held a soft, hand-sewn doll with short black hair. My hair? She then took one of the leeches and squeezed it like a tube of toothpaste, its bloody black pulp got smeared all over the doll. Then she took another leech and squeezed all its juices between her teeth. I cringed.

Licking her lips at what had to be the most disturbing meal I'd ever witnessed, she took one last living leech. Together with the two dead and flattened leeches she held them over the fire. All three burst into flames. The fire licked all around her fingers but she didn't seem to care. Nor did the fire appear to hurt her.

"It is done." She smiled with wicked mirth as she turned to face me.

I don't know how, but she knew that I'd been watching her the whole time. "What is done?"

"You know."

At the same time three leech bitten scabs started to heat up. The burning entered my bones, then followed them to my back where it ran up and down my spine. My stomach nearly crawled out of my throat. I knew. Sick with shaking dread, I knew.

She took the doll and bent its knees. Involuntarily, I collapsed to my own knees. "Me owns you now," she said. "You be doin' what me tells you do, for now and always."

There on my knees, I emptied my belly of the eggs and meat and milk of my recent meal.

"Haya!" She screamed. "You's wast'n me food, foolish by! You serves me, you needs be stronger." She thought for a minute tapping the doll against her chin. I felt every tap, it gave me a headache. I could even smell her breath.

I wasn't just terrified, I was violated in the most evil way I could image. My very body was no longer mine. I could feel the thick tendrils of evil, weaving their searing strands around my bones. Invisible strings tied me to this witch like a puppet for her to perform her darkest pleasures. This was the end of Iddo. I could hardly imagine what she'd want of me. I wanted to die before I had a chance to find out, but even that choice was out of my reach to control.

Suddenly, she had an idea. I didn't like the malicious grin she gave me either. Taking the doll in each hand, she began to stretch it.

I screamed, but not from pain. Her intent wasn't to hurt, but whatever evil she'd woven into that thing, it was affecting me. I felt my stomach burning. My considerable gut was transforming. I can never explain how it feels to have your body cannibalized over the course of minutes and turned into something else. At first I thought I was suddenly slimming, but then I felt my clothing get tight all around me. Then it ripped. I had grown from five foot tall to over seven feet tall in that horrific moment.

I fell to the ground, exhausted, as if I hadn't slept in weeks. Hungry too. All I could hear was her laughing. In my dizziness, I saw that my arms and legs were skinny. It hadn't just been my gut the growth had robbed my bulk from, but every part of me. When I woke up next, I ate what felt like a whole goat. She slowly stuff that doll with sawdust and me with food over the next week, and my strength returned and then some.

The horror of my predicament was short lived. Being

a slave to a witch was nothing like I'd thought. The first month passed. I did everything from taking care of her animals to chopping wood. Contrary to what I would've guessed a witch to prefer, she was a stickler for cleanliness. In fact, she was more concerned with cleanliness than even my own mother.

My mother. I should have been home weeks ago. I knew she couldn't help me. Not here. What was she thinking right now? She knew I was supposed to come home for the summer break, but if I was late, what could she do other than place a call to the college? They wouldn't know anything and they certainly wouldn't send any search parties into the woods. Would she even recognize me if she saw me now?

Today I was dusting. Dust was never present here. I think some magic spell kept it away. Still, every minute I wasn't busy chopping wood or fixing meals, I was supposed to be dusting. And spiders—if I found a single spider, no matter the size, I was to smash it to a pulp and add its gooey remains to the other invaders of her territory that she kept ringed around her home. These creepy bugs, like dust, seemed repelled by that ring of dried remains. Still, a spider or two would occasionally find its way past that mystical circle. Probably by floating over it on a strand of silk. "Scustin' creatures," she called them.

Rarely did she openly display her religion. Aside from that terrible doll which transformed and bound me to her, plus that healing she'd first performed on me, she never did anything within my sight or hearing. I think she was afraid that I'd learn something that I could use against her.

Aside from her unusual jewelry, she seemed pretty normal. Well, hermitic and demanding, but not supernaturally weird. Even her speech wasn't all that different from some people I knew. They were usually older than this woman, but they had learned English, if only out of necessity. Many of them resented that their native tongue was disappearing from our culture altogether.

I wanted desperately to get away from this place. But every so often, more at the beginning than later, this self-pronounced Laidy of the Woods, or Laidy for short, would jab her doll with a needle, or flick it with her finger. One flick felt like being slapped in the face by a heavy door. The needle, oooh the needle! Imagine being impaled by a fence post. Just the memory of it makes me tremble. I wondered if the hangman was out there somewhere. Did even he dare venture near these witches? I dreamed of him coming in with that thick righteous rope of his to sever the grasp that Laidy held on my soul. I don't know when I started thinking of his rope as righteous, but if this was hell, I'd happily live in his paradise.

That was dangerous thinking though. It brought back memories of Midnight. With every memory of the hangman, or every comparison I made of a girl, my thoughts always came back to her. Even if I did love her, which I didn't, I was never going to see her again.

Occasionally, when Laidy wasn't in easy view of me, I'd get the idea to run. Then, as if she had magically read my mind, I'd feel my sides pinch in, as if a giant had taken hold of me with two massive fingers. I could almost imagine her holding my doll and playing with it like a little child. "Me owns you for always," she'd say.

One morning after I'd woken up, I set to work making her breakfast. I felt different that morning. It wasn't just that my arm had fallen asleep. Laidy had fallen asleep on my doll's arm again. No, I felt frustrated and rebellious. I wanted to see my mother. If I remained here, slave to the cleanest witch in the world, I'd scream till my throat bled. Also, I wanted to go back to school. Laidy might be able to smother my hot head with just the threat of her sewing needle, but I was determined that she wouldn't see my hate for her. I had to get that doll away from her.

I watched her finish her porridge, waiting for any opportunity. Then it happened. As if Providence had opened a way, she stood to take a walk in the woods. The doll fell from her lap onto the ground. I felt the fall like one who wakes from a fall in a dream. I also felt the slap of the earth. My whole body jolted. But it was over in an instant, just a dream. In the seconds following, I bent over and picked up the doll.

"Give me here, boy," Laidy warned, stretching her arm out.

"I will not be controlled by you anymore. I have the doll now and I'm leaving."

My heart froze as she laughed with a wicked smile. "You think me needs a doll? You see me drink black blood of sucker yes. We three be one."

Then, to my horror, she lifted her finger to her mouth and clamped her yellow teeth so hard that her finger snapped in two places. I knew this because my finger suddenly broke in two places. I screamed in pain. She screamed in exultation.

I clutched my finger, a useless attempt to ebb the pain. Then I watched in horror, as she grabbed her broken finger with her other hand and commenced churning and grinding the broken pieces of her own bone together in a circular pattern.

I howled and recoiled, falling to the ground. I wanted to bury my hand in the earth. I wanted to cut it off. The grinding shot lightning bolts of pain up my whole arm. Even my teeth ached with each gyration.

When she finally let up, my jaw ached and I could just make out the taste of sweet copper in my mouth. My teeth had been clenched so tight with the pain that that my gums had bled. My teeth would be fine, but I would never forget the feeling of my finger as its bones were intentionally grated together.

When her shadow crossed over mine, I looked into her eyes. They were both hard and soft, like that of a dark souled parent, disappointed for having to discipline a child. She held out her hand and I passed the doll up to her. She clenched it tight in her fist; my sides ached with the squeeze. But her broken finger was miraculously whole again. I looked at my own finger, expecting it to be good again. But no, mine truly was broken. Somehow hers had healed, and mine had been the one that broke for real. I even had teeth marks in my skin. It was exactly as if she'd bitten my finger, not hers.

"Dis pain is much worse when done it dis way. You learn. You be mine for always, boy."

That night I could barely sleep. I had nightmares of the most morbid self-mutilating tortures that Laidy could do and physically transfer to me. The whole while I could see her grinning and laughing, with her own blood dripping from her mouth. I imagined the blood changing to mine, not the normal red, but that same black ooze she'd sucked from the leech after healing me of the snake bite. I could feel it dripping around her teeth as she laughed at my agony. Then I finally fell asleep.

I expected nightmares, but that's not what happened. In my dreams, I was filled with light. I re-experienced my day back in journalism prep and how I'd seen some peers chanting and piercing their tongues. The memory of my epiphany at the time resonated in my mind. *If evil has power, then the Devil is real. If the Devil is real, then God must be real, too. And if God is real, then he too must have power. Not just any power, but power over evil.*

I woke early. My mind was at peace. I examined my finger. It was still broken. Somehow the pain was less. The swelling had gone down in the last couple hours of sleep. I took it for a sign that my dream was telling me a truth that I needed to heed. Sitting up, I struggled to firm up my resolve. Already the impact of my epiphany was fading. I knew that if I didn't act soon, my newfound faith would abandon me all together. But how to act?

I could take the wood axe and drive it into Laidy's chest when she wasn't expecting it. No, I was no killer. I don't think I could even kill a dog, let alone a human. Not even if that human was some wicked hag that had no qualms about hurting me. Besides, even if I did work up the will to slam that chopping wedge into her chest, like my finger, she'd probably laugh it off, and I'd be the one with the hole in my heart. There was really only one thing I could think to do.

I would do it. I took one last look at my finger, a twinge of fear curled in my gut. I pushed the feeling away. It's funny how even when evil is so evident, faith placed in righteousness can seem more daunting. I had to keep reassuring myself as I got dressed and gathered my few belongings. I made one last meal for Laidy of the Woods, picking up my money clip that was stashed in her room as I delivered her food. She would have seen me reach for it if she was looking. But she was seated at an odd angle, and couldn't have seen what I'd taken.

"You not be thinkin' to take me doll today, boy?"

"No, you can keep the doll. It's not important to me anymore."

She eyed me suspiciously as I left the room.

After exiting, I walked and didn't stop. Even after I heard her shriek, I didn't turn back. My mind was focused on hope and the power of Him to deliver me. Even when she sent her snakes after me, I kept walking. The slithering serpents barred my way as they had done the first time, no doubt intending to bite me and force me back to the witch. But my faith rendered the voodoo ineffective. Even the throbbing in my finger ebbed to a dull nothing. I wondered if Laidy's shriek had been because her magic wasn't working, or because the pain of my finger had somehow transferred back to her.

In any case, I just lifted my eyes to the tree's canopy and let the morning heat fill my heart. I walked right through the snakes, not caring where my feet landed. I had tapped into the merciful power of the Almighty. He protected me from the poisonous fangs of the Laidy's reptiles.

In my mind, I thought on everything I'd ever been told. There was truth in what people preached about witches. The Believers on the other hand, they were different. I had just defeated the power of this witch. Was the ability to do this, the same power that Believers relied upon? Duy had admitted that some of his people really did have miraculous powers. He'd refused to demonstrate. I almost think he couldn't show me, even if he wanted to.

What I was feeling right now, it felt so pure and good. Duy had been experimenting with his freedom. He was away from his family, and subsequently anyone that would disapprove of his actions. He was testing a life of deeds that were in conflict with his people—with his god.

I leaped over a log and experimented with my new freedom, and knew it was a much better freedom. I stretched out my arms. For the first time in a good long month, I felt so alive and free. Free from the clutches of evil. Free from the fog that filled my mind, not just from this last month, but for most all my life. I almost felt like skipping and jumping. So I did, at least for a minute. Eventually this strength and power left as did my breath.

Finally, out of breath, as the exultation of the moment faded, I knew in my heart that Laidy's control over me was permanently severed. Yet I would forever be scarred in more ways that one for my experience there. For one, my finger, though it no longer aches, has healed in a slightly crooked manner. Even more noticeable, was the fact that I was a giant now, maybe not for an American athlete, but definitely for any natives here. I had the height, and I had the muscle.

I also felt as though I understood the fierce rivalry between the witches and Believers. Witches would use the power of the devil. Believers, well, I know evil can't defeat evil. Plus, what I felt was definitely not evil. If anyone could tell the difference, I could. Evil was in the power of Laidy. Evil was the motivation that led men to dispose of their babies in the woods. Evil was in so much of the subtleties daily life. But there was good in the world too.

Even the hangman, by comparison, was good. In his own way, he waged a one-man war against the bad that invaded his realm. Despite Duy's weak resolve to follow his own beliefs, he wasn't a bad guy either. At least I didn't believe he was. His choices were increasingly leading him in that direction though.

Unfortunately, even though I'd already made some progress this year, changing my perspective on the Believers would be challenging. I had some real truths to work out for myself. I wasn't ready to run out and join their ranks. But there are powers in this world that go beyond normal reasoning. I knew this now. Because of this, I had to figure out how they all fit together. If they indeed were attributed to God, then perhaps there was life after death also. If that is the case, then I would be supremely stupid not to search for a better understanding.

I had time though. I didn't want to procrastinate for too long, lest I lose my zeal. But for now, I was free. I knew for sure the source of my freedom and I would treasure that miracle forever.

Chapter 16

Daddy Smiling is not a criminal. He may be a form of vigilante. But if our fuzzy law permits bribery and corruption in all levels of government and law enforcement, what right do they have to condemn this man? For years now they've turned a blind eye to murder of the youngest and most innocent. Their deliberate ignorance created the hangman. He hunts down the cruelest of our society, adopting their young into his band. Only with Daddy Smiling do they stand a chance at life. Live they do, and wonderfully too.

I walked for the better part of the day. Normally I would've been a little concerned, but some of that light optimism stubbornly clung to my mood. While I had a general idea of what direction to pursue, I was also aware that I had a lot of jungle to navigate and no clear path. I hadn't thought to bring any food for my journey, as escaping Laidy had been my only goal. Maybe I should've thought things through a little. Of course, if I'd done that, I wouldn't have attempted it. Even still, while my mind told me to worry, my heart assured me that all would be well.

Toward late afternoon I stopped to rest. My heart might be light, but my stomach had no problem voicing its complaints with constant grumblings. A quick survey told me that none of the trees or plants held anything worth eating. At least nothing that I knew could be eaten.

There was nothing else to be done. I stood up to continue my hike. I looked up at the sun to check my bearing. My shoulders fell, pulling my heart with them. Now that the sun was drifting more to one side of the sky, I saw that for the last couple hours I'd been going the wrong direction. I wasn't backtracking, but I'd gone a little perpendicular to where I wanted to be heading.

A twig snapped in the distance. Someone or something was out here. Could that be Laidy, or one of her animals? I hoped I hadn't gone in a large circle! I couldn't risk walking on like before if someone was following me. I needed to know who or what was out there.

Slowly and quietly I crept toward where the twig had snapped. It was probably just a rodent on a dry branch. There were no more noises and nothing living to be seen. By the time I figured that I'd gone beyond the snapped twig, I gave up. There was nothing out here. I turned around, determined to be back on my way—then froze.

Before me on the ground was the distinct imprint of a shoeless foot. Did Laidy wear shoes? I think she did. At least sandals. Judging from the size, it could've been her foot. I walked a little further and found another print. This one was smaller but clearly human. A smile touched the corner of my lips. I sped up, nearly running along the tracks. A charlie horse brought me back to a crawl and I had to limp along until the pain faded.

At times, the tracks were hard to follow. After an hour, I had no problem. The tracks were joined by others, until eventually there was a nearly packed-down trail leading to their camp. I walked into the clearing just before sunset. A few heads turned my way, but I kept on going until I found Midnight. She was eating alone.

For the last hour, I'd forgotten much of my hunger. Not all, but enough to let my mind think about her. Now, as I stood in place and watched her gracefully dine on her humble meal, I couldn't help but lose all the confidence I'd acquired over this incredible day.

My heart thudded, dragging my heavy nerves with each pounding beat. Why was I so nervous to walk up to her? Would she even recognize me anymore? And where was Chirp-chirp and Grub? At least they could help make this easier on me. Slowly, she found herself aware of the attention directed at her. Her eyes lifted to meet mine. Her head raised, followed quickly by her smile. She stood as I approached. She looked more beautiful than I remembered, stunning me anew. Before I knew it, we were in each other's arms. We held each other close for several seconds. How had that just happened? She was taller than me before, now she was shorter, but she felt so good in my arms

"You came back. I knew you would, yes I did," she said as she let go of me. You've grown up, yes you have. Big and strong, like Daddy Smiling."

My chest was pounding and I couldn't think of how to answer. I hadn't ever planned to come back; it had just kind of worked out that way. Yes, I might have day-dreamed about it a little, but fantasizing about it wasn't the same as actually doing anything about it. But I was glad to see her!

My heart palpitations weren't quite settled when I asked, "Chirp-chirp? Grub? Where are they?"

Her gaze dropped to the ground. Was it because I asked of them instead of telling her that I'd missed her? "Grub is Daddy Grub now. He helps Mommy Flor with new baby."

"Grub is raising a baby now?" I was shocked. Not just because Midnight held a small grudge against Flor, but he was just a little kid himself. I knew that these kids were given high responsibility early on, but it was hard to fully assimilate.

"Daddy Chirp-chirp is with Mommy Darling. They have new baby, too, yes they do."

"What about you?" I asked. "Are you going to get an-other baby and find a boy to help you raise him?"

She looked at me for a long minute, her eyes probing mine before my belly—no, not my belly, I couldn't really say that anymore, as it had been replaced by a muscled core. My stomach interrupted the moment with a gurgle of hunger. She laughed. "Big strong man needs big food." She stood and jogged over to the cooking area. My eyes never strayed as she went. She didn't have any of her own food left, but there was plenty of food left over from other pots that she was able to scrape together. It wasn't great, but it sure eased the pain in my stomach.

That night we walked and talked for hours. I told her of the witch, my schooling, and my work. She told of how Daddy Smiling was bringing in so many babies that some kids were even adopting two. If there was that many new babies, I wondered why Midnight hadn't taken on another one herself. But every time I raised the question, she deflected it. I think we were the last ones to go to sleep that night.

I hadn't meant to stay long. My mother was probably worried sick. I'd only planned on staying for a meal or two. The normal Iddo would have been right on my way home to ease my mother's concern. But a meal or two turned into a day or two. Then that turned into weeks. Each night I would tell myself it was time to go home. Then I'd spend the evening talking with Midnight. There was something magical about this place.

This camp was as primitive as could possibly be. Aside from the occasional sound of a distant airplane, were completely cut off from the rest of the world. I loved it. The air was cool and fresh. Down by the small lake, the canopy parted to show more stars in the heavens than I'd ever noticed before. Just like the witch's cottage, this place cast a spell of its own on me. And of course, there was Midnight.

My nostalgia for this place and the children's way of life was great enough that after a day or two, I'd taken to waking early in the morning. I'd follow the other boys into the woods for a day of gathering food. The first few times, Chirp-chirp or Grub helped me learn what to look for. After a week, I was doing everything on my own.

When I came back to the hangman's camp each night,

Midnight would be waiting with a warm smile to greet me. I was gathering for her and me. Some of the older kids teased us, calling us Mommy Midnight and Daddy Iddo, raising "Baby Nothing." Normally, this might have bothered me. Now, as long as Midnight was by my side, I was invulnerable. I could talk to her about everything and anything. Well, anything that is, if the language barrier didn't get in our way. We were both growing accustomed to each other's limits and we were adapting remarkably.

She even sympathized with my newfound feelings on Deity. I got the distinct impression that she had a deeper relationship with God, even if it was as primitive an understanding as my own.

Daddy Smiling still went out every day, sometimes bringing back a young child or infant. Most days he came back alone. When he wasn't doling out stewardships for the new arrivals or actually saving those children, he'd walk around the camp. He rarely said anything. With that huge toothy grin, he'd walk by, putting giant tender palm on each person's shoulder. His expression hardly ever changed. But there was something in those eyes. They were often squinted, but when he laid his hand on my shoulder, he no longer seemed such a giant in stature to me. He didn't seem to look at me like he did to the others. Rather, he opened his eyes to me, almost willing me to see into the wide depths of his heart. Though we were nearly the same size now, what I saw inside him was larger than life. Everything within him was giant, but especially his compassion for his children.

I loved this place and I loved the hangman. I have to admit that I quickly grew to love Midnight, also. And to think she saw something in me before, when I was still as unattractive and round as a melon, and now that I was freakishly big, like Daddy Smiling, it was hard to believe. But I knew that she loved me, regardless of how I looked, too. Every time we were with each other, we moved as close together as we could. Our shoulders or hands were always touching. My daily foraging was blissful, but even with the satisfaction of finding a living from the woods, my work was done in haste so I could return to be with Midnight.

I hadn't been keeping track of time very well. I'd allowed myself more distraction than I should have. I must have stayed for close to a month. What had I done to my mother?

For the last couple of weeks, I'd thought more and more about this. I was being selfish and I knew it.

I was on one of our evening walks when Midnight turned to me, "What's wrong? Are you Mad? Is my poor Iddo sad?"

"Midnight--I," I squeezed her hand, trying to think of how to say what needed to be said.

She looked at me, her eyes wet. Somehow, she knew what I was thinking. "You need go to Mommy Mother." That was what she called my mother, since I always referred to her simply as Mother.

I nodded.

"Daddy Smiling brings new babies. He needs new mommies, yes he does."

Where was she going with this? "Why haven't you gotten a new baby yet?"

"You came once and I feel not same. You here now and I am not same. I like not same. I want be Mommy Midnight with Daddy Iddo, but for always. I want be-"she struggled finding the right word, "-wife Midnight."

That caused my heart to skip more than a single beat. I pulled her close to me and hugged her. I inhaled the scent of her skin so close to mine. I wanted to hold her so tight that she'd be a part of me, never to separate.

"I want to be with you, too," I whispered in her ear.

"Stay," she begged.

"I can't. I have to go."

"Then I go, too."

I thought for a minute. There was no way. Not at this time. I would need at least a year. I had school to go to. I had an apartment already reserved for that year. I had a busy job. I had no way of supporting this wonderful girl.

"I have to go for a few days to visit my mother. I'll come back here for a few days. Then I'll need to leave again for a year. Just like I did last time. But I will come back."

"Then you stay?"

"Then I will take you with me, away from here. I will make you Wife Midnight." My stomach filled with butterflies as I said this and I knew that I wanted it to be so. She might lack my formal education, but there was nothing stupid about her. She would adapt quickly. Young as I was, I would have her for my wife.

Her smile, glistening with teardrops, filled me with warmth. "I wait for you, yes I will. I—love you, yes I do."

"And I love you." Then, for the first time for either of us, we kissed. Never was any moment so sweet as this. Never did I feel so weightless and happy. This was, without a doubt, the best day of my life.

The next day, she packed me enough food for the remainder of my journey home. We walked together, just far enough to be alone. After all, while boys and girls paired up to raise a child in this camp, none had ever actually fallen in love, at least not to my knowledge. Their families were just a temporary arrangement to help raise babies to the bare minimal point where they could in turn take care of a baby. Midnight was among the oldest here and her feelings were maturing beyond her peers. She wanted a real partner, with a real family. The others might not be able to understand. So we kissed one last time, away from their curious eyes.

Turning to walk away was the hardest thing I'd ever done. I wanted her to come with me, but found comfort in my resolve to visit again on my way back to school.

Chapter 17

Some wicked men accuse him of stealing children out of their homes. This lie only serves those who escape his noose. How else could they save face when confronted about their missing children? This deed is practiced openly, still they lie about it. Their own conscience condemns themselves. Yet they would rather harm this mentally challenged, disfigured man, who gives his all to provide a second chance at life to the innocent. If nothing changes, then one day you and they will look up and beg "Have mercy on me, and send this Lazarus, that he may dip the tip of his finger in water and cool our tongues; for we are tormented in this flame."

I'd grown used to spending the first several of hours of each day away from Midnight. But this time, for the first two hours of my hike away from her, I felt a heavy longing to return. My mind replayed our conversations. Had I really just proposed marriage to this girl? Well, maybe she proposed to me. But it had happened!

The thought made me giddy. The more I imagined it, the lighter my steps felt. Before long, I was practically skipping through the forest. The very idea of a life with Midnight had been unimaginable only a year ago. Now I could hardly wait to be with her again.

My biggest dilemma was, of course—should I tell my mother? I was young. Too young to even be thinking of marriage. I'd lost track of the exact day, but in another few weeks I would be seventeen. By the time I came back for Midnight, we'd likely get married at eighteen years old. Young still, yes, but not unheard of. The bigger shock to everyone would be that I, Iddo, had found such a beautiful and sweet girl who was willing to marry me. Of course, maybe that wasn't going to be the biggest shock, but it would surely rank high. So, no. I wouldn't tell my mother—yet. I might tell her that I had a girlfriend, but I would leave it at that.

Late that night I arrived home. Our humble home was dark and I knew my mother must be sleeping. Not wanting to wake her, I lay outside in front of the house and fell asleep. I anticipated dreaming about Midnight, but my subconscious had other things to sort out. Of all things, I dreamed of Duy. In my dreams, he and his fellow Believers were using their powers to battle the witch from the woods, with all her dark magic and poisonous serpents. The witch was strong in her power, but the Believers were stronger. Stronger, that is, until Duy was expected to contribute. Once he got involved, the witch gained the upper hand.

For some reason, Thing Two was there encouraging and criticizing him. The witch just smiled. Her snakes bit Thing Two then turned toward Duy. "Dere aw no ways you can serve both masters," she hissed. "We chosed we own path. You make yous choice and, me own you now. You be doin' what me tells you do, for now and always." The snakes all reared back then lunged to strike Duy—I woke with a jolt.

The sun was just peeking over the horizon. The morning heat was about to wash over me. The familiar smell of a cook fire drew my attention to the side of the house. My mother was already awake, heating a small pot of rice. Her smile was the sort that couldn't be removed, not even with a metal pry-bar. Not counting the extra wrinkles brought on by her grin, she looked much older and smaller. Wet puddles of tears had yet to dry from several creases that I'd never seen in her face before now.

"I'm so sorry, I wanted to let you know I was all right, I-"

She didn't let me finish. Her arms were around me in seconds. Apparently she hadn't exhausted her crying. Her breath came in ragged sobs. "What happened Iddo, where have you been? Are you okay? You grew up on me." She laughed, as if she couldn't believe her own words.

My mother, my wonderful mother. She looked radiant. Fresh tears leaked from her eyes and I couldn't help but let some of my own squeeze out too. Her cheeks were flushed, and her eyes glistened. But she was happy. Then without warning, she grabbed a ladle from another pot and smacked me on the top of my head, though given my size now, it hit closer to my forehead.

"Are you trying to kill me?" She scolded. "I was so worried for you! You better have a good explanation."

I rubbed my head. I could still hear the metallic thump of steel on skull. Over two months had passed since school let out. I'd had two months to figure out how to explain my delay and I was stumped. The nauseating sludge of guilt oozed into me, filling me with a sickness I never thought possible from a simple emotion. She stood in front of me with fists on her hips, that ladle still clutched in her right hand. That large steel spoon hurt and it threatened to give me another good whack if my story wasn't good enough. Maybe she would give me one anyways just for good measure.

I couldn't tell her about the witch. She'd never let me go back to school again. Still, this was my mother and I couldn't lie to her. I thought quick and hard. It was insanely difficult. How were other boys able let their mothers down so often and still go on living?

"I'm sorry. I didn't mean to make you worry. I just had a few extra lessons to learn after school ended. I didn't mean to be so late in coming."

They say that the best lie is one with some semblance of truth. Well, I did learn some lessons. I'd learned that there is a God, though I didn't know much about Him except that He's more powerful than a devil woman. I also learned that I loved a girl who would one day become my greatest treasure. I even remembered the dream that I'd just had. It was so vivid, almost like I had something to learn from it also, but I couldn't figure out what.

"You could have written. We may not have a phone, but your uncle does. Why didn't you call him? Iddo, I thought the woods had swallowed you! You can't do this to me."

"I'm sorry, I was so caught up in everything, I didn't even think-"

"That's right. I sent you to college and you still can't think!" The ladle raised in the air again. My hands shot up to defend myself but it didn't come down. Instead my mother pointed it at me as if it were a dueling sword. "You may have moved out mister, but that doesn't give you the right to ignore me. I called the police and the school. Nobody knew where you were. I nearly charged into the woods myself in search of you. If it weren't for you uncle, I just might have. And don't you go telling me that you enrolled in any summer classes, I already asked the school about that. Your newspaper hadn't heard from you either. So what were you up to?"

"I was staying with friends and I lost track of time." I felt bad for not telling her everything. I felt even worse that she caught my little fib. I felt bad for admitting that I'd been selfish. I felt so bad that I didn't even try to stop the ladle as it came down hard again on my forehead. Wow, she was strong when she was angry.

"I'm still mad at you, but I am relieved that you are safe. I don't care if you delay coming home. But next time you better write, even if you make it here before the letter does."

"Yes, Mother," I said through a growing headache.

While breakfast was cooking, she sat down on the ground in front of me, her flare of rage returned once more to the loving smile I'd known all my life. How could she still love me after that? "So I want to hear all about it."

"All about what?" Did she suspect something more?

The way she sat with that new glimmer in her eyes made me suspicious. Was it that obvious that I was in love?

"Your schooling. You've wanted this for a long time. How's it going? You found work at a newspaper—how was that?"

I sighed. Of course, school. I should have guessed.

"And who is the new girl in your life?"

I jumped in surprise. "Girl?"

She smirked. "Do you think I can't see the glow in your eyes? You can't hide something like that from your own mother."

I smiled. No, I guess I couldn't. But maybe a few details could still be hidden. At least until a more appropriate time.

We talked all through breakfast. I told her about my roommates, my job, schooling, and a little bit about Midnight. Luckily my mother got hung up on her name and didn't pry too deeply beyond that. She found it difficult to believe that any adult would name their child Midnight. I didn't tell her that it was probably other kids who'd given her that name.

Talking with my mother was nice. She even left for work a little late. Since there was nothing for me to do at the house, I took to wandering. Maybe I could find some small jobs to help her out while I stayed. Mostly, though, I didn't want to be bored sitting at home. There were plenty of neighbors to visit and I did talk with some of them. Somehow, I was drawn toward the marketplace and onward to the school of journalism that I'd attended not so long ago.

For maybe the first time in my life, I noticed the smells of my hometown. Obviously I'd smelled them before, but this was different. From the dried fish market to the lime dusted streets near the Tusk plant, my hometown was welcoming me back.

As I looked at my old school, despite my dislike for the profession, I couldn't help but admire the building with a sort of nostalgia. I didn't go in. Classes were out for the summer here, as well. I turned back around, retracing my steps in the direction of the marketplace. On a whim, I turned up a street I'd rarely walked. It took me through the richer neighborhood where Krystal lived. Surprisingly her father's house was among the more dilapidated homes in the neighborhood.

I heard a commotion coming from inside the home. A woman in her thirties came running out of the house. Her tight skimpy clothing suggested a profession meant for the most desperate. Krystal's father followed not far behind. He was missing a shirt; his hairy chest was slick as if he hadn't showered in weeks. He held a nearly empty bottle in one hand; I couldn't tell if he wanted to drink out of it or throw it at the retreating woman. He was shouting something that was so slurred, I could only grasp about every other word.

The woman kept quiet and quickly walked away, trying to avoid attracting any more attention. I turned around to ignore her. Any eyes following her would only add to her shame. I felt bad for her. I felt even worse for Krystal. I couldn't imagine coming home to such an environment. I remembered how I'd treated Krystal in the time I'd known her. Yes, she'd annoyed me, but she had a tough life too. At least I came from a good stable home. I should've treated her better. Despite my own insecurities, I now saw that she probably had a mountain of her own. She was the one who needed a good friend.

I hoped to see her now. She wouldn't be home, though. Not with her father in this state of angry inebriation. She probably didn't spend any more time at home than absolutely necessary.

I wouldn't.

Where would she be right now?

The next two weeks passed without much excitement. I never did see Krystal. I found a few odd jobs to help pay for meals while I was at home. My mother's health seemed good enough and I enjoyed spending time with her. But after two weeks, I was ready to leave. School would be starting again, and I wanted to be there at least a week beforehand, mostly to guarantee that nobody else came and took my journalism job. I'd also promised to see Midnight on my way back to school. I couldn't very well let her down.

Chapter 18

Do you consider yourself a good person?

Leaving home again was hard, but not as hard as last year. Home was welcoming and warm. I just didn't belong there anymore. It was strange to feel like a guest in the house I grew up in. On the other hand, my mother was sad to see me go. She treated the whole event as if I'd been leaving for the first time. But after packing me enough meals with portions large enough to last a full week, she released me to the woods.

The extra food weighed heavy on my shoulders. Its physical weight wasn't the issue. It's just that, she needed it more than me. I couldn't turn it down. Not without spurning her gesture of love. Soon I was back in the woods. Those mysterious trees held many secrets, but I'd grown much more confident in my ability to navigate them. Sometime tomorrow I'd see my Midnight.

The next morning, I woke early to raindrops. The sky was still dark, the sun an hour or two from rising—or at least I thought so. The trees always hid the stars, but I could usually find some, just not right now. It was a sign that they were all blanketed over by clouds. Thunder surged nearer, like the crashing waves of an ocean. It would be a large storm. I wondered if I'd found sufficient cover under this tree. The blackness of the sky, combined with the tree canopy, made seeing anything impossible. My eyes wouldn't tell me anything, but I would find out soon enough.

Soon enough came in about five minutes and no, I hadn't found adequate shelter. The lightning that skittered across the sky every thirty seconds offered some illumination when it was flashing. Already I was soaked and no place looked any better than where I sat. I could have stood, but I'd have been just as wet. Besides, I was cold and tired. Misery more than anything kept my butt planted in the soft mud.

With my arms wrapped tightly around my legs, I tented my shirt over my knees, hoping to bounce some of the water off the fabric. I tucked my head as close to my core as possible. With eyes squinted shut, I tried to find escape from the soppy shivers by falling asleep.

It didn't work. There was nothing to do but wait. For hours I sat, my mud hole getting softer and slimier by the minute. The impression my body made in the soft earth, kept me a little warmer. After the first hour, I tried standing. The mud was like a suction cup. Since my body had warmed the mold, I only stood for a few seconds before I was compelled back down into its relative comfort.

Eventually, though not soon as I'd have preferred, the sun climbed to its place in the morning sky. It remained hidden above the storm clouds, but at least some of its glow filtered through the towering dark clouds. The sheets of rain were the only limiting factor in how far I could see.

Now I marveled, not for the first time, at how the thick canopy of the trees was insufficient to stop the rain. The blanket of leaves couldn't even divert it into manageable curtains of water. Instead the drops kept falling, going straight through the foliage as if each tree was nothing more than an illusion.

I ate a quick breakfast. Thankfully my mother had packed it in a plastic bag. But the short few seconds between leaving the bag and entering my mouth made it dripping wet. With a sucking pop, I stood from my mudhole. My ankles ached as only wet cold joints know how. Like an old arthritic man, I limped and hobbled for a good ten minutes until my knees limbered some. Even after that, every few steps felt like my feet were carrying twice their weight. Little pinpricks explored every spot where one bone connected to another. It was going to be a long day.

Every fifteen minutes of hiking felt like an hour. I hiked twenty-four hours that morning. By noon I found the hangman's camp. It had been particularly hard to find in the rain, but something was wrong. Not a single person could be found.

At first, I wondered if I'd stumbled into an older camp. Maybe they went somewhere else during bad weather. But that didn't seem right, either. There were no more shelters, pots, or clothing anywhere. I walked around quickly to make certain that I was in the right location. Everything about the place was right. It was the same camp I'd spent a whole month becoming familiar with. That was only two weeks ago. All was the same, except everyone had moved on.

They couldn't have left too long ago. I hadn't left that long ago. But there were no tracks leading anywhere that I could discern. Their footprints must have been washed away by the storm. I had no means of following the large group of children. I sank to my knees. How was I ever to find Midnight? I looked around again, hoping for something from her that could tell me where she'd gone, but she couldn't even write. There was no way I'd ever find her.

One broken thatch roof had been left behind. It leaked badly, but it was the best form of shelter left. I took refuge under it and stayed, feeling sorry for myself. I didn't have the energy to go on. I remained there for some time, maybe from a vain hope that someone might return and let me know where everyone had gone. More likely I was just too tired to press on. Angry, wet, and alone, I cried.

Afternoon came, then evening. All the while the rain beat down.

After what had started out as a restless night, I blinked awake. The sun was up; for how long, I had no idea. The rain must have stopped during the night, allowing me to drift into an exhausted sleep. Now the cold wetness was replaced by a hot and muggy midmorning.

My mouth felt like cotton and tasted like I had a week's worth of morning breath. I took off my shirt, hoping to walk in more comfort without the sticky damp thing on my back. But the mosquitoes quickly compelled me to put it back on. Putting the soggy garment back on was a trial of discomfort all its own. I felt disgusting as I slowly rolled the cloth back down my fleshy body. Mosquitos turned into skid-marks as my damp shirt disturbed their feast. Thoughts of getting to my comfortable apartment dominated my will. Even Midnight was pushed to the back of my mind. I had a single-minded purpose of finding comfort again. If I didn't find dry clothing soon, I'd never shake this dreadful state.

Like yesterday's storm, the one in my mind soon passed. By noon I had dried out. The weather was still intolerably hot and humid, but my head was clearing and I was able to hike on noticing trees and birds rather than mud and fallen sticks. I knew that I had a full day-and-a-half walk from the hangman's now former camp to civilization. Midnight would be disappointed that I didn't see her again this summer. But she had to understand. I vowed that before next summer came, I would find her again. My first opportunity might be around Christmas, when school generally gave us two and a half weeks off between semesters. If I had to, I would use most of the break to find her again.

That next afternoon I was in my new apartment, washing mud-stained clothing in the kitchen sink. After hanging the last of it to dry, I wanted to plop down on my bed and sleep for a couple days straight. That wouldn't do. I needed work, which meant that I had to re-secure my job at the New District Times. I changed shirts one last time then dragged myself out the door toward the publisher's office.

The interview went well. The job was easily mine again, even though the main editor accused me of sloppy work. He told me that I'd need to write better this year than I'd done last year. It was the same story he told every journalist to negotiate lower pay. "You're not a high rolling journalist yet. Don't expect to be paid like one." The degrading comments were just a part of the job as far as I was concerned. He might lowball my articles, but even then, I could manage to pay my bills. So, while that didn't surprise me at all, what—or, rather, who—I saw when I left his office nearly knocked me onto my rump.

Krystal had just turned a corner and happened to walk right in front of me. She stopped, her eyes widened, and her jaw dropped, if only for a moment. "Iddo? Is that really you?"

I could barely answer. She was every bit the girl—woman—I remembered, but my, how she'd changed, and only in a single year. While her face retained a healthy plushness, she somehow looked thinner, more radiant. She didn't look like a girl, that much was clear. She had the voluptuous maturity of any American woman I'd seen in the movies. Unfortunately, her personality hadn't bloomed nearly as much as her figure.

I opened my mouth to respond, but in true Krystal fashion, she cut me off and began her own story.

"Iddo, I can't believe I'm seeing you here of all places, oh my gosh, did you hit your growth spurt? I thought you quit studying journalism! You're probably wondering what I'm doing here. Well, yes, I'm not quite done with my schooling yet. I mean, sort of. You know how it is, I've got some college credits, but I've still got a good three years left of actual college. But I was offered a chance to leave for an internship here and of course, I couldn't pass up that opportunity. Besides, it was a good excuse to get out of my house. My dad can be so difficult sometimes. But you know how dads can be. The bus rides around the woods took so long and . . ."

She droned on for some five minutes. I remembered why I'd found being around her such a struggle. Not only was my body tired, but now my mind was going to be drained just from keeping up with her. I didn't want to offend her again, especially since she'd now be working here. I was sure she would eventually tell me all about her soon-to-be responsibilities as an intern, but she was only to the part of her story where she found an apartment. Until I understood what she was doing here, I didn't want to burn a bridge that might negatively affect my own employment.

Over the next week, I saw Krystal two more times. I learned that her new responsibilities involved helping edit and review all articles that came in for publication. She and my chief editor worked closely together. He needed a free laborer to keep up with the work. Krystal was just financially secure enough to not need the income for living on. At least I suspect she didn't need it, not as long as her dad was still willing to pay her living expenses. Whatever cost it took to get his daughter out of the house was likely well suited to his preferred lifestyle. Then again, Krystal wasn't completely devoid of income. She was still allowed to do some freelance articles if she had any spare time. Knowing her, she'd find the time. Her goal was to be the face of news someday. In her mind, she saw everyone recognizing her. From what I could tell, her looks alone would significantly help with that.

Like before, I was the first one to settle into the apartment. Jhon and Charles came next. Their parents still drove over in the same cars. The vehicles were just as immaculate as they'd been last year. If I hadn't known better, I would've assumed they were brand-new.

We exchanged brief welcomes. Jhon and Charles were still a bit aloof around me, but I didn't mind. They were amiable enough to call them good roommates. After hearing some of the horror stories about other people's roommates last semester, I could easily live with two guys like these, even if one of them always made a mess around the toilet.

The day before classes began, Thing Two burst in the door. He looked as though he hadn't slept in a week. Still, he radiated energy and commenced with overzealous hellos. Behind him I expected to see his sage-like friend, Thing One. But Duy was the only one returning with him.

"Happy birthday," Duy said with a hard slap on the back. "How was your summer?"

"Good. I'm surprised you remembered."

"You're seventeen now, right?"

"Yep." I said, silence following. What else should I say? I had so many questions to ask him about the Believers, but this wasn't the time for it.

"So young. But better than sixteen." He hobbled past, luggage in tow. I wondered if Duy and Thing Two had spent some time together over the summer, or if they both just happened to arrive simultaneously.

An irrational jealousy crept in on me. Not that I would have cared to spend any time with either of them over the summer. It would have been impossible, anyway. Still, it felt like a mild jab at my own social awkwardness. If they could have developed a good enough friendship to hang out over the summer, why couldn't I have done the same with Thing One? Did this mean that Duy would no longer want to room with me?

The jealousy was quickly replaced by hope. Maybe they would room together, and Thing One would have to room with me. Then I might actually get to know him better. The man did intrigue me. Without a doubt, he would be a better roommate than Duy.

But aside from the two arriving at the apartment at the same time, nothing else really changed. Duy still roomed with me, and Thing Two took over the last remaining room.

As for Thing One, he didn't show up until the following week. I went to class on a Monday morning, and when I returned late that evening he was there. Since I didn't need tutoring from Duy this year, I hoped that I might be able to develop a better friendship with Thing One.

Thing One wasn't as cooperative. He was still the same guy I remembered, but he had to catch up for missing his first week of school. When he wasn't working on his schooling, he seemed to disappear. I could swear he was nearly as busy as I'd been last year, maybe even more. His tone of voice reflected that sage-like friend I'd grown accustomed to, but his brow was constantly wrinkled with some unshared stress. Maybe it was his job, maybe it was school. Whatever it was, it weighed heavily enough on him to show despite his amiability.

No matter. This school year was shaping up to be a great one. Nobody could bring my spirits down. I was learning something I was passionate about. I had a good job. Most of all I had a wonderful girl waiting for me, that is, if I could ever find her again. Many of my free moments were spent daydreaming about her. Countless hours of wistful planning were exhausted. One day I'd bring her out. I'll need to have a way to provide for her. For us.

Chapter 19

Good times often breed complacency. We relish these breaks from turmoils we've lived through and squalls that are sure to come. But all too often, we nap in the glory of our ease. Then when we're in trouble, we can't see beyond our misery. In truth, looking beyond ourselves is impossible at any time unless we consciously make the effort today, regardless of where life has placed us.

"Hey Iddo." Krystal punched me in the arm as I entered to turn in my latest two articles. Yeah, she was just being friendly, but she still packed a punch meant for a tough guy, something that I still hadn't fully gotten used to. People did look at me differently now. I sometimes wonder if I would have grown this big on my own, and Laidy had just brought on my potential early. I guess I'll never know that. I guess there's silver linings in just about anything.

I rubbed my bicep anyway, more out of habit, than

anything else. "As always, it's nice to see you, too." Why was she wearing such a conniving smirk?

I soon found out.

I could always e-mail my articles rather than delivering them in person, but I chose to hand delivered most of my stories. I'd found that I had better commission leverage if I stopped by in person. For some reason my boss always felt it easier to cheapen my articles if he was communicating across the Internet. As I stepped into my boss's office, he took my articles. After one quick glance, barely enough to read the title, he handed them back to me.

I eyed him suspiciously, sensing he had something else on his mind today. "Iddo, I've been thinking. I've got this really good intern who needs a little more responsibility." He waved a hand toward the door. "Have you met Krystal yet? She's been with us for about a month."

I shook my head. I guess I should have nodded to his question, but my mind kept saying, Oh no!

She always looked good. Today she looked like an elite businesswoman. That smirk that only moments ago I'd seen on her doll-like face had disappeared and was replaced by a much more mature and professional smile. Her normally self-absorbed air was replaced by a confident stature. Even her fruity lotions had been replaced by a subtle perfume. Had I not known her before, I might have found her attractive.

"You could say that we've met," I ventured carefully. I didn't want to insinuate that we knew each other, just in case he knew about Krystal's pompous layer beneath this radiant facade. I didn't want him to associate her character flaws with me. I had enough of my own. The last thing I needed was to be further stained by association.

"Good, because you two are going to be working closely together from here on out." My jaw dropped. I snapped my mouth shut, hoping he hadn't noticed. Could he hear my teeth clicking together as audibly as I could?

From his swivel chair, he raised an eyebrow. A mischievous smirk touched the edge of his lip. I couldn't believe it. He was amused. Not by partnering me with this girl I'd grown to like and loathe at the same time. No, he was delighted to play matchmaker with someone as quiet as me with such an attractive American girl.

I had to admit to myself that if I hadn't grown up around her, I might have been a gushy pile of boiled cabbage in this situation. As it was, I was easily able to regain my composure.

Somewhat disappointed in my reaction, he continued. "Krystal is going to be editing all your articles from now on. Don't think you can slacken your quality, you hear me? She's a bright one and she'll catch you on it."

I had no doubt about that. If there was one thing I remembered clearly, it was Krystal's undeviating ambition to further her own self-interest. "Thank you," I said, only because I didn't know what else to say. I turned and handed her my articles. "One is about the upcoming school pride dance. The other is a biographical interview with the dean of the medical school."

She took my papers and gave me a wink that only I could see.

I gave my best congenial smile back. She waited until I left the room before discussing something more with my boss. Maybe it wouldn't be so bad reporting to Krystal. I was still employed, but no longer under the constant scrutiny of the chief editor. I imagined the move was in part to give Krystal the experience she needed, but I like to think I was chosen because he'd come to trust my work enough that he didn't need to personally keep tabs on me the whole time.

It could also have something to do with the fact that campus news wasn't as big a part of the publication as some of his other sections. Most of those sections dealt with the world outside this community and many articles couldn't have been written by any of our reporters.

Still, for many people, especially students, the college section was the most read part. Not a big deal. As long as I could keep my job for two more years, I'd be able to get a paid internship in a hospital while I started my fifth year of school.

I had it all planned out. Money would be tight, but in the past week I'd been visiting different apartments. If I budgeted very carefully, and submitted a third article occasionally for the news, I could afford my own apartment with Midnight. It could work. I would make it work. After all, I was used to being poor and knew how to get by on very little.

Midnight was used to getting by without any money at all. Of course, this would be a different environment for her, but I felt confident that she could adjust.

October was nearing an end. Duy found me at our deeply gouged writing desk, also known as our kitchen table and occasionally as a downhill grass sled.

"Put your pencil down, Iddo! It's time to par-tay."

I sighed. "Do I really have to? Can't I just go by myself? I'm a much better reporter when I'm alone and able to focus on observing." That wasn't the real reason I preferred to go by myself. When Duy had returned from his family, he'd gotten some of that Believer zeal back into his life, but it was already eroding again. I didn't trust his judgment in friends right now.

"You're not getting out of a good time that easily. Plus, you work too much."

"Oh-kay." If I had to go anyway, maybe it would be better to go with people I knew.

I stood and followed him out the door. Thing Two was already waiting for us outside. We took an energetic walk about a kilometer down the road before detouring into another apartment block. These were high-ticket apartments, the type that Jhon and Charles would have been more apt to attend; that is, they would if this wasn't also considered the party block. Duy and Thing Two rushed into the second building on the right. I trailed a little less enthusiastically.

"Come on, Iddo, don't be such a stiff," Duy chided. "Thing Two said you'd be a lot of fun tonight."

Thing Two? Why would he want me here? The guy was just as incorrigible as Duy, but crankier. While Duy knocked on the girls' apartment door, Thing Two fell back to talk to me.

"Yeah, I told him I wanted you here. Duy is a good

guy, you know that, but I need help tonight keeping him out of trouble. I'm worried about the company he's found to take to the dance. Girls and drugs. You know. All the stuff that trips up a good Believer. He respects you, you know?"

I stared at Thing Two for a moment. "Since when do you care about Duy forsaking his beliefs?"

He gave me a hurt look. "What are you suggesting, that I like his new lifestyle? I run with this crowd so I can keep a good eye on Duy. I don't want to see him trip up his life the way I've done."

"Okay," I said with some trepidation. What I meant, but didn't dare say, was that you can't lead from behind. That's called pushing. It's the whole principle of you have to stand on higher ground if you're going to raise anyone else up. Like I'd ever say that to his face. Thing Two had a temper, which I've been known to set off, though I doubt he'd go so far as to get violent, not any more at least. I was no fighter, but I was big and strong, and I'm pretty sure that Thing Two didn't want to test me much further than a little verbal assault every now and then, which was still unpleasant, so I kept my thoughts to myself.

The girls who answered the door were gorgeous. Not just good-lookers, these were unrealistically attractive. How in the world had Duy befriended them? Then I realized that he hadn't. They had brought me along for show. I was immediately swarmed by attention, and that attention was quickly and expertly leached away by Duy and Thing Two's sharp whit. I felt so used. I don't mean to be mean, but while Duy wasn't necessarily unattractive, neither was he up to their standard of beauty. In total, there were five girls. Two of them already had guys hanging on their arms. One latched on to Duy and another to Thing Two. The last girl eyed me warily. She was a cat who'd just found out that she had a chance with the main attraction. She wasn't the type who wanted a relationship either. She wanted to play. She was the mischievous sort that enjoyed toying with men before carving out their kidneys. That's just what I needed tonight. What I really wanted, was to find a way out of this.

"Hi, I'm Iddo." I extended my hand.

Her grin grew wicked and she grabbed my hand, yanked me down close, and nearly sucked my tonsils out of my throat. She let go and I staggered back, tripping on the threshold. I came down hard on my butt.

Laughter erupted all around me. Oh boy, here we go. This is going to be a very long night.

She told me her name. It could have been Lien, Lainey, or even Wilber. It was hard to concentrate on introductions with the hurricane of mirth that everyone was having at my expense. I was the only one who wasn't about to roll on the ground from laughing so hard. This coming from me, the only guy who seconds ago actually was rolling on the ground. How on earth was I going to make it through the night?

I should've just walked away right then and there. I didn't fit in. I didn't want to fit in, not with this crowd at least. I could've endured Thing Two's chastisement later. I tried to tell myself that my article took precedence over my embarrassment. Even then I knew it was a stretch. I think, if I was even thinking at all, that deep down I wanted to prove my maturity. If I was going to marry in under a year, but couldn't handle one stupid dance, how was I ever going to handle raising a family? If I'd truly been thinking, which the fog of humiliation clouded, then the true test of my confidence would have been to leave.

Somehow, we all found our way to the dance. My mind was drowning in a bath full of embarrassment the whole time. Time itself became an abstract. One minute I was getting a tongue hickey, the next I was her puppet at the dance, even while my mind was still stuck on the short walk to the Student Union building. It's hard to concentrate when the most gorgeous woman you've ever met is dressed in skintight clubbing silks and won't let go of your arm. I'm sure I inhaled more panicked perfume laced breaths in that ten-minute walk than in all my activities for the past decade or more.

At the dance, I could feel every eye on me. This girl was attractive enough to have any man in the room. Her confidence extended beyond her need to be with an equal. Tonight, she was just having fun and I was her big pathetic toy. She wasn't shy about it in the least either. She made sure everyone saw us together. The more smiles and laughs she produced, the more of a show she made at my expense. I had to get away.

"I need to go get a drink. I'll be right back."

"You know something?" she said soothingly. "I could use something to moisten my lips, too." She then ran a finger up my chest to my chin.

I gulped and spun around, making for a quick walk to the refreshment table. She kept stride; the first awkward thing I'd seen her do all night. It must not be easy running in high heals.

After choking down a cup of water, I turned my face away from hers. She never took her eyes off me, unless she was accepting someone else's humored giggles. "I need to visit the bathroom." Really I did. I needed to visit any place, alone, that would let me catch my breath and settle down. This girl was going to give me a stroke before the night was over.

She put her arms around my waist. "You're too clever. Okay. I'll come along with you," she said with a seductive wink. Then she started leading me toward the bathroom.

This girl was crazy. She was acting like she would follow me into the bathroom.

I flashed my head from side to side, looking for any excuse to escape her. "Where's Duy? Maybe we should join back up with them."

She feigned a hurt look. I wanted to scream. Just then a light-skinned finger tapped her shoulder. She turned around and met my saving angel. "Mind if I cut in for a dance or two?"

Lien gave me the largest fake frown I'd ever seen. She was probably grateful for the break, herself. Only I knew that once she had a moment with her friends, she'd come back more vicious than ever. Thankfully, though, she did release me to this new American girl.

"Thank you," I nearly cried.

"Please," Krystal said pathetically. "Do you really think I'd let that girl just keep trying to corrupt you like that? Why don't you stand up for yourself? Even if you just tried to make a move or two on her, you'd probably scare her into quitting."

"Listen, I just have to get out of here."

"Okay, okay. Let's just dance for a minute, and we'll slowly make our way toward the exit."

Krystal was true to her word. It took about a song and a half, but we made it out of the dance hall before Lien had a chance to track me down.

"Mind if I walk you home?" Krystal asked.

"Just like going home from school, like we used to do," I reminisced.

She laughed. So did I. For minute, I forgot my disgrace. I was glad, for once, that Krystal could carry on such a good one-sided conversation. It took all the pressure off me. There was something else to her, also. Either I hadn't noticed it before or maybe her personality had matured a little, but she was pleasant to be around. I even enjoyed our slow walk. We got to my place and then we just lingered outside for almost an hour. Talk was easy. We both exchanged genuine smiles.

"Krystal," I said, just as she was about to leave.

Her eyes looked openly to me, inviting me to continue.

"I've been wanting to apologize for how I treated you when we were still at school together. You always were trying to make me happy and I don't think I ever gave you any credit for it. I think I even spurned you on more than one occasion. I've felt really bad for it."

She leaned over and gave me a gentle kiss on the cheek. "You're sweet, Iddo. Stay away from trouble, okay?"

"If by trouble you mean Lien, trust me, that's the last thing I ever want to get close to."

Krystal smiled. Her eyes lingered a moment too long on mine before she walked away. I stayed outside for a few minutes till she turned out of sight. Those eyes seemed to be telling me something but didn't want my ears to actually hear. Whatever it was, maybe we might be good friends after all.

Chapter 20

When your life unravels and nothing fits the way you would have it, will you stubbornly hold to your perspective? Maybe you don't think you have goals. You do. We all do. We may not write them down at the start of each new year, but we have them, even if they are simply to maintain your status quo. Is reaching so difficult that many of us just give up?

The next morning, I woke up alone. It was a Saturday morning and Duy never did come back from his night of partying. Jhon and Charles were sleeping. They tended to sleep almost till noon whenever they could get away with it. Thing Two wasn't here, and oddly enough, neither was Thing One.

Maybe that wasn't so odd. Thing One had become unpredictable lately. He would disappear for days at a time, only to return and lock himself in his room to catch up on missed schoolwork. He blamed his absence on work, but even I knew that the New Tum Police Department didn't keep those kinds of schedules. Thing One wasn't even an official police officer. He was just one of many social workers who dealt with the logistics of moving troubled youth from one home to another. I don't think he ever made any of the trips himself. He just coordinated the activities.

Not my problem, though. What he did with his time was his choice. For that matter, same went for Duy and Thing Two. Duy was the one who'd put me in that awkward position last night. Well, sort of. Where had all my courage gone? During the summer, I could've done anything. Maybe my mother's ladle had whacked some sense out of me. Anyhow, if Thing Two was so concerned about Duy's immortal soul, then why was he trying to get me to do all the heavy lifting? All I could manage to shoulder was a giant yoke of embarrassment. Both Duy and Thing Two thought it was hilarious.

If I was to be honest, I did care about Duy forsaking his God. I was finally coming around to the opinion that Believers might be onto something. The faithful ones took their devotion of God to a higher level than most religions I knew of. I was only just beginning to realize the importance of faith in my own life. It was something that I'd experienced firsthand over the summer. It was something I was about to experience on a completely different level over the next couple months.

Despite my concern for Duy, he was a free agent, and probably understood God better than I did. What choices he made, he made purposefully, in contradiction to his own knowledge. I'm sure the black-and-white lines he was toying with were somehow gray in his head. Still, he was the one smudging those lines.

I cleared my mind of him and tried to think past Lien and her mocking seductions last night. I pulled out my notepad to write about the dance party. I had a hard time finishing. I kept wondering why I'd allowed myself to get sucked into that degrading situation. It felt wrong from the beginning.

Was I slipping? I put down my pen and closed my eyes. My zeal from the summer had diminished some. I wasn't pursuing truth to the degree that I'd wanted, so the light was leaving me. This caused a shiver, and I told myself that during the next month or two, I needed to start focusing on finding the truth about God, if the truth could be found.

When I put down my pen for the second time, my article was finished. In actuality, the story was more about last year's party. I'd attended that one, also. Both were basically the same. The only difference was that for this one I couldn't focus on anything aside from my humiliation.

Maybe now that I was finished with my article, I could move beyond that night. Of course, I'd need to proofread it before turning it over to Krystal for publication. I wondered if she would marvel at my ability to surmise the party after having needed rescuing by her.

Oh well. Let her think what she would.

Just then the front door burst open. Duy came in laughing with Thing Two. They seemed in good spirits until Thing Two locked eyes with me. Duy continued to the bathroom, but Thing Two walked up to me. He looked down and saw my draft of the news article. He ripped it from my notepad, crumpled it up, and threw it across the room.

"What was that for?" I protested.

"You ditched us last night. I needed you there to help me keep Duy out of trouble. Do you want to know where he spent the whole evening?"

"I'm guessing it was at the same place you did," I ventured.

Thing Two slapped me across the face. I don't know where it came from, but I slapped him back and he fell backward, landing hard against the wall and the floor. I had never been violent before. I didn't know what to do next, so I did nothing, I just watched him, to see what he would do next. I could see the anger simmering in him. Was he going to fight me? He stood, stared at me long and hard for an unflinching moment, then stormed into his room, slamming the door behind him.

My skin tingled with hot anxiety. The slap to my face was nothing compared to the slap on my dignity. Shaking, I walked over to the wall and picked up my crumpled notepaper. My heart thumped in my chest and my breathing came in gasps. Why did Thing Two assume that I was the only one responsible for Duy's transgressions? I went back to my room, sat on my bed, and hoped I wouldn't see Thing Two for the rest of the year.

Duy came in. His hair dripped with water and his eyes were ringed in dark circles. He looked over at me as he pulled on some fresh clothes. "You okay, Iddo?"

"Yeah, I'm fine," I muttered.

"Look, sorry about last night. I didn't mean for Lien to be so—well, you know."

Thanks for being a real pal and bailing me out! I wanted to accuse. "No big deal," I said instead. "It seems that Thing Two didn't have a much better night, either."

"What are you talking about? We had a crazy-awesome night. We went back to—"

"Stop." I raised my hand. "I really don't want to hear about it."

"Riiight. I know you've got your reservations about Believers, but sometimes I think you're closer to that lifestyle than I am."

"Do you actually believe everything they tell you?"

Duy studied me for a moment. Or was he studying himself? "Yeah, I suppose so."

"If you consider yourself a Believer, then why last night? Doesn't that kind of conflict with how Believers are supposed to act?"

Duy shrugged. "Why are you asking me that?"

Because I'm curious and want to know more, but I don't know if I can even ask you about that way of life anymore. "I'm just a little concerned for you is all." Maybe that was the wrong thing to say. Why couldn't I ever just say what I really meant? I hoped he wouldn't give me one of those *who-are-you-to-judge-me* sort of reactions. Luckily that didn't happen.

"Don't worry. I'll be fine. I haven't stopped believing. I just—just don't you worry about me."

I shrugged. I could almost sense his guilt, like he

was more worried about me associating his actions with Believers than with himself. He was trying hard to suppress it, though. The more he grayed the black-and-white lines of his moral conviction, the more easily he could get away with living loud and reckless. He knew what he was doing.

As it turned out, over the next couple months, Duy fell more and more away from the Believers' way of life. He still claimed to be a Believer, but nobody believed him anymore.

The semester break finally arrived. Those who celebrated Christmas went to their homes for the holiday. After sending a card home to my mother, explaining a possible delay, I packed a bag and went into the woods. All previous attempts I'd made before had ended in disappointment.

Granted, I didn't have much time to search the woods on the few weekends that I'd been able to break away. I'd get into the woods, search for a day, then come back exhausted, just in time to sleep off the hike before school the next day. Now I had two full weeks to search for Midnight.

I was more prepared for an extended stay in the woods than at any other time before. Not that I packed a lot of extra food. The hangman's orphans had taught me how to forage. Mostly what I brought was a good knife and a light pot with a lighter to start cook fires with. I'd have no problem as long as I could stay away from the dark cottages that I now knew speckled the deep woods. I had no desire to spend another stint with a witch.

I printed an aerial photo of the woods and used it

to find the prominent lakes that pocketed the region. The hangman's last big camp had been by a lake. It stood to reason that he'd search out another similar location. Large ponds or small lakes could often be relied on to supply fish. Not only were they a good source of protein, but the small streams or springs that fed them were good for drinking water.

I could either hike to the northwest of the hangman's last camp, or I could go to the southeast. The woods stretched on much farther to the northwest, over two hundred kilometers, and contained more little lakes that would work well for another camp. To the southwest, the trees and brambles got thicker and were harder to travel through. After about a hundred kilometers, they met a rough and rocky seashore. Considerably fewer lakes and ponds populated the terrain in that direction.

Since the northwest appeared to be the most likely spot for moving a large group to, I decided to focus my search in that direction. I started by hiking to their last camp, which became my first camp for this trip. In the morning, I took out a cheap compass and set my course toward the next closest lake—or, rather, pond.

That day I hiked several kilometers, visited two lakes, and skirted around one suspicious cottage. That home might not have belonged to a witch, but who else would live out here? I didn't care to chance it. Day two was much like day one, except I found no sign of people and I got lost for half a day before finding the pond I was hiking to.

On the third day, I rolled my ankle while crossing over a fallen log. Nothing beats hiking alone through a vast jungle with a crippled ankle. Nothing that is, except for just about anything else. It hurt, really bad. Each step felt like a spiked spring expanding in my joint.

I struggled onward, limping heavily for the first hour, but the more I walked on it, the less it pained me. Of course, continuing to walk on it was extremely stupid, but I pressed on until I reached my next pond.

The next morning when I woke up, my foot looked like I'd filled it with compressed air. It was swollen like a latex balloon and I couldn't even put my shoe on over it. I had to soak the bloated thing in cool water before it was small enough to fit back in. Since I wasn't going anywhere fast, I used that soaking time to bathe in the pond I'd camped by that night. I'd neglected bathing to this point, and I sorely needed it. Every time I moved, a whiff of pungent air billowed from my shirt to my face.

Late that morning, I debated hiking some more, or catching fish and letting my ankle rest for a few more hours. I chose to stay put. I was also a little depressed. I'd hoped that I would've found some sign of them by now. Afternoon came, but I decided to stay in place. I slept one more night. There wasn't even any fish. I was reduced to eating stale bread and whatever roots I could claw out of the dirt.

The next morning, I set out again. It was a Friday and I covered three more small lakes, none producing any results. My discouragement deepened. According to the printout I'd made, I still had over a hundred and fifty kilometers of zigzagging to go before I exhausted this side of the forest. It would take months, and I wasn't even sure that I'd chosen the right direction to search for them.

Late Sunday afternoon I exited the woods on the west

side. I was tired and frustrated. Part of me wanted to continue searching. But I had spent a whole week without seeing any clue as to where they were. I caught a bus and rode it for two and a half hours as it slowly made its way to my hometown.

I arrived at my mother's house late that night. My mother was still awake, and very happy to see me. It was Christmas Eve. We didn't celebrate the holiday in the same way that an American or Christian might. For us it was mostly just a time to spend with family.

"I wasn't sure you'd make it here."

"Well, I spent a little extra time hiking through the woods. Did you get my letter?"

"Yes, but it didn't really explain why you'd be late. Why spend any more time in the woods than you have to? Is everything okay?"

"I'm fine," I began. Then, whether due to exhaustion or just needing to talk, I told her all about the hangman and the orphans he'd adopted. I even told her about Midnight and my commitment to her. Unloading this all to my mother felt incredible, like shrugging a bag full of heavy rocks. Of course, I still left out the part about the witch. Mother didn't need to know everything.

I don't know exactly what my mother thought of it all. If I were to guess by her stiff posture and tight-lipped expression, she disapproved. She continued to listen quietly, keeping her own thoughts to herself. I figured she'd have some reservations, it would be hard not to. The whole time we talked, I kept a wary eye out for her kitchen ladle. Eventually it became clear that she wasn't going to scold me for making a foolish promise to a strange jungle girl. At least if she was, she was going to use sugar instead of a rod to change my mind. Really, she seemed like she was trying to accept my decisions.

Christmas Day started nicely. A faint smell of cinnamon from the neighbors drifted on the morning air. Childhood memories flooded back to me. Like so many times before, I longed for my father to be back with us. I imagined that if he hadn't died, that somehow Mother would have convinced him to let me change schools.

I took in a deep breath, savoring the best memories and ignoring the unpleasant. I'd always loved these kind of mornings.

"Well?" My mother asked.

She'd started mining me for every little detail before even kindling a fire on the stove. She wanted to know all about Midnight. She must have been upset, because she was trying extra hard to be nice. I think she was trying to convince herself that I was smart enough to make a good decision. Her way of doing so was to learn as much about it as possible. She hung on every word as if my tale was fascinating. In a way, I felt a little awkward with the degree of attention that she focused on it. I'd already told her much of this last night, but she wanted it all again and in as deep of detail as possible.

The more I told her, the more she wanted to hear. Neither of us worked that day. We just stayed at home or went on small walks. Mostly we talked. Eventually, she would exchange a story about her younger life for stories of my new life. In the space of only a year and a half, our relationship had completely changed. She was still my mother, but we were also like two adult friends. I learned stories from her that I couldn't imagine her doing. They weren't bad, it was just that she hadn't told me much about her life before she married my father. The whole day was fascinating in a way I'd never anticipated.

The next day she had to go into work. Her situation upset me a little because of her health. A year and a half ago, she had a cough. Over the summer she'd masked it well enough, but I could tell that she was weak. Now it took all her energy just to hide her poor health from me.

As I watched her walk off to work, she carried herself as well as she could until she thought I might not be watching anymore. She was several hundred meters away, almost far enough to be obscured, when I saw her nearly collapse. She caught herself against the side of a building and paused for a minute. Standing straight again, she sneaked a glance back at me, to see if I'd noticed her lapse.

I pretended to have my attention elsewhere. I could almost feel her relief at not letting me see her infirmity. She continued on. I wanted to rush out to her and bring her back. She needed caring for. Tears came to my eyes as I thought of my own selfishness. I hadn't once considered my own mother's needs. For my whole life, she'd taken care of me. I loved her with all my heart and she was slipping away. I couldn't think of what to do.

My mind raced through every diagnosis that a second-year medical student might know. The top contenders were tuberculosis or cancer. Neither were good. Then a thought entered my mind that scared me even more. What if she was being so good about my decision to marry Midnight because she knew she wouldn't be around much longer to see me happily married otherwise? Is that why she'd asked to see Midnight if I could find her before my classes started up again?

I couldn't think about my mother dying. I resolved that I needed to find a way to take care of her and Midnight together, but how could I do both and still go to school? I sat down, staring into the distance. Even if I could find a way to take care of all of us, how would I bring my mother to New Tum District? She wouldn't survive the hike. I couldn't afford to bus her around the woods. Even if I did scrape the money together, she wouldn't allow me to use my college money for it.

The only other option was to quit school and come back home to be with her. But we couldn't afford a doctor, and if I didn't finish my schooling, how could I even hope to take care of her? Being a doctor might not make me much money, but I would gain the skills to help her. Unfortunately, I was convinced that by then, it would be too late.

Chapter 21

There is the world in whole, then there's the smaller world we inhabit. The little overlap we find between the two may seem small, but it's larger that we know. Sometimes we think we're helplessly bound to our own sphere and can't imagine reaching out to the larger realm. In those times, all we can do is focus on our own place as best we know how. The truth is that our little world greatly overlaps many other people's little realities. As we influence all of them, we exert a greater influence over the grand world in a way we may never realize or even think possible.

December 27 was a Saturday. My mother left for work and I too went in search of any odd job for the day. I ended up cleaning gutters at the local market. That was a job I hope never to do again. I don't know when the last time those narrow concrete foot traps had been cleaned, but they seemed to have more than just debris flowing through them. They smelled of sewage and pig guts. There was close to a half kilometer of the zigzagging trench snaking through the grounds of the market. All of it contained at least three centimeters of sludge. In some spots the crud dammed the system and water spilled over the top of the drainage trench.

I made an honest day's wage. By honest, I mean that if you had no other work, and your employer knew you were desperate, they could pay you the bare minimum required to keep you working for a day. Another day of this and I could donate the money to my mother for bus fare to New Tum. The only problem, as far as I could see, was that I wouldn't be around long enough to work that much. I had a bit of money saved up from my normal job, but that was dedicated to paying for my next semester of school and rent. I wondered if anyone we knew could loan us the money to get my mother to New Tum. She was tough, but I was pretty sure she couldn't handle an extended hike through the woods.

I got home about the same time as my mother. She was going to make dinner for us, but I insisted that she rest and I prepare the meal. My body ached from the manual labor, but I could only imagine how worn down she must've felt. In the back of my mind, I wondered if my hands still smelled of guts and rot. If they did, I hoped they didn't infect dinner with their unique flavor.

"If I can find a place to rent over by my school, do you have enough saved up to get a bus ticket to New Tum District?"

My mother's drooping head shot up. "Why would you want me to come live with you?"

"You've hidden it pretty well, but you're sick." I hated being so blunt with her, but I didn't know how else to broach the topic.

"Iddo, I have a good job here. My boss understands my situation. There's no way I'd be able to find work again."

"Maybe it's your work that's running you down. I'll find a way to support both of us. If you had a chance to rest, you might get over whatever's bothering you. Plus, there's a lot of doctors at the college. Maybe-"

"No. I can't do that. You have too much going on. I'm fine, really I am. I may have my moments, but I'm doing okay. Besides, there's no way you can support both of us, go to school, and eventually support your bride. While you're at school, focus and work hard. I'm not going any-where. Just, when you find Midnight, bring her here so I can attend your marriage. Besides, Iddo," she smiled in amusement, "you can't even take care of dinner without burning the beans."

I raised an eyebrow, wondering what she meant by that. The acrid smoke woke my nose. Looking down, I realized I'd been so wrapped up in my concern that I was burning our dinner. I quickly stirred the food, trying to salvage the meal. Luckily I hadn't completely ruined it, but it would be a little more charred than either of us preferred.

My mother laughed heartily. I couldn't help but laugh, too, until a coughing spell quieted her. My eyes bored into her while I pulled the pan away from the heat.

"Don't give me that look, Iddo. You can't afford to take care of us and go to school."

"Then I'll quit school and stay here to help you." For a second, I considered threatening her with her ladle. But I left it alone.

Her eyes sharpened and her face hardened. "No! We've all sacrificed too much to get you where you are now."

I wanted to argue that currently I was here at home, but I held my tongue. Maybe I really should give her a whack on the head with that ladle.

"You're going to big things, Iddo. You've always had a bigger heart than you've had brains to hold. Don't let that heart talk you out of the right choice. You have a good future ahead of you, but you have to stick to it. Stay in school. If this Midnight really is good enough to deserve you, then find and marry her. I've had a good life. I found a man I was able to share it with. He was a hard man, but a good man. I loved your father. Together we raised you. I'm so proud of you. You're better than either of us ever were. What more could I ask from my own son?"

How could I respond to that? "But if I can make it all work out, would you come?"

She thought hard for a long moment. I almost thought she'd concede. "No, Iddo. I wouldn't. My life if here. Yours is over there. I have family and neighbors who can help me if I need it. Really, don't worry about me."

That night I lay awake, searching for a fix to all our problems. My mother, once so meek, had turned into a stubborn woman. I couldn't just leave her alone. She truly did need help. I decided to consult with her brother—my uncle.

Sunday morning, I fried an egg to put over rice for breakfast and left it for my mother. She would sleep later today. Sunday for her was not a day of worship. Sure, she spent an hour or two on her knees. But unless worship is kneeling by a tub of water, scrubbing clothes, she had an empty day ahead of her. For a sick woman who worked six long days each week, she needed her one true day of rest.

I walked the two kilometers to my uncle's home. He was married to a cranky lady. I doubt my aunt had always been such a shrew. Someone as good natured as Uncle Kim wouldn't have chosen his wife if she'd been such a nag when they'd first met. Though I rarely saw him, especially now that I was going to school so far away, I always felt welcome around Kim, even if his wife tempered that welcome. They never had a kid, and while they seemed content with that, I think Uncle Kim always wished he had.

Being Sunday, Kim and his wife were home when I showed up.

"It's Soportevy's son," my aunt called over to Kim, a hint of irritation peppering her abnormally low voice. I don't think she was upset, but she was so used to being ornery, the tone had become a permanent landmark of her personality.

Kim appeared more quickly than I expected. His wife's bellow apparently wasn't meant to call him from a distance. I think that if divorces were more common around here, she'd be a lonely woman.

"Iddo! Welcome. It's nice to see you. How's your schooling?"

"It's hard work, but I really like it."

"You'll be a great doctor someday, I know it. So what brings you here? I haven't seen you for a long time."

"It's my mother."

Kim's wife snorted and mumbled something under her breath. Kim ignored her, his smile never wavered.

"I'm just worried about her. I wanted to see if you could give me some advice."

He put an arm around me and we stepped outside. A cheap wooden bench was fixed in front of his home, and we settled onto it. The hot morning sun was slightly tempered by the shade of a large tree and a cooler breeze. I felt relaxed as I explained my mother's condition.

"You're right to worry," Kim said after solemn hesitation. He was thinking. "I don't think I can tell you what to do, but I can offer you a little advice. If you quit your schooling now, not only will your mother still be sick, but she'll also have a broken heart. You'd never get back to school, either. You should see how proudly she boasts of you when you're not here."

"Boasts? Of me?"

"You're being a man, Iddo. You have an honorable dream and you're working hard to realize it. Your father may not've liked the choice, but your mother couldn't be more pleased. If you throw that away because of her, how do you think she'll feel?"

I thought long and hard. "But her health. What if I go back to school and she doesn't live long enough for me to see her again?" I choked up a little at this question. Thinking it was one thing, admitting it out loud was much more difficult.

"I think she'll be fine. She has good months and bad ones. She's probably just doing poorly this month, but next month, she'll be feeling much better."

I wasn't so sure. My face must have said as much.

"Listen, Iddo, even if she doesn't make it, which I'm sure won't happen, do you want her unhappy?"

"Maybe, if it's better than being lonely."

"You really think she's that bad off?"

I shrugged. I didn't know. The thought threatened to break me down into sobs.

My aunt, who'd been listening from the doorway, stalked up to me. With a loud harrumph, she planted her fists on her ample hips. "You listen here, young man. Whatever happens to your mother, I guarantee, she won't be alone."

Even standing, she was still at eye level with me, even though I was sitting, but it still felt like my reddened eyes had to look up to meet hers.

"You do your part by going to school. It'll lift her spirits to know you're where you ought to be. We'll visit her weekly, won't we, Kim."

Kim just smiled and nodded his head. I wasn't sure, but for a second I almost got a feel for how my aunt and uncle's odd relationship worked. He was the face, and she was the driving force. But that didn't really matter. "Would you really do that?"

"Iddo, when my wife sets her mind to something, don't ever second-guess her."

I studied her face for a moment and almost saw the tinge of a smile. She stifled it before it could show, no doubt she had to keep up appearances.

She would visit my mother weekly. In fact, I could tell that she would likely visit daily, except when it was truly inconvenient. Maybe she wasn't so bad after all.

They gave me more reassurances that all would be well, then changed the subject to school, work, and girls. I elaborated plenty on school, work, and my roommates. I kept vague when pressed about girls. They didn't need to know about Midnight. However, I did tell them about the girl Duy had set me up with. My aunt's scowl deepened, my uncle laughed. It was still a painful memory, but gradually, I too found the humor in it. It's funny how time can let you laugh.

I stayed long enough that they fed me lunch. After eating, I went home. School would start up next week. If I was to go, I needed to leave tomorrow. I made up my mind to spend some extra time searching the southeast side of the woods. I still believed that the hangman would've gone northwest, but I wouldn't have time to travel and search any farther in that direction.

When I arrived home, my mother was pleased to hear my decision. I don't know if her health improved with the news, or if she faked it well, but she did seem better after I told her. I'd like to think she wasn't just suffering a smile on my behalf.

Monday morning, we shared breakfast together then said our good-byes. She seemed to be holding back as many tears as I was. I was tempted to reconsider my decision to leave because I had a sinking dread—the kind that hollows out your gut and tells you to soak up the moment, because you'll never get the chance again.

I swallowed my fear and walked toward the woods as my mother walked in the opposite direction. I only turned once, fearing that if I looked twice I'd see her steps waver. If that happened, there was no way I'd ever make it to the tree line again.

Chapter 22

Never trust your own opinion completely, it's far too biased. You are the sum of your experiences. You are not the complete sum of your neighbors' experiences. Finding wisdom is finding that you're not the smartest person around. This requires that you don't just admit your inadequacy, but that you believe it. I made a move against my better judgment and it caused me to find exactly what I was looking for. It just goes to show that we are all imperfect. Sometimes we must stand back from ourselves in order to move forward.

The woods were no different on this trip than any other. The sun was still blazing hot, but not enough to dry the sticky humidity. There wasn't a cloud in sight, but that meant very little. Some of the biggest storms I'd encountered, had no clouds the day before. I could easily find myself in bad weather again on this trip.

While I didn't expect to find the hangman's new den, I methodically plotted my course through the lower half of the woods. I placed my compass on the crude Northern arrow I'd drawn on my aerial photo of the woods. A quick turn of the map got me pointing north. Then I turned the compass to point in my desired direction and adjusted the plastic dial. This was getting easier all the time.

While the low-resolution aerial only showed the largest of the lakes and ponds through the dense trees, I was confident that I could cover enough ground between bodies of water to check off the entire area as I searched.

My payments for classes were due on Friday, and Krystal told me that she wanted to see a couple of articles ready for publishing when school started. That left me with just over four days to cover the ground that I wanted to search before needing to be in New Tum. It was plenty of time to search, even if the place was where I had no hope of finding Midnight.

After three days of hiking, I learned two things. First was that this side of the hangman's original camp was full of witches. I passed by two or three of their wicked huts each day. I had to be extremely careful. I knew that my developing faith in God would help me avoid the worst of their sorceries, but even witches know how to use a club, machete, or even a gun. I had no illusions as to how far my faith would protect me from something like that.

The second thing I learned was that hiking around these parts of the woods was painfully tedious. The trees were thinner, allowing more undergrowth to cumber the way. The snagging shrubs were so thick that I lost a good half of my time trying to push through them. By the time I'd reached the first lake on the second day, I looked like I'd been in a fight with a band of wild city cats. This was taking far too long. I realized that I needed to push straight on through to New Tum. I'd intended on taking a meandering course that would cover more land, but my original plan would take over a week and a half in this itchy maze.

Not a big deal. At least it confirmed that the hangman wouldn't have come this way. He knew the woods better than anyone. There was no chance he'd risk all those kids falling into the hands of so many witches. Nor would he likely be able to get all the younger ones to hike through this mess.

Around the middle of day four, I emerged. It only took around two hours of walking the edge of the woods before I was back in the familiar college district of New Tum. On one hand, I was relieved to be out of that nasty section of forest. On the other hand, I'd spent a great deal of time and effort looking for Midnight, only to be disappointed.

For the next few months, I was in a funk. I'd have to wait for summer to search the woods again. But if the hangman continued being mobile, what was there to stop him from moving again, even back to a spot I'd already searched? The more I thought about it, the more depressed it made me. Maybe this was some weird twist of fate. Maybe I really wasn't supposed to marry Midnight.

The March weather was particularly uncomfortable. Maybe it was just me getting used to the air-conditioned apartment. Today, though, I'd decided to wait until evening to deliver my news article to the press. The sun was almost at the horizon and already I could feel the temperature ebbing from its blistering high. In another hour, the evening air would be downright refreshing.

Usually at this time of day, Krystal and my former editor would be gone. Still, somebody was always around, because the press printed in the evenings. I'd planned on going in, putting my articles on Krystal's desk, then leaving.

As I walked around to the cubicle that Krystal claimed as her office space, I stopped dead in my tracks. My breath caught and I eased a foot back. She hadn't seen me yet, and maybe if I got out of view and made a little more noise before coming back into sight, she'd have a bit of warning to compose herself.

Her head was on her desk, but before I could duck out of sight, she sniffed once, held her breath, and raised herself up. "It's all right, Iddo. I know you're there." Wiping a tear from her cheek, she turned around to face me.

I don't know how she'd known it was me. All of a sudden, though, the two articles in my hand felt weird. What's wrong? Is there anything I can help with? Lay it all on Uncle Iddo. These might have been the right things to say. Instead, like usual, I just muttered the wrong thing. "I just came by to drop these off."

She took them and pretended to glance at them before placing them on her desk. "Thanks," was all she could say.

"Yeah, anyhow, I'll go now." I turned around, took a step, then stopped. One heavy breath, then another. Fine. When I turned back to face her, she had a sort of pleading look in her wet-rimmed eyes.

I didn't even say anything before a drip of the salty fluid broke the dam. No sooner had that first trickle leaked out, her eyes and nose spouted. Each breath came in four or five inhaled gasps for every short exhale. I should've kept going. I didn't know what to do.

Apparently, I didn't have to do anything. In classic Krystal fashion, she stole the whole show. I hardly had time to find a chair nearby before she expounded in a torrent of emotional baggage. And I thought I had problems.

Mostly I just listened. Sure, like any guy, I might have had an idea or two that I wouldn't mind pitching, but Krystal was too quick to let me have any real say. She jumped around from her daddy issues to growing up here, where everyone looked at her differently. She talked about dreams, fears, regrets. She even spoke wantonly of career and disappointment in love.

I must have listened for a good half hour before I suggested we go for a walk. I don't know if I was hoping that she'd settle down a little if she got some fresh air, or if I would settle down. In either case I was getting mighty uncomfortable just sitting there. She agreed.

Not long after we'd been walking, I found that we were on a path that skirted the edge of the woods. The sun was down, but the sky hadn't darkened enough to show any stars. My eyes looked longingly at the woods, wishing that I could see through them to where Midnight might be. Though, even if she were close to the edge of the woods, I didn't think she'd be around here. I was walking in a southeasterly direction, the direction that I doubted the hangman would've taken his troop.

I'd lost focus only for a minute on what Krystal had been saying, but suddenly found her arms wrapped around my elbow. I was now a good head or more taller than her, which still seemed weird to me, as she'd always been taller than me growing up. I was sure she weighed more than me back then too, though I don't know why that would matter, other than she seemed to be leaning into me now, and I could barely feel her weight. Another reminder that I had grown both bigger and stronger.

Certainly, I'd never entertained any ideas about a romantic relationship between us, but having her lean on me felt satisfying. I couldn't pull myself away. She fit with me, not like two peas in a pod, but more like a large shoe on a padded sock. Obviously, she couldn't be attracted to me. Neither was I attracted to her, pretty as she might be. Clearly she just needed a friend to talk to tonight. I could do that. Still, oddly enough, I had to keep reminding myself that I wanted to be with Midnight.

We walked for what must've been a solid hour before we turned back. We were just about to find a lower road, since the woods are no place to be near in the evening, at least, not if you can help it. This stretch was especially bad, as I knew, there were so many witches. As we gradually wandered away from the trees, we saw some lights coming out of them. It was a group of men, perhaps ten strong. No, make that eleven. While most of them were carrying ropes, clubs, machetes, or even the occasional gun, the eleventh man trailing several meters behind, struggling to keep up, just carried a notepad. I recognized him. He was one of our senior reporters. If I remembered right, his name was Biahn.

Seeing this group unsettled me a little, but Krystal

and I kept going on. If Biahn was chasing down a story, we had no place interfering. The nice thing, though, was that their appearance gave us something else to talk about. Krystal's mood cheered like a rare blossoming moonflower. I remembered the one I'd seen before in the woods and how it had inspired a sense of peace in me, even then its blossom hadn't been open. I'd only seen one whose flower was fully opened before. It had been in a neighbor's garden when I was young. So delicate and pale. Moonflowers had a fragile beauty that could melt the hardest of stone, while threatening to wilt at the slightest touch.

I looked at Krystal's beautiful pale face. I was glad that her spirits were lifting. At the same time, I knew she could wither and fall to pieces if I wasn't careful.

When it was finally time to part company, we stood awkwardly for a minute. Krystal then leaned over and gave me a lingering kiss on the cheek. I froze in place. We looked at each other for another second. She must have misinterpreted me, because she leaned in and gave me a warm and gentle kiss on the lips.

Finally, I withdrew and blushed. She smiled. Then with a wave good-bye that had a few too many fingers rippling for my comfort, she left. Before her eyes parted from mine, she seemed to wink without even fluttering an eyelid. Inwardly the two halves of my brain matter ground at each other.

I would not sleep well tonight. "Women," I half cursed once I was out of earshot. What had I just done? Was this, me, giving up on Midnight?

Chapter 23

Don't believe everything you read, unless of course you're reading it from me. I'm not trying to pad my wallet with money. My sole aim is to improve the lives around me. Maybe you'd expect most journalists to believe in their work. Well, they make a good show of it. But give equal weight to my version of the story too, as you make up your mind about the truth.

It took a whole month for the news to leak out. I hadn't forgotten seeing Biahn in the woods that one night with Krystal. Something about his little mob reminded me of a witch hunt and I could only hope that they were trying to clean out the forest from those evil soothsayers.

It's almost ironic—no, it is ironic. The group they should be hunting down was left alone. The title of Biahn's first article on the subject that the paper published was titled, "Mass Murderer Makes Widows in the Woods." It was by no means front-page material, but for our periodical, it found its way there. I happened to find it on the printed version, since I never felt comfortable in front of a computer.

You had to look deep into the printing to find my story about the ringworm outbreak in the college gym, even if it carried more truth than this slanderous article about the hangman.

The title had a memorable ring to it. I usually ignored what I considered the bad-news articles. Somehow, just knowing Daddy Smiling, I was inspired to look for the good in everything. Well, most everything. Reading bad news tended to make that exercise a little more difficult.

The news was as grim as I could've imagined. Not one hint about Devil-worshiping hags I say hags, but that's just because I don't know what to call the men of the same persuasion. Anyhow, Biahn made plenty of mention about being on the trail of a dangerous man with a rope who kidnaps children for who knows what purpose. The innocent fathers were strangled to death. This hangman preyed on all who dared enter the woods.

Of course, the article made no mention as to why the fathers were taking their young babes into the woods in the first place. Nor did it mention that all these children were seconds or thirds in a family that was allowed only one.

Few details were given. Just enough to confirm to me that these men actually were on the path of the hangman and that he truly was hiding on the southeastern side of the woods. I'd been wrong to dismiss the inhospitable landscape. It made some sense, though. If he was being pursued, where better to hide than among dangerous witches and hard-to-hike-through brambles? If these men had been pursuing the hangman for several months, which it now appeared they'd been doing, then living in that part of the woods was the only reason he and his children hadn't been found yet.

I finished my last class for the day, then half ran to the publishing house. As I walked in the door, Krystal eyed me coldly. My gaze fell to the floor. Ever since that night I'd walked with her, seen Biahn and well, I'd avoided her. I'd promised myself to Midnight and I truly did like her over Krystal. The fact that I hadn't told Krystal why I'd been avoiding her only made things more awkward between us. In the last month, she'd become increasingly critical of my work, even snippy with me on the occasions when I did have to converse with her.

"Is Biahn here?" I asked, still staring at her shoes.

"Yes." But the ice in her voice said that I had no hope of speaking with him.

"I've really got to talk to him. It's about the story he's working on."

"Your job is to report on campus life. Leave the real stories for the professionals." Krystal planted her primly manicured fists against her waist.

"Krystal," I begged, "this is important."

Krystal's lush lips puckered. Not in the way that would suggest a kiss, or another kiss I should say, but more like the kind that was wetting itself for an indignant verbal assault.

Just as her finger lifted and her lips parted, the suave tone of Biahn's voice broke the tension. Waves of static washed away from Krystal's defense as the senior reporter asked, "The mass murderer? You know something about the hangman story?"

"How much time do you have?"

Biahn was a professional. His ego wasn't important, at least, not while chasing a story. Any lead he had on a story was time worth spending. I admired that about him. He ushered me into his little office. It was surprisingly clean. I thought that with all the firsthand research he did, he'd have clutter everywhere. Krystal didn't join us. She stalked away. I got the impression that my audience with Biahn, against her will, would soon come back to trouble me.

I told Biahn everything about the hangman. His only sources up until now had been the extremely biased lies from that posse hunting down the unusual foster parent. Biahn sat silently. One hand massaged his chin. The other gripped a pen that went first to his lips, occasionally down, jotting notes in a form of shorthand that I didn't understand, then back to his mouth again.

"Iddo, my good man, you are wonderful!"

"So, how close are these men to actually finding the hangman?"

Biahn's hand lifted from his chin to wipe at his eyes, then rested back on the table. He was careful to answer, clearly concerned over my feelings for the hangman. "To be completely honest, Iddo, I think it won't take long at all. The hangman-er, I mean, Daddy Smiling—he keeps moving his camp around, but from what you've told me, with all those children, he won't be able to move very quickly. My guess is that in another couple weeks, these men'll have tracked him down once and for all."

"But you know the truth now. Isn't there anything you can do?"

"These men hunting him don't care about the truth. If what you've told me is true, they're just as bad a bunch of murderers as they accuse the hangman of being. They've all lost either a brother, a friend, or a child to this guy."

"Yeah, but if they lost a child, they're lucky they didn't lose their life, too; something they really deserved."

"Look, Iddo, I agree with you. But I've spent time with these guys. I can tell you of a surety they'll not relent. Not till the hangman is dead."

"That's not fair!" My fingers ached and I noticed that I was gripping Biahn's desk, trying to wring the slick, un-malleable laminated-wood top like a sponge. I relaxed my grip and tried to calm down. "Isn't there anything we can do?"

I knew I wasn't making the best impression. I'm not especially good at being angry. I would sooner be mistaken for nervous, not the most helpful of expressions.

Biahn leaned back in his chair, clasped both hands together, and raised them. A few gentle taps against his lips as he contemplated, then his eyes lit up. He was still careful with his words as he voiced his thoughts. "As I see it, the real issue has nothing to do with the stories I publish, but everything to do with finding and saving this so-called hangman and his children. I don't usually participate in the stories I follow, I merely observe. It's one of the main reasons I'm allowed access to so many good digs. In this case, maybe I could bend my rules just a little bit."

He puzzled in his chair for a few seconds. His eyes were distant, staring through me, through the wall beyond me. Slowly, one eyebrow at first, then the other raised. I'd never taken much time to know the reporter, but I could see in his calculating features that he was more than a man with a pencil and a knack for being where the stories were happening. He might not have hit the big-time reporting yet, but he would someday. Finally, he opened his mouth.

"I'm going back into the woods tonight with those men. I'll—"

"What! You can't be serious, after what I just—"

He raised his hand to silence me, but it was the hardness of his face that froze my speech. With all the coolness of a shrewd general he said in measured tones, "I'll go with them tonight, but I'll be more than just a spectator. I'm going to join their hunt."

I wanted to cry. How could he join them? His hard stare kept me silent, though.

"I'll increase their trust in me. I'll learn what I can. Everything I learn about their hunt, I'll pass on to you. It'll be up to you to find the hangman first. Once you find him, I'll help you keep him at least one step ahead of this mob."

I exhaled in relief. "What about your stories?"

"Don't get me wrong, these men are dangerous.

While they aren't exactly the smartest bunch of guys, don't think for a minute that they're alone. The ones tromping through the woods are just the tip of the spear. They're the muscle behind the real power. There's many men, smart, too, who'd notice if my articles took on an opposing stand to their activities."

"Who are you talking about?"

"Let's just say that if the hangman is ever captured, there'll be no fair trial."

I swallowed hard. I had to find Daddy Smiling first.

"Meet me here tomorrow around noon. I'll let you know everything I learn. Can you take time off school to start searching the woods?"

"I'll talk to my teachers. I'm sure I can work something out for a week. Two might be a stretch, but if I need to, I can make it happen. My job here is another thing."

I looked out the door. I thought Krystal had completely abandoned us, but she was there, eavesdropping. Our eyes met. She sensed my nonverbal intentions.

"Oh no you don't." She threw her hands in the air as she stepped closer to the doorway. "You can't drag me into this. This romp of yours would put me on the line, too. If I lose this job, I'll have to go back home. That is not happening!"

"Krystal." Biahn pouted, his lower lip not quite protruding. "Couldn't you cover for this young man, just a few days? a week at the most? It's not like his work is all that difficult or important, anyway."

That stung a bit, even if Biahn was arguing on my behalf.

"No way. I'm not getting involved in this. I don't owe you any favors, Iddo."

"Then do it for me," Biahn begged gently. "I'll have a talk with the bosses. They'll be more than happy to lend me Iddo, if I tell them it's for a big story I'm working on. He'll be my temporary partner on this. Think about it. If Iddo's story is true, how big would you imagine this story could get once I expose it for what it is?"

"Why not just do that now?" I asked.

"Evidence. We can't just make outrageous accusations. Like I said, this little mob has powerful backing. I'll need more time. I'll make sure you get some credit for this too, Krystal."

"So tomorrow at noon?" I confirmed.

Biahn nodded his head then turned to Krystal, eyes locking on hers.

She threw her shoulders down with a huff of frustration before storming out of the office.

"You must've done something to that girl. I've seen that brand of anger before."

I just shook my head. How could I explain what I had yet to understand?

"Don't worry about her," Biahn assured me. "She'll come around."

For the rest of the day, I wrote article after article.

They were the plain vanilla sort of stuff that the company could use as filler material. I had every intention of taking as much pressure off Krystal as possible. After seven articles, enough to last a whole week, I crashed onto my bed. The little hand on my cheap clock was pointing at one o'clock. Reluctantly I got off my bed again to flip off the light.

Duy wasn't home yet. He was probably still out partying at some girl's apartment. If he was out there this late, he probably wouldn't come back until the sun was up again. Even if he did come back, I doubted he'd wake me. I was asleep before my head even hit the bed.

I woke up early. Still tired, I knew I wouldn't be able to sleep. Nightmares had plagued my head all night. I'd imagined all sorts of evils done to Daddy Smiling and his children. None of my professors would be in yet, so I cleaned myself up and cooked a hearty breakfast. Might as well start the day right. I reviewed all my articles from last night and realized how horrible they were. I spent the next hour editing them. They still weren't great, but Krystal could touch them up for me, even if grudgingly.

My first class started at eight thirty and I was there at eight fifteen to visit with the professor before class started. The professor basically just pointed me toward the syllabus from the beginning of the semester. She told me to keep up on the reading, and that the final test would make up for any small quizzes I missed.

Most of my other classes were similar. Missing two weeks irked some of my professors a little, but only one took some real persuasion to give me leeway with my assignments.

By noon I was running to the publishing house. I'd be late in meeting with Biahn. Not a great way to start things out, but at least I'd accomplished what I needed to this morning. I was all ready for two weeks of catching up to the hangman before someone else did.

Biahn was even later than I. After I waited in his office for nearly an hour, he strolled in. His face was a passive display of good humor. I could almost think that he forgot all about our meeting. I had no intention of accusing him of such. Not only did I fear confrontation, I needed his willing participation.

"Is it noon already?" he asked, smile and charm never wavering.

"Uh, sure."

We stared somewhat awkwardly at each other for a minute. I'd just opened my mouth to fill the void when he said, "Iddo, my boy, are you sure you're ready to tackle this thing?"

I straightened my back. "I've never been more ready. Someone's got to help, and it would seem that I'm the only one who cares enough."

"I care too, Iddo, don't forget that. I want you to return to me every day or two to report where you are and what you've found. I'll lead the hunters to areas you've already searched, and let you know where else they might have looked or are planning on looking. Together we'll stay just a step ahead of them. We'll find the hangman first, I promise."

I smiled for the first time since our meeting had

started. It was still a serious, measured smile, but I was pleased with where the conversation was going. Pulling out my small aerial photo from my last crossing of the woods, I asked, "So, where do we begin?"

Biahn scrutinized my crude map. "We start by going over the areas that have already been searched, but not with that." He reached under his desk and produced two expensive looking fold-out maps. Fully opened and flattened, the maps were each close to a meter wide and about two-thirds of a meter tall. Everything about them was identical, including the yellow and red highlights that Biahn must have penned in.

As I studied the map, Biahn pointed out the few red marks first. "These are where we discovered remnants of the hangman's band. They're stealthy, but it's impossible to move that many kids without occasionally dropping some evidence of their passage." The numbered marks zigzagged all over the forest, but clearly moved in a lazy southeasterly direction.

"As you can see, there's a little overlap. They're trying to make it real hard for the hangman to backtrack," Biahn said. Eventually the hangman would have to attempt to backtrack, or he'd get cornered on the sea shore. But that could take up to a month or two at their current pace.

A month or two wasn't very much time. If I was to help, I needed to find them either this week or next. Silently I examined the map for a minute.

"Well, what do you think?"

I looked up at Biahn. "The map shows very few lakes or ponds between your searched area and the sea. There are plenty of small streams, but not enough to catch a lot of fish in. I've spent enough time with them to know how they forage for food.

"Most likely what they're doing is moving every evening before dark, even if just a little. Then they'd need to camp for the night. In the morning, they'd send the boys to gather food. Since fish will be scarce, they'll need to search a little wider in the woods to find enough food to bring back to the camp. By late afternoon or early evening, I'd guess they'd be on the move again.

Instead of combing the woods like your hunters are doing, I think I should be able to find them by hiking perpendicular to your search patterns. If I go from your search area to the sea, then zigzag back about a kilometer or two farther, I should be able to find them. That is, as long as I do most of my hiking during the first half of the day."

"Why the first half of the day?"

"Like I said, that's when all the boys will be spread out looking for food. Your hunters are just looking at night when they're all huddled up in a group. During the day, while they're foraging, they'll be spread out over a much larger area."

Biahn nodded. "Iddo, you'll make a great investigative reporter someday."

"I hope not. I want to be a doctor. I want to help people in need."

"Well, you have a good head on your shoulders in any case. I'll look you up on that day when I need a doctor.

Shall we plan on meeting here again tomorrow after-noon?"

"Let's plan for three days from now. Those woods are hard to hike and I might not move as fast as I'd like. I'll plan on meeting you here around five or six in the eve-ning."

Biahn extended his hand. "Good luck, Iddo."

I grabbed his hand with one of mine, reaching my other to grab the map. "I'll see you in three days."

I started at the edge of the forest where the band of men chasing the hangman had ended their search only one night ago. As tempting as it was to continue the mob's search pattern, I didn't want them to find the hangman first. I was wary of witches, but no longer afraid of them; I knew how the hangman's children moved and foraged.

After the first day of hiking, I realized that it would take a whole week to get all the way down to the sea. Instead I decided to hike only one-and-a-half days in that direction before coming back about two kilometers deeper into the woods.

All day, every day, I searched for any sign or footprint that might suggest a foraging party. Nothing. No sign of the children, the hangman, or even the other searchers. I refused to slow my pace. When darkness fell, I was nearly exhausted. Even my bones felt as weary as an overworked muscle.

I almost collapsed just making a campfire to cook my food. I couldn't remember the last time I'd pushed myself so hard. Sleep would've come quickly, but I forced myself to study and do homework by firelight for at least an hour or two each night.

At the end of day three, I was only an hour away from the college town again. If I hadn't been ready to collapse from fatigue, I might've finished the hike to sleep in my own bed. Three days of the hardest hiking I'd ever done left each muscle feeling bruised and worn into knots. There was no way I'd ever be able to hike that last couple kilometers tonight.

In the morning, like each morning before, I ate a light breakfast before starting my hike back. Like the morning before, the first kilometer was just as hard as the last kilometer from the night before. Bones felt like splintering and muscles were so tight that my feet dragged with every step. What should've taken an hour, took two. By nine in the morning, I was pushing my way into the publishing house.

Biahn wasn't in yet but Krystal was. She said little, mostly she just eyed me. Whether she felt spite or curiosity, I was beyond worrying about it. I waited until noon, catching up on my homework, then Biahn finally came through the doors. After a quick stop in the break room for a porcelain cup of coffee, he entered his office.

"So the cavalry returns. You're a day late."

"Yeah, I think meeting every four days is a little more reasonable. Any news from your friends?"

Biahn gave me a sly, knowing glance. "Same story." He pulled out his map. I pulled out mine. "I updated this last night. You can scratch about two more kilometers from your search area."

"They covered that much ground already?"

"Remember, you were gone for four days."

I showed him the area I'd covered. Together we went over the anticipated search area for the next few days. When we were done, Biahn offered to buy me lunch. I was delighted; I never eat out. It's one of those luxuries reserved for people with money, not people struggling to get by or save up to care for a sick mother and possibly a new wife.

He took me to a grill shack. It was a dusty, open-air shed roof over a hot grill and two televisions. Meat, pickled cabbage, and cheap wine were the top menu items. I think wine was usually ordered more often than the meat. Not really surprising. The food was subpar compared to what I could cook.

I opted against beer, choosing an orange soda instead. It was one of only two flavors of soda they had. But, it was a free meal and I guessed that Biahn could easily afford it. In my estimation, he would soon be leaving our small-time publisher and make a break for some of the bigger outfits in the region.

"Listen, Iddo, just so you know, my schedule is booking up pretty fast for the next couple days. I need to know that you'll be able to make an appointment with me at noon in three days."

"Three? Not four?"

"Like I said, I've got a busy schedule coming up. Watch your time better, don't push so deep into the woods. Do whatever you need to do, but I want to plan on three days."

It wouldn't be easy. But I figured it was possible. "I promise. I'll be there on time. I have a much better idea of what I'm doing now." At least I hoped I did.

I finished the last bite of skewered chicken. No, the golden-brown chicken wasn't great, but it was salty, and that was something I'd been craving for the last day or so. Hiking three days straight can really drain a guy.

A few more words of encouragement from Biahn, then we parted again. It wasn't like I needed a pump-up speech. I was already motivated far more than Biahn was. But he was older and had a take-charge attitude. This was going to be a good story for his career, but I wasn't thinking about my career. I was worried about my future wife and a good-hearted man trying to protect so many children.

I didn't set straight out that afternoon. I went to my apartment first. My muscles were still sore, but I still had some time and energy left in the day to work on my schoolwork. Still, as soon as I sat down, it took all my self-control to keep from falling asleep. Somehow, I managed to get all caught up before Thing Two walked through the door.

"Have you seen Thing One today? I need to talk to him."

I looked up from the kitchen table. My blank face told him everything before I said, "No."

"What about Duy? Is he in?"

Again, a slight shake of my head.

Thing Two slammed his fist down hard on the table. I jumped, my eyes suddenly popped wide open.

"I don't have time for this!" Thing Two shouted. "Argggh!"

I leaned back ever so slightly. I wanted to sneak off to my room, but caution held me steady. Thing Two's mood swings were getting worse every month. The last thing I needed was to trigger an outburst directed at me.

Even Duy was trying to avoid the guy. Somehow, much to Duy's displeasure, Thing Two always found his way to the parties that Duy was at, even when Duy flat out tried to ditch our roommate. It looked like this was one of those days when Duy succeeded in sneaking off without Thing Two. Usually when that happened, Duy would show up hours later, drunk or high on who knows what.

It always surprised me that he could find his way back here at all when in that state. Usually he couldn't even remember where he'd been once he sobered up. At least he didn't own a car. He'd be long dead by now if he ever got behind a wheel.

Luckily, Thing Two vented his frustration quickly before slamming the door on his way out of the apartment, grumbling about missing out.

He didn't seem to notice that I'd been gone for the last three days. Oh well. Not like I wanted him to notice. Talking to him was like talking to someone who only wanted something out of you.

My old hard futon mattress had never felt more inviting. The sun still hadn't settled, but I did. Before I completely drifted into dreamland, something Thing Two had said struck me. Thing One had been gone quite a bit this semester, but I couldn't remember even seeing him in the past two weeks. I wondered what could be so time consuming. If there really was anyone that I'd enjoy a talk with, it would've been him.

Morning came quickly. The chirping alarm on my cheap digital watch woke me at four in the morning. An hour later I was rubbing sleep out of my eyes as I walked down the quiet street.

There was a chill in the air and smells from burning cook fires were clinging low to the earth. It was both refreshing and a little ominous. I hoped it wouldn't rain. I could warm up quickly just by hiking. Not only was hiking in wet clothes annoying, but the day after a rainstorm, the extra humidity would make an unbearable sticky hot day to follow.

Dark clouds shaded the morning sunlight, but passed on by late morning. By that time, I was already hiking along my previously planned route. Well, maybe not exactly along my planned route. This early in the day, I felt comfortable in stretching the space between my hike yesterday and my path today by nearly a whole kilometer. The boys in the hangman's group would be out foraging and they often wandered more than that in a day. If they were near, I might find them.

At the end of day one, I found nothing. Day two was about the same, but I lost too many hours dodging not one but three witches' homes. They could have just been hermits; well, at least one of them could have been a hermit. The other two were definitely dabbling in evil arts. If the creepy bones, runes, and weird idols weren't dead giveaways, the dark mood of the surrounding area was. I assumed that the third shanty was a witch's home, also. It didn't have the same unnerving decor scattered around the home, but it was so close to these other two.

The delay meant that I didn't reach my turnaround point until late in the second day. I could smell the salty water teasing me from a distance. I knew I was still too far away to find it, but the scent of the sea made me feel that if I could just see beyond the next the trees, I'd have an open view of waves lapping against the distant shore. That was just wishful thinking on my part. I was simply catching the smells carried on the wind.

Instead of pressing on, I ate a hearty dinner. I'd found plenty of roots and berries earlier in the day. The berries were especially good when eaten with the last of my bread. How I'd like to push on till I got to the water's edge, but that wasn't practical. So, I started my next leg back. All of this hiking was exhausting, but my endurance was improving. I hiked for a few more hours, until it was too dark to go on.

When I finally did stop for the night, I didn't collapse immediately to sleep. For the first time in my life, I offered a quiet prayer to a God I'd never really known. If there truly was an omnipotent being of righteousness, which I'd slowly been coming around to accept over the last year or more, maybe I should try this prayer thing I'd heard about. I wasn't sure exactly how to go about it. If He could read my mind, then maybe it didn't matter how I addressed Him, as long as I was sincere.

I spoke, then lowered my voice to a whisper, my words feeling lonely in the vast still night. I pleaded my case, and remembered to thank Him for the faith to overcome the witch of last year. I also thanked him for any help he may have lent me with the witches I'd passed last night. Mostly I asked Him to help me find Midnight and Daddy Smiling. I figured that God would rather I call him Daddy Smiling instead of the hangman.

When I was finished, I sat there for a long time, wondering if I was being silly or if my petition had even been heard. Finally I drifted to sleep. Early in the morning, I was wakened by the sound of a light drizzling rain. It didn't last long and I was able to stay dry, but it did hit the ground enough to dampen it. Before the sun lit the sky, the cloud passed. I'd eaten all my food last night, so I didn't worry about breakfast. I could gather a thing here or there as I walked.

I felt more refreshed than I had on any other morning this week. Occasionally I looked down at my cheap compass to make sure I was still heading in the right direction. I didn't think I'd find the hangman today, but I did have a good spring in my step. Around midmorning I realized that I needed to start back to the town if I was to meet Biahn. I went for one more hour, or at least until I reached a small pond that was a key landmark on my search. I found the pond at ten o'clock. Still there was no sign of anybody around. I had just two hours to get back to the publishing house for my follow-up with Biahn.

I knew that I'd be late, so I tried to jog. Obviously, that didn't last long. I was just slowing down when I tripped on a branch and did a face-plant. I wiped damp twigs and dirt from my body, then my eyes caught the faintest imprint in the ground. The footprint was smaller than mine. I would have missed it entirely if I hadn't fallen. The print had to have been made this morning. It was so light that, if there'd been no rain earlier, the footprint wouldn't have even been noticeable.

I wanted to ditch my meeting with Biahn and track down the boy who'd made it, but I was late already. At least I had a good idea where to start looking tomorrow. I had to consider that it might take me another three days just to track them down. So I made a mark on my map, then continued on until I exited the woods.

I found my way to Biahn's office around three in the afternoon. He was just working on touching up an article when I burst through his door.

Chapter 24

Also, you may have heard this before, but remember to choose your friends carefully. They can help you, or they can destroy you.

"You're late, again." Biahn's gaze didn't even leave his desk. His attention remained glued to the article he was working on, his pen changing a word here, deleting one there. His brow was slightly scrunched down, wrinkling as it neared his nose.

"I'm very sorry, it's just that—"

"You may have no problem finding excuses, but excuses are like butt holes. Everyone has them and they all stink!"

I'd heard that saying before, but it surprised me coming from Biahn. I thought he'd be delighted to see me. I also wondered if my own butt hole really would stink. I was pretty sure I kept it so clean that it wouldn't. I had to shake the thought away. "But I'm only a few hours late."

"You're a whole day plus a few hours late," he accused.

A whole day? How—then it hit me. I hadn't even thought about it. We'd talked about meeting in three days, I knew that, but in my mind, I'd thought three days of searching. I'd spent that first night sleeping in my apartment. So really, I was a day late. Maybe I could still salvage this encounter. "I think I've found them."

This time Biahn did put down his pen. The hard shell of his disappointed eyes thinned quickly and I wondered where the Biahn of thirty seconds ago had just vanished to. The only explanation I could think of was that he was simply a good-natured person. Cruelness wasn't something that came easily to him, so it must also leave him more easily than others.

He laced his fingers together, then smiled. "Well, Iddo, this might be good news after all." He reached behind him and took hold of his map. I brought mine to the table, as well. I unfolded mine as he unrolled his.

The hunting party was still a good three, maybe four days from where I'd found the tracks. It looked like they'd done a fair amount of backtracking, just to be safe. Even if they did stumble near where I'd found the footprint, it would probably take them another day or two on top of that to find the hangman's camp. I felt more optimistic about my chances of finding them first.

"I'll see what I can do to buy you a couple extra days," Biahn said as he shook my hand. "Are you going home to your apartment tonight, or are you going back out today?"

"Everything is still so fresh. If I leave now, I should

be able to find those footprints again, then track them down."

"You kind of stink, you know that, right? If I were you, I'd go home for an hour or two. Get clean, pack a few new meals. Besides, what would your friends there think, if you suddenly show up smelling like three or four days of sweat?"

I thought of Midnight running up to greet me, then stopping short to plug her nose. Not a bad idea. I hadn't noticed my smell before now—or at least not much. If it was bad enough for Biahn to smell from a few feet away, I'd hate to repel what might be my best hope of winning a bride. "Thanks for the tip. I think maybe I will go home and shower first, but I'm still going out right afterward. I want to find those tracks before it gets too dark to see them."

"Good luck, Iddo. I'm sure you'll find them soon. I'll do what I can to stall the mob. What're you going to do once you find them?"

I hadn't thought about that. I'd been so engrossed in just locating them first, I hadn't considered what to do once I found them. "I don't know yet. Do you have any good ideas?"

"Wish I did, son. My only idea is that you have them cross back on their retreat to a place the mob won't think about searching again. Eventually, they'll have to give up."

"Thanks, Biahn." I got up to leave, but he stood also. A little confused, I asked, "You're not coming with me, are you?"

"Oh no. Remember, I told you that I was very busy today. You're lucky you even found me here. If I'm going to help you, I've got to run a few errands and get my work done before I meet up with the mob. You need me to stay behind, delay or misdirect them while you find and get your people to safety."

I looked down at his article that he'd been so absorbed in only moments ago. He followed my attention. "Oh, that. That can wait. It was just busywork till you showed up. I've been impatient for you to return. I was worried; didn't expect you to be this late. By the way, sorry for getting after you about that. I tend to lose patience easily."

Biahn losing patience easily? No, that didn't feel right, but I acquiesced. If I was as busy as Biahn surely was, I'd be a little annoyed with tardiness too.

Once out of the building, I jogged back to my apartment. That was another thing I'd noticed. My endurance had drastically improved over the year. I sometimes had to remind myself that I was no longer a short fat kid.

After six long days of hiking, I had no clean clothes. The last three days had plastered a thick coating of dust and pollen all over my face and yes, I did stink. Before showering, though, I cleaned three shirts, two pairs of brown jeans and enough underwear to match. I wanted something fresh to climb into after I washed myself and shaved. In the heat of the mid-afternoon sun, my clothes would dry quickly. I packed a few meals then cleaned up. By the time I put on a second-hand t-shirt with the faded earthy colored jeans, they were nearly dry. They'd been sitting out in the sun for almost an hour, and were only just a little damp around the seams. I could live with that.

By five o'clock I was back at the edge of the woods. With my compass in one hand, I tried to orient myself so that I could find my way back to the tracks as quickly as possible. I folded the map and stood upright. Here I go, I better not get lost. I suddenly had a feeling of grave responsibility. What would I do once I found them? How dangerous was the mob? I mostly wanted to find the hangman and his children for Midnight's sake. But I couldn't just take her back with me and leave the rest of them to the mercy of the mob. They would—what would they do?

I turned in a slow circle, trying to imagine a group of men with torches and poles coming to torture or capture what I could only describe as my future in-laws. I sighed deeply, then started into the woods.

I'd only gone a few hundred meters when I thought I heard a stick break behind me. I stopped and spun around. Nothing. Thinking about the mob must have put my senses on high alert. They weren't behind me. I was alone. Biahn had said they wouldn't be showing up for several more hours. I heard noises like this all the time while I was hiking. I think the added pressure of this evening was just making me paranoid. Besides, even if the mob was going to search tonight, Biahn was going to be with them. He'd keep them searching in the wrong spot for a good week while I helped the hangman escape.

After a few hours, I knew I was close to where I'd discovered the footprint. Even with the help of my map and compass, I couldn't find it. I should've tied something to a tree so that I could more easily find my way back. Especially in this fading light, everything looked different. I zigzagged around until it was too dark to see.

Finally I made camp. I'd been so naive to think that I could just stroll on back, find the footprint, then follow them back into Daddy Smiling's camp. Sleep was hard to come by. I tossed and turned. I knew I was close. I also was afraid of not actually finding them. Then there was the mob. Every noise of the dense forest made me think that the mob was surrounding my camp. From the creaking of trees to the patterns of insect noises, I imagined the worst.

I fell asleep at what I guessed was three in the morning. I awoke as the sky was shifting from black to dark blue. The sun would be up in less than an hour. I wanted to sleep longer, but decided against it. I splashed a little water onto my face, then thought of something. Looking at the canteen, I realized that there wasn't any lake or pond around here. Daddy Smiling would need water for all his children and they had very little to pack it in.

Pulling out my map, I studied it for a moment. With all my zig-zagging and no clear point of reference, I could only guess my location, but as I studied it, I noticed a faint, almost invisible crease snaking near my position. I hadn't noticed it before. It was easy to miss, but it could be the beginning of a small stream.

If that's what it was, I definitely hadn't crossed it yet. A stream should eventually feed into a larger creek. I traced my finger along it. Yes, several kilometers away it met with a thin blue line. Daddy Smiling had to be somewhere along this first little stream.

I ate as quickly as possible before leaving. I felt so sure about this morning. I would find them at last. By noon I was kicking up damp clumps of sod. I'd found that tiny trickle of a stream. It wasn't any wider than my hand in most spots. It was good clean water, though, and I'd hiked most of it. I didn't see a single footprint. Frustrated, I collapsed on a rock several meters from the water. I didn't want to see or hear the trickling reminder of my morning's failure. As I sat in silence, I suddenly picked up on the faintest of sounds. It was still far off in the distance.

At first, I worried that my paranoia of last night might have been justified. Maybe some of the town's mob had followed me. As I strained to listen, I could just start to make out the words. My heart sped and I listened with excitement. "If you get there before I do / Coming for to carry me home . . ."

I jumped to my feet and ran toward where I thought I heard Daddy Smiling's voice. I paused, then listened. At first, I couldn't hear anything above the sound of my own whistling breath. Then I heard it again. "The brightest day that I can say / Coming for to carry me home . . ."

I sprinted for another minute or two, then paused. This time I heard nothing. Not even the birds were chirping anymore. Not a single sound except for my own wheezing lungs and the occasional groan of a tree. I pulled out my map again, trying to keep an ear tuned for any sounds. I couldn't see anything on the map that indicated anything special about this area.

I hadn't imagined that deep melodic voice. Maybe it had bounced around, and I'd run the wrong way. I felt so close, but was terrified that I'd lose my chance. When I remembered how well Daddy Smiling knew these woods and how much ground he seemed to always cover, my spirits sank even deeper.

While I was folding my map, I dropped my compass. As I bent over to pick it up, I noticed that the dirt had been disturbed. It was a footprint of a smaller child. Quickly stowing my compass, I followed it to the next set of prints. Soon they were joined by more. By this time, I was grinning. I was finally on my way. Half an hour later, I couldn't distinguish the tracks anymore because there were too many. They led all over the place in every direction. Daddy Smiling's group had been here. Now, nothing. Just a lot of packed earth. My enthusiasm drained as reality sank in. I'd finally stumbled close to them, but they were on the move. It might take me days to catch up to them.

I knew I was hungry, though I had little appetite for food at that moment. I wanted to find their tracks away from here. At the same time, I wanted to lie down and feel sorry for myself. I'd been so sure I would've found them by now. I decided on something in the middle. I would have lunch, then resume looking for them. I was just about to unzip my backpack when I heard a twig snap.

I looked up into the branches about three trees away. Two innocent-looking eyes were staring back at me. I smiled and waved. "Hello there. I'm Iddo. What's your name?"

They continued to stare, not answering, but then I heard other branches snapping. Before long, little heads were peering down at me from every tree and up from every shrub.

"Olly olly oxen free!" someone shouted, and they all came out from hiding to greet me. My head swiveled from side to side until my gaze rested on the most beautiful face ever. Midnight was shyly stepping closer through the crowd of small children. She paused about five meters from me, then we both ran to each other and embraced in a long-overdue hug. She cried and I kissed her face.

We held each other for a long moment before other kids, Grub included, pulled me away and laughed as they squeezed my muscled arms.

For the first time, I was something of a celebrity. Nobody clung tighter to me, though, than Midnight. "I'll never let you out of my sight again," I promised her. For ten good minutes I endured the attention from everyone. At last I asked, "Where's Daddy Smiling? He needs to know what I know."

"Daddy Smiling looks for new home. We play hide-and-seek, yes we do. Bad men seek. We hide. Daddy Smiling keep us safe. We love Daddy Smiling, yes we do."

"I know where the bad men will be looking for you all. I can help."

"Daddy Smiling knows where bad men are, too. He follow them every night."

It hadn't occurred to me that Daddy Smiling would be following the men. Why not? He knew these woods better than anyone. He was more prepared to help his children than I could ever be. Maybe I really did know this, deep down. Maybe in my selfishness, all I really wanted was to make sure that I didn't lose Midnight forever.

No! My intentions were good. Yes, I wanted to find Midnight, but I also wanted to help Daddy Smiling in any way I could.

I'd rarely heard any words from his deformed mouth other than that repetitive song. In truth, I knew that he suffered from some mental disability, but I hadn't the slightest clue as to the extent of his mental ability. What was really going on in his mind? I was starting to suspect that there were depths to him that neither I, nor anyone else, would ever understand.

"Is Daddy Smiling near?" I asked again. "I want to let him know that I plan to bring you back with me. Will you come back with me?"

"Silly Iddo. I will come with you, yes I will. We be Mommy Midnight and Daddy Iddo forever. I love you, yes I do."

I hugged her tight again. "So, where is he? I want to let him know."

"You not tell him now. He just come back, now he sleep. He need sleep for finding bad men tonight."

"Okay, Midnight, I'll wait till he wakes up."

Dinner came early. I guessed that the hangman wanted it so. That way he could leave with enough time to find the mob before they got too far into their search. As he ate, I approached him. I hadn't expected to feel nervous, but every one of my bones felt like jelly. Fear of the hangman had nothing to do with it. Fear of asking permission for Midnight's hand from her adopted father was the real knee-trembling experience. I tried not to stare at his head-splitting mouth as he took a bite of a large fruit that seemed dwarfed in front of his massive teeth.

"D-daddy S-miling, I know you're being chased down by some bad men." My words came more easily as I skirted the main focus of my topic. "I know where they've been looking, but I guess you already know that. I wanted to see if I could help, but I don't know if you even need my help. I guess what I really want to know is, if you'll let me take Midnight with me. We love each other and wish to be married."

There, it was out. A little convoluted, but I'd said it. A huge but gentle hand touched my arm. I realized that my eyes were focused on the green ground cover by my feet. I quickly raised my eyes up to meet his. They were eerily gray but at the same time warm and accepting. Suddenly they took on a sharp wariness. My throat seemed to swell shut, until he diverted his eyes and slowly searched the surrounding trees.

"Don't anybody move!" came the loud order as a dozen men, each armed with machetes, encircled the camp. With them were at least three guerilla fighters. Those aging mercenaries, still clinging to their wartime ways, were always recognizable. The last place you wanted to be was on the unpaid end of their attention. In a sense they were like the journalists whose loyalties aligned perfectly with the highest bidder. Given my foreknowledge of the journalists' attitudes, I shouldn't have been surprised to recognize one other man.

We locked gazes for a moment. "Sorry, Iddo," Biahn said with a half-smile. "I know how much you like the hangman, but this was just too good of a story to let pass."

The feeling of betrayal was nearly impossible to describe, even if I should have known better. "You followed me?" I could hardly believe it. Anger, mixed with sadness and despair, exchanged a rapid struggle for my cognitive focus.

"Why should we wear out our shoes when you were perfectly willing to do the legwork for us?"

"Round them all up," one of the men ordered. "And be careful with that beast, he looks as strong as a truck."

"Which one, they're both huge."

"The older messed up one."

I swept my gaze around. Frightened children cowered close to one another. Midnight dug her fingers into my arm, as if anchoring herself to her only hope of safety. Five men with ropes confronted the hangman. He must've known that he was beaten. He didn't even put up a fight. I pried Midnight off my arm and stepped between the men and the hangman. Time to see if my newfound strength was up to the task of protecting everyone.

I raised my fists, uncertain as could be, and opened my mouth to protest. Then I felt one of his massive hand on my shoulder. I looked back through wetting eyes. I wanted to tell him how sorry I was. Instead there was a reassuring softness to his hideous countenance that told me all was well.

As gently as he would cradle a newborn, he pulled me to the side and stepped forward to greet his captors. Within a minute he was bound so tight that his hands took on a shade of purple. His feet were left free, but a slip knot was fastened around his neck to lead him along.

"If you don't want to be bound or beaten, grab hold

of this rope and don't let go!" shouted a man as he and another uncoiled a long manila rope. Girls with babes in arms and boys alike all joined in a line along the rope. A few stragglers were slapped with the flat end of machetes.

Midnight tried to fight off a rough-shaven skinny guy who smelled strongly of wine. His hands looked like rusty vises as he dragged her over to the rope. I jump up to him and tugged at his other arm. He was surprisingly strong and swatted me in the face, a reach for him, but it stunned me none the less. Before I could react, I was kicked and clubbed by two other men. "You're no hero, boy. If you aren't one of us, you're one of them."

They pulled me to my feet and then the machetes started whacking me in the back and the butt. Each blow with the flat end of the blade brought a burning welt. I had no illusions as to what my back looked like. The edges of my zebra stripe welts were accented by bloody lines where the edge of the knives ripped into my skin. Each time one of those blades smacked flesh, my eyes lost focus in a daze of bright stars. They weren't just beating me; they were trying to break me.

Just when I thought I'd fall to the forest floor, never to rise again, I found my hand clutching the line of rope. Midnight was ten children in front of me, but I hadn't the strength to press closer to her, a lot of good all my newfound size and strength afforded me now.

Then the rope tugged. My wobbling legs followed as we were led away, all the time, me feeling a failure.

Chapter 25

Likewise, there are worst things than being a prisoner of a jail. I was held against my will, but I was free. You are free, but are being led gently to a prison from which there may be no escape. That Evil One whom the witches worship, he will bind you tighter than any rope. He will trap you more surely than any steel door, but he starts with the subtlest of snares. Both powers of good and evil have gentle leashes. It's not always easy to see the final destination beyond the moment.

The moon was full when we finally exited the woods. Morning wouldn't be far off. Even with the brutal men prodding us faster with their machetes and clubs, a hundred and fifty children or more are hard pressed to make a speedy march. We didn't go directly to the New Tum police station, at least not all of us. They couldn't have housed so many people. They did lock the hangman in a cell, but the rest of us were herded to a nearby lot where two massive and drab looking army tents had been hastily erected and stood waiting. Their faded tan canvas effectively sucked hope from anyone near them.

Small family units were broken up as the boys were separated from the girls. Huddled and squatting inside the boy's army tent, I found the once confident Chirp-chirp. He was crowded in a mass of other boys including Grub.

I'd nearly forgotten that he'd taken on the role of father figure for one of the newer babies. Grub, not even ten years old, was cradling his own little boy. His limp arms never dropped the babe despite his complete exhaustion. How he held onto the sleeping child was beyond me. He looked ready to roll his own eyes into the back of his head and collapse.

All these children were beyond terrified. Beyond that, the long hike to this unfamiliar place had left them drained. Tears that had been shed freely on the trail now dried up. Exhaustion and sleep took the younger ones. Shock, curiosity, or something else kept the older ones awake. Like trapped feral cats, their eyes stared wearily from one end of the tent to the other.

For so many children, most of whom couldn't remember ever living behind a wall, this tent must've felt extremely confining. I could see the horror in their faces and I knew that it was more intense than my own. In a way it comforted me. I wasn't the worst one here. At least I had a better hope of release. My lack of fear turned into a form of confidence that the others noticed. While I might have been responsible for leading the mob to these children, they didn't look at me as a betrayer. They looked to me for hope and possibly leadership. Now I really couldn't look scared, for their sakes.

Morning came. I was suddenly aware of the tent being brighter and much hotter. A faint odor of ammonia clung to the increasingly humid air. The urine was quickly overpowered by the more pungent odor of human feces. There was no bathroom in here. Even if there was, it would be as foreign to these kids as a car. Little babies without any control of their bodily functions were the least of the problem. The older kids turned one corner of the tent into a steaming pile of refuse.

Suddenly I realized how quickly the living conditions of this tent would deteriorate. Over six thousand kids die each day from diarrhea. If these kids didn't get a more sanitary environment, they could easily get sick and start dying. I had no doubt in my mind. I walked over to the tent opening. Two drowsy guards were standing watch.

"I need to help these children in here. Who can I talk to about their needs?"

One of the guards ignored me. The other turned only halfway to face me. Indifference shaded his expression. "We're just the night watch. We should be replaced any minute by someone else. You'll have to talk to them."

"But these kids need—"

The guard just raised his hand and turned away. Nothing I could say would make him care in the least.

As if on cue, they both looked up as two fresh guards came over to relieve them. My eyes nearly bulged when I saw who one of the guards was.

"Thing One!"

He looked at me as if expecting to see me. "Hey

Iddo." Then, as if it was the most normal thing to do, he took one peek inside, then planted himself in the former guard's position.

I wrinkled my brow. "What's going on? What're you doing here? You need to help us."

Thing One sighed. "Listen, Iddo, I know things look bad right now. In fact, things might get a little worse before they get better. But trust me, everything will work out fine in time. You might need to just steel yourself for a couple of really rough days."

"What are you talking about? Since when were you part of this mob? You've got to do something to help!"

"I'm not part of the mob, Iddo, I'm doing my job. The kids will all be handled by committees tasked to this. I'm on those committees. I know they're not the best, but they will do what's best for the children in time."

"What's best for the children is to give them back Daddy Smiling and to let them go back to the woods. Do you seriously think the courts will let that happen?"

"I can't say, Iddo. And there's little I can do to help you right this moment, but trust me when I say, you'll soon be out of here and these children will be taken care of. By the way, I do have a bit of bad news. I'm sorry, I opened the letter and read it. You're not going to like it."

Thing One reached into his back pocket wond pulled out a folded envelope. The top seal was ripped, and he handed it to me. His hand shook a little as he passed it to me. I looked up into his eyes and for the first time noticed that they were bloodshot. Maybe I wasn't the only one who'd had a long night. "It's from your uncle. I'm really sorry, Iddo."

My stomach suddenly dropped to my feet, leaving a hollow pit just under my chest. I pulled the envelope from his grasp. He had a hard time letting it go. Fear gripped my heart. There was only one thing it could say. Believing what I thought it to be, made the task all that more difficult.

Dear Iddo,

Please forgive me for not coming to tell you this in person. I would have called, but didn't know how to reach you. By the time you get this, we will most likely have conducted the funeral for your mother. Her only wish was that you finish your schooling, to become that man she knew you to be at heart. She believed in you more than anything else in this world, which is why we think she was able to go on as long as she did . . .

I found myself sitting on the floor. Folding the letter, I let the impact of it sink in. I would finish reading it soon. For now, I didn't really care what the rest of it said. My eyes were too blurry and wet to finish.

"Why you sad? They not let us go?"

I rubbed my eyes and looked up to see Chirp-chirp. Fear still rimmed the edges of his face, a face that looked gaunter than I remembered. Despite his own fears, concern for his brothers and me were evident. Raising Grub had helped mature this young man well beyond his age.

"I don't know," I said honestly. "I know one of the guards, but all he could say was that things would work out well enough for everyone here."

"This is good, yes? So why you crybaby?"

I snorted and smiled. It was a genuine smile, though I don't know how I managed it. "It's nothing for you to worry about. I just got sad news from home."

Chirp-chirp looked down at his surprisingly calm, but awake baby. "All home is sad news now."

That was true. I had my problems, which I could do nothing about, but these children all had a problem too. Instead of wallowing in my own grief, I could help them. I felt guilty for pushing my mourning aside. Doing this would probably make it all that more difficult to bear later on, but I had to pull myself together. Now was not the time to shut down. These children needed help and I couldn't do much for them unless I got out of here.

"I need to find a way out if I'm going to help you," I told Chirp-chirp.

"We will seek, we will find—yes we will," he replied.

The tent didn't have a canvas floor, so sneaking under the wall might work. He walked halfway up one side of the tent. Every meter of the sturdy fabric was staked down and tied securely. I'm sure we could have worked at loosening a stake, digging under, or just tearing the wall to escape, but I wanted to survey the remainder of the walls for an easier weakness. Before I could continue, every head swiveled toward the front of the tent.

I turned my gaze to find the focus of everyone's attention. A medium-built man with a slick comb-over had just entered the tent. He was dressed nicely in a button-up maroon shirt and dark formal wool slacks.

"May I have your attention, please," he said slowly in a deep, slightly British accent. He paused, then lifted a cloth to his nose. I'm sure it did little to dampen the fecal stench attacking his senses. It just gave him an air of arrogance. Lowering the cloth to speak, he went on, "I know you are all scared. I also know that you have a deep love for the hangman. He has, however, committed crimes and he must be punished for them.

"None of you have done anything wrong. You are all considered orphans. The youngest of you will be taken to homes, where new families will care for you. Those of you who are older will be taken far from here where there is a school for orphans. They have been advised of your coming and are preparing to help you integrate into normal society.

"Please don't be afraid. You've been hidden from the world for too long, but we will help you return to it. It will be new and different, but it will be good for you. In just a minute, food will be brought in for you. We will not let you starve. We are your friends. I would expect that you need only wait here for one day, two at the most, before we help you find your new homes."

The man looked around, maybe trying to judge whether or not he'd been understood. Then, as if he was suddenly assaulted by another whiff of the horrible smell that clung to the air like a mist of aerosol poo, he snapped his dark-patterned handkerchief to his nose and held it there like a gas mask. Without further discourse, he shook his head in what could have either been pity or disgust, then turned and left.

I needed to get out of here. But even my own room-mate and friend, the one I knew to be smart and wise, wouldn't let me leave. I'm sure he was just doing his job and that if he could turn the other way, he might. Surely these people wouldn't send me off to some reform school to reintegrate into society, would they?

It's not like I was a—my mind suddenly took another turn for the gloomy—I was technically an orphan now. I tried to imagine the complication this might create in getting myself free. I had to consciously force the thoughts away. It was as difficult as telling gravity not to pull on the Earth.

I was relieved from my prison of worry when Chirp-chirp grabbed my arm again. "We seek more. You find way out now."

"Yes," I replied. "We find way out."

We continued to survey the tent walls. For such a thin material, the tent could have been made of steel and not been more secure. The once or twice that Chirp-chirp or I leaned into the wall, we were met by a heavy blunt cudgel from the other side. I didn't know how many men they had watching the tent, but it had to be a lot if they could keep such a close eye on every square meter of canvas.

With a newly bruised shoulder, and a wrist that was almost cracked, I walked back to the center of the tent with Midnight's former parental partner. "I think we're both stuck here," I said.

"Iddo," a hard voice boomed.

I looked at Chirp-chirp, confused, then turned to

face the opening of the tent. A tall, healthy built man in a police uniform was standing with his billy club in hand. "Iddo, you're coming with me!"

Chirp-chirp took a step to follow, but the officer's club raised in warning. "No, not you! Just Iddo."

Chirp-chirp paused; I could see a flame of rebellion in his eyes. I'd never seen any of Daddy Smiling's children display anger before, but my friend looked ready to take up the hangman's cause. I placed a hand on his shoulder. "Don't worry about me. I'll do everything I can to help you all."

"Be careful, buddy. You are good boy, yes you are." Chirp-chirp's anger was replaced by concern. Concern for me, I realized, not himself. Chirp-chirp was as self-less as anyone I'd ever met. I knew right then that he'd place me or any of these other children before himself. As young as he was, he was already a man's man. I shouldn't be surprised. I saw it every time I glimpsed the advanced maturity of these kids. Daddy Smiling may have had lit-tle choice in how he raised them, but they sure proved themselves. Still, I got the impression that they didn't sac-rifice too much of their childlike wonder and fun for this premature state of mind. At least they didn't used to.

The officer motioned for me to walk in front of him. "Follow the sidewalk to the court building just over there." He pointed a finger.

I did as instructed, aware of the short heavy steel rod, still clutched firmly in his hands. When I looked back, I saw the outside of the tent. I expected to see guards ev-erywhere, but there were only a few. However, under a small awning, there was a man in front of a computer screen. They had a camera inside the tent. How had I not noticed it before? They didn't have to surround the tents with a hundred guards. Two or three would be adequate. They'd know every time one of us went near the sidewall and just direct one of the guards to that area. I was stupid for being so ignorant.

My momentary distraction earned me a shove from the officer. Thankfully he didn't pound me with that steel club. I already had enough cuts and bruises to last a month. The court was air conditioned, but had a stale and depressing echo to it. A small peppermint aroma clung to the air around one of the clerk's desks. The smell reminded me of a sweet older lady and I had the feeling that if any place might find a just and compassionate resolution to this whole mess, this place might. Only there was no nice lady behind that desk to greet us. The whole building was empty.

I was confused, then realization dawned on me. I'd completely lost track of the days. This was Sunday. Nobody would be working today. So why was I being dragged in here? We walked past the reception area and entered the actual courtroom. Apparently Biahn hadn't lied about everything. Any thoughts of mercy evaporated immediately.

The comforting smell of peppermint was replaced by the pungent odor of sweat mixed with tobacco and alcohol. The judge was sitting in his black robes. Chubby and regal, except for a perpetually oily face, he fingered a gavel near his right hand. "Is this the boy?" he called out.

"It is," someone confirmed. I didn't see who. There weren't many people in the room, but I didn't dare look away from the judge. I knew that if I let my attention wander, I would find that I'd walked into a den of conspiratorial mobsters. For some reason that scared me more than keeping eye contact with the judge. Maybe I could convince him. He was the law here, even if he'd put himself in league with these ruffians. If anyone could see reason, it would have to be him.

"Is it true; boy; that you wanted to warn the hangman about our coming?"

He referred to himself as we. I was in trouble now. I could see it. This wasn't a legal meeting. It was intimidation in a legal room, opened by a criminal with a key to the courthouse.

"Look at me, not the floor!" the judge yelled, spittle spraying from his lips.

My head snapped back up. I couldn't look him in the eyes, not anymore, but I gave a resigned nod.

"Pathetic." He paused, then asked, "Why would you care so much for this monster and murderer?"

What do you hate more, that he looks like a monster, or that he protects the innocent children from monsters like you? That's what I should have said. What came out was, "He saved me once." Even this feeble attempt to speak well of the hangman came out as barely a squeak.

The courtroom filled with laughter—drunken, vile laughter. "Get him out of here," the judge said, "before someone misses him. He's no threat."

Strong hands grabbed me and pulled me toward the door. I tried to squirm and turn. "No wait! You have to listen. Those kids, Daddy Smiling, he—"

Nobody listened. I was thrown onto the street. "Get going, boy," one of the men said. "If it weren't for the fact that you led us straight to these guys, we might not let you go at all. Watch yourself. Don't go stirring up trouble, understand?"

I didn't respond. I couldn't. I scrambled to my feet and ran. I didn't stop until I was well out of sight. That next twenty minutes might have been the longest foot dragging walk to my apartment that I'd ever taken.

Chapter 26

I've done all I can. I'm no leader, but my conscience is true. What does your heart tell you?

"Let me guess, Thing One didn't even try to help you."

I peered into the dark room the two Things shared. The arrogant voice of Thing Two carried a little more bitterness than usual. I wasn't in any mood to waste my breath. I just wanted to go to my room and think for a while.

I was edging for the hallway when Thing Two added, "Don't you even want to know how I knew about your little romp with the police?"

"Half the town already knows." I was sure of it. A reporter like Biahn would have seen to that. I realized that I'd be lucky to walk the streets without getting assaulted.

"Hey Iddo," he laughed with a touch of rude hysteria. "Hey, don't ignore me, you self-righteous jerk! You think you're so much better than me or Duy? You don't like who we spend our time with? At least I don't worship a murderer!"

I was at the end of the hallway. I stepped into my room and slammed the door before Thing Two could say anything more. I collapsed onto my dirty old mattress, curled into a ball, and filled the futon with a sticky stream of tears.

"I heard what happened, Iddo. For what it's worth, I'm sorry."

Startled, I sat erect. I used the sleeve on my shoulders to wipe my eyes dry. I hadn't even glanced at Duy's bed. He'd been gone so much that I hadn't expected him to be home, let alone in our room.

"I've been nursing a headache all morning," Duy said casually, as if making an excuse for his intrusion on my privacy. He was still lying on his bed as he talked. "I really should stop partying so much. Eventually I'm going to regret it. But this is college life, eh? Enjoy it while you can, before you need to be responsible, you know, that sort of thing."

"I wish it were that easy," I mumbled.

"Yeah, tell me about it."

"Well, I've got to find a way to help the hangman out. He saved my life, you know. He's not what the newspaper is portraying him as. He's actually a really good man, if not a little different."

"When I said tell me about it, I meant that as an expression." Duy paused.

I didn't know what to say.

He laughed. "Sorry, I couldn't help it. No, seriously, you can go on. A good man though? I heard he strangled hundreds of men."

I sighed. Duy was trying, but I wasn't in the mood. "He has killed a lot of men," I admitted. "But every one of them was out in the woods to murder their own second or third kids to avoid paying the surplus child taxes. Then he takes those little babies and raises them. He's got over a hundred and fifty kids that he's saved."

"No way—he's like the destroying angel. You know, kills the wicked and saves the innocent."

"I-I don't know." I shook my head. "All I know is that he's going to be tried and killed. Then there's Midnight. She's about my age and I promised to marry her. Only problem is that she's going to be taken away somewhere. I have to get her before it's too late, but I don't know how."

"Dude!" Duy exclaimed, then put a hand to his head in regret. "Oh, I hate hangovers. Seriously, Iddo, you're engaged? Why didn't you tell me?"

"Sorry. The circumstances are a little—different. Besides, I didn't think you'd be interested. I didn't want you to give me a hard time over it."

"Do you seriously think I'd give you a hard time over anything?" Duy asked with a playful tone.

I didn't want to point out his lifestyle choice; how could I do that without offending? "Maybe not, but if I were you, I'd think it odd to find my roommate engaged to an orphan girl who lived in the woods and was raised by a killer. Especially when you're enjoying your bachelor status as much as you seem to be."

"Well, anything sounds absurd when you put it that way—but are you kidding, Iddo? A fling with a savage sounds really exotic!"

"It's not like that!" I knew Duy was just trying to sympathize, but his humor was pushing me in the wrong direction.

"Okay, okay, but you're a reporter, why don't you write some articles in defense of this hangman?"

"I'm not a real reporter, I just write campus filler news for the paper to pad their college life section. The real reporters, like Biahn, are already slandering the hangman anyway. There's no way my editors will let me publish anything that contradicts their star reporter."

"No, that's the beauty of it. Don't you see?" Duy sounded serious, maybe even a little conspiratorial. He rolled over on his bunk, linking his arm over the edge of the bed. I still couldn't see his face. "Okay. Imagine this, Iddo. You pitch to your boss another take on the story, a sort of battle of the wits, as it were. The paper would be showing both sides of the story, creating a little drama between writers that would make the audiences follow the story even closer. You could even throw in some details about your love story to gain support. They could sell more papers in a single week than they would in the whole year otherwise."

I rolled off my bed and stood. "Maybe not the whole year, but you might have a point." The idea was novel. Maybe, just maybe, I could pull it off, save the hangman, and find a way to be with Midnight again. The more I let the idea sink in, the more I liked it. I looked up at Duy, who was taking a break from massaging his temples. His bed-matted hair looked perfectly styled for the big crooked grin now cemented on face.

"Duy, some days I could just kiss you."

"No-ho-oh," he said playfully. "I don't swing that way. I prefer—"

"I don't need to know. But all the same, thanks. I gotta run."

"Good luck, Iddo."

I ran into the bathroom, splashed some water on my face, then ran out of the apartment. Thing Two tried to shout some profanity at me, but I was gone before he could finish his line. What was his problem, anyhow? I'd never offended him in any way that I was aware of. Not a big deal. I'd worry about that later, if ever. Considering the bigger picture, Thing Two was low on my list of worries.

Not daring to waste any time, I jogged. Well, I jogged for about one block. Then I walked at a more sustainable pace. Either my memory was poor, or I was always overconfident. Every time I felt like jogging or running, I was reminded that my body was worn down from the beatings. My throat whistled with heavy breaths for the next two blocks. When I finally reached the publishing house, I was covered in sweat, but otherwise in good control of myself. I was confident and energized. I was going to make a difference.

Even on a Sunday, the publishing house was open. The news never stopped, so neither did they. Of course, there were fewer people in on a Sunday. The Monday paper had to come, even if it always tended to be lighter. The news never rests.

The front door hadn't fully closed behind me when my excitement got a cold wet towel thrown onto it. There were a few people in view, not like on a weekday, but they were all busy going about their tasks. Only one person noticed me walk in and her hesitant eyes made me wonder what the bad news could be. Of all people I actually thought she'd have the day off.

"Hi Krystal, are you okay?"

"Yeah, I'm fine. I didn't expect you back so soon."

"So you heard what happened?" I asked.

"I'm so sorry. I know what Biahn did to you. He used you to find those people, didn't he?"

"That's what I'm here to talk about. I need to speak to the chief editor."

"I don't know if that's a good idea right this minute," Krystal warned. As I passed her, she gasped. "Iddo, your back!"

I stopped and turned my head. Futile, I knew. There was no way I'd be able to see my back. But I knew what she was looking at. Yet again I'd become so obsessed with an idea that I'd forgotten to think. In this case I'd forgotten to change my clothes. Not only was that unprofessional, but the back of my shirt was ribboned with cuts and blood. Though I'd been aware of the aching pains and crusted scabs, my shirt had seemed unimportant next to freeing Midnight, Daddy Smiling, and all the kids.

Krystal must not have been aware of how wide her mouth was open, because she looked a little silly and uncommonly disheveled. She was peering below my ruined shirt at the long slashes, bordered in thick black-and-blue strips. Since I hadn't cleaned the blood off, it probably looked worse than it was. Maybe it really was worse than I thought.

"Did Biahn do this, too?"

"His posse did this to me. Don't ever trust him, Krystal. He's just like they teach you to be in journalism school. His loyalty and beliefs lie with the best story at any given time."

Krystal shut her mouth. I wondered if she remembered advocating a similar mentality back in school. Well, haggard or not, I was going to speak to the editor. Maybe my battered appearance would help win my case.

Before Krystal could stop me, I pushed the office door open and entered the chief editor's office. He looked up from his computer.

"I need to go over something with you," I blurted.

"Iddo, you look terrible. I'm guessing you didn't like what Krystal had to say?"

"She hasn't told me anything other than the fact that I look like a rag doll. She can't help me, anyway. I need to go over this with you."

The chief editor folded his arms and leaned back in

his chair.

I laid out my plan. "That's pretty much it. I know you're going to publish Biahn regardless. Just let me do some stories from the other point of view. I promise, people everywhere will read about the controversy. It'll be good for the paper. It might even go international."

The editor rocked in his chair for about five seconds. "I suppose you'll want a small raise for this, too."

I couldn't believe it. I needed a raise. This would make renting a place for me and Midnight so much easier. I should have said, *I don't care about the money. I'll do it for free. This is just a story that has to be told!* Instead, what came out was, "Thank you, that would be great."

The chief editor tossed a pen onto the table. "I told Krystal to tell you this and I still stand behind it. You're fired."

With eyes bulged and mouth agape, I was at a loss for words.

"Biahn is one of our best reporters. If you sympathize with a murderer, then we don't need you here. Not for your current pay, not for a raise. I wouldn't even keep you on for free. You disgust me, Iddo. Get out of my office now and don't come back!"

My jaw hung limp and I just stared at my former employer. He picked up his pen, turned to the other side of his L-shaped desk and said over his shoulder, "You may leave now." As if he'd called me in for a minor editing remark. I stood, then dragged my feet out the door. I looked back once, but his back was still to me.

When his office door clicked shut behind me, I looked up to see Krystal. She was standing not five feet away, biting at her knuckles. Had she been listening at the door?

"I'm so sorry, Iddo. I tried to tell you. It's just that when I saw what they did to you—then you marched into his office so fast—I just, I'm sorry."

Still in shock, I walked right past Krystal, failing to acknowledge her with more than a brief nod. Her pity bored into my back as I silently exited the building. The aches and pains of my lacerated back seemed to attack with new vigor. My body acted as if it too, were betraying me. I walked only two blocks, far enough away that the publishing house was out of view. With no more willpower to put one foot in front of the other, I sat on the curb next to the street.

Crying was out of the question. Not only had I already spent my tears, but also it now seemed pointless. I'd been betrayed, beaten, ridiculed, fired, and on top of that, my mother had died, my fiancée was going to be taken away, and there was nothing I could do to stop it or save the hangman. Even Krystal had come full circle and now pitied me again. This seemed only to put an official stamp on my dejection.

I had nothing left in me. If someone were to come along and pick me up by my leg, I would probably not even change position while they turned me over and shook the rags off my back. They could place my naked body right back on the curb, and I doubt I would've even blinked once. I felt completely and unsalvageably defeated.

After an hour, maybe two, I stood and walked. I

walked so long that when I lifted my gaze from my feet, I didn't recognize where I was. I'd moped my way into some border town I'd never visited. I wasn't exactly lost; it's hard to get lost when you know the direction you just came from. Showing less reluctance than I felt, I turned around and placed one foot in front of the other. I didn't know how long I'd walked to get here. I didn't know where I was or where I wanted to be. I was beyond caring at this point. Though I knew how to find my way back home, I was lost more deeply than any map could help with.

As each step took me closer to my apartment, the smog filling my brain only thickened. For a long time, I kicked stones down the street, imagining that each rock was my body bouncing irregularly as it rolled along the rough asphalt.

At other times I don't remember seeing the street. I just remember seeing Midnight's pleading lips as they trembled or accused me of betraying her. She'd be gone. Everyone would be gone. How could I just pick up my life and go on again like nothing had happened? I didn't think I could. If I couldn't do that, then I'd let down my mother also. I imagined her telling me how I'd disappointed her.

Somewhere deep inside I could see that I was becoming my own worst enemy. I knew that the self-loathing was tearing me down and I shouldn't let it happen. Still, I felt powerless to stop it. When my feet felt too tired to continue, I untucked my chin from my chest long enough to realize that I'd walked past my apartment by at least ten kilometers. I was at the edge of the woods again.

Night had fallen and I could see the yellow glow emanating from so many little lights of the college town. It looked inviting and warm. I turned to the woods, which seemed dark and engulfing. My feet hurt. I'm sure blisters had formed and broken. Instead of working my way back home, I stumbled the last few hundred meters to the base of the woods, where the dark blanket of trees seemed to fit my mood much better. There I let myself collapse next to a thorny bush. It poked at my shoulder, but I didn't move away. I just let it bother me to sleep.

That night dreams of everyone I loved plagued me. Thing One became one of the whipping mobsters. Duy joined Thing Two in bullying me. My mother chose to ignore me. Daddy Smiling tried fastening his rope around my neck. The only one who didn't turn on me was Midnight, but in my dreams, she kept reaching for me and I couldn't even lift my arm to help. Last of all, the Laidy of the Woods screamed, "Me owns you now, boy! You be doin' what me tells you do, for now and always!"

I startled awake. The sun was just rising above the horizon. All was calm. Hidden birds were singing the morning in. My thumping heart slowed in relief, then, it nearly stopped.

Something was on my leg. I lifted my head. The prickly bush I'd fallen asleep next to dug into my cheek. Then I saw it, the largest krait ever was slithering across my leg, warming itself on me. The deadly snake brought back every memory of the witch from my dream. I choked back panic. Was this the work of a witch? The snake remained calm. No, it was just a wild snake looking for a warm rock tc sun itself on.

Something about my unsettling dream and this snake

brought back a resolve that I'd allowed to diminish. I remembered that I'd escaped the witch's snakes through faith. Faith in a God I still barely comprehended. Faith in a God who'd protected me, despite myself.

Light from the rising sun pushed away the shadows. As the morning rays warmed my skin, the light of understanding filled me. If faith could protect me from a witch and a mess of serpents, why couldn't it support me in a good cause? What better cause was there for me than to help Daddy Smiling and his children?

I'd heard of people striving to accomplish their goals, referencing God as their supporter. During the war that was staged around my broken country, I'd heard that both sides fought in the name of their god, not to mention many of my people in the middle, pleading to the same god for protection.

I doubt I could ever say whose side, if any side, God had been on, but I felt something now. I had a reason to go on. I had a reason to fight for my convictions. I would save Daddy Smiling. I would marry Midnight. I would help the children of the woods find refuge. I would find the means to support myself through college. Most of all, I would not give up.

Another thought entered my mind, as if someone else was hinting deeper truths. *Are you only going to turn to Him when you need Him most?*

I drew in a deep breath. No, I couldn't. I was growing beyond that. If I was to call on His grace and actually expect to receive it, I would have to finally commit. I'd told myself more than once that I'd learn of God, but I'd procrastinated. I made a promise to Him right then and there that I would not pursue him so idly any more. I would turn my life over to Him. As I made this commitment, my heart burned with joy. A calling as it were, started growing within me, though I couldn't fully see it yet.

I half laughed. *So is this what faith feels like?* Duy might not be the best example, but if this feeling of unearthly confidence was the same that supported his people, then I might actually become a Believer after all.

Gently I reached under the giant snake. *The sun is coming up, my friend. It's time for you to find a warm spot someplace else.* The poisonous reptile allowed me to lift it off of my legs and place it on the ground next to me. It took one look at me, staring unwaveringly into my eyes. That steady flickering tongue was the only movement between us. To me it almost felt like it was saying, *Good job, Iddo. I came here to get you thinking. You'll be just fine.*

I'm sure it was just trying to decide why its warming stone had just picked it up and moved it. It might have been wondering if I was a threat. If it did consider me dangerous, it must have decided that chipping a fang on such an unusual rock was riskier than just slithering away.

For my part, I stood, stretched, and brushed myself off. My back felt swollen, and I wondered if I should worry about infection. But the morning was fresh. I was fresh. However my body ached, my mind was invigorated. The road ahead might be difficult, but I was bursting with holy resolution. God was on my side. There were many things that could stop me, but nothing would. I would see to that.

296

Chapter 27

I sympathize with innocence. Ask yourselves, is it better to condemn a man who punishes the wicked, in order to save the smallest of children from a brutal death? Or is it better to applaud such a hero and strive to improve our culture so that parents prioritize the family?

It's a common belief that all cultures are good and that we should respect them all. I heartily disagree. There are successful cultures, and there are unsuccessful cultures. There are cultures that encourage kindness and cultures that tear apart the fabric of decency. Daunting as it is, we live in an unsuccessful and immoral culture. If we are ever to live the life we dream of, then we have to make that leap from our comfortable norm.

Whatever your beliefs or disbeliefs in a higher power may be, don't stand idle while our culture punishes a hero.

Today, Tuesday, the man, lovingly called Daddy Smiling, known to most of us as the mythical hangman of the woods, will go to trial. The trial won't be fair. It's being done in haste to prevent sympathy from spreading. This vigilante that our murderers have created will be put to death. Only with considerable persuasive pressure from us will he stand a chance. I will be at the courthouse to protest from sunrise until sunset. If you maintain any shred of compassion for these children and their protector, you will join me for a peaceable protest. By standing together we can make a difference.

It was still only Monday and I signed my name at the bottom of my article. On the off chance that it would get published, I knew my signature wouldn't make the final print. Still, it felt good to scribble my own name at the bottom. It was like I was sealing a pact with myself.

All morning as I labored at one of the school's common-room tables, writing my petition to the masses, I kept getting interrupted by strangers. This wasn't surprising, because I'd hoped this would happen. I was on a crusade and I would do anything to advance my cause.

This is how my morning began:

After rushing back to my apartment, since I smelled very foul, I showered. As the water cleansed my body, each drop of stinging water revealed how badly my back really was hurt. Then I put on a fresh pair of pants. Just as I contemplated how to pull a shirt on without having to endure agonizing pain, I had an idea. I threw the shirt back into my room and walked to campus bare chested, or, more important, bare backed.

The school generally frowns on shirtless students,

but I resolved to park myself at one of the most heavily trafficked hallways in school. Stealing a small desk, I was definitely too big for it, but that wasn't bad, because drew attention to my larger billboard back for all to see the abuse heaped upon me. Just above my belt line, I'd scrawled in poor handwriting, since it's really hard to write on your own back: "Ask me about it." I'd tried to tape a paper that said as much, but the tape kept falling off. Maybe a string to hold it on like a necklace, but by the time I thought of that, I'd put the ink on my back.

That whole morning, amid interruptions, I composed my article. Many people did ask me to tell them about my experience, but few lingered. I've heard that the only people who are crazy enough to think they can change the world are the ones who actually do. I had no sure way to publish my article and I doubted that enough people would get my message in this hallway to make a difference, but somehow, I would publish it.

I read my article one last time before standing up. I still had other things to do today. Since I was on campus, I went ahead and visited my professors, turning in my homework for the past week.

"Mr. Iddo, what are you doing here without a shirt?" my first professor asked as I stepped into his office.

I told him everything. He paid rapt attention. "If you have any suggestions that might help me, I'd love to hear them," I finished.

"Sounds to me like you have your work cut out for you. I'm sorry I can't help, but it's a compelling story. Perhaps, though, I could recommend a topical cream for your back. I'm not good at social movements, but I am a doctor."

"No, thank you. I'll heal eventually. For now, I'll let my back stand as a testament against those men."

"You're a brave young man, Mr. Iddo. I hope, though, that you don't let this whole thing keep you from your studies. You will still attend to your schooling while you fight for this vigilante's life, won't you? Promise me you will. You're too good a student to drop out of becoming a doctor, regardless of which outcome befalls your friend."

"I promise," I said. Dropping out of school had crossed my mind yesterday during my bout of depression, but I'd already dismissed the idea. Life would go on no matter how things turned out. At least for me they would.

My meetings with my other professors went similarly. With each, I had another opportunity to share my story. Each professor skirted the subject of offering any real advice that could help the hangman or the children of the woods. I got the impression that the professors didn't want to be involved. They were more concerned about my back healing faster than about saving a man's life.

They had their reasons, I'm sure. They hadn't experienced what I'd been through. I couldn't blame them. They lived in a different world. They might talk about it for weeks or years to come, but it would be an academic exercise to them. A distant ethical event and debate.

Afterward, I walked back to the only place I could think to go. I couldn't publish this article by myself. Yes, there was the Internet, but I didn't know enough about it to do my own publishing. Besides, I couldn't imagine how my article could go viral in time to make a difference. I should have learned how to use the social media tools available there to voice my concern over a year ago. That had never crossed my mind. Anything I'd ever wanted to say or write always got published, anyway.

There was only one person I knew who could help me get this article published.

"Absolutely not!" Krystal emphasized in a hushed tone. She didn't want the chief editor to hear her talking to me. She showed me out of the building so we could talk more openly.

Passing ahead, she led me across the street. When she felt we were far enough away from the company, she stopped, turned around, and just as I approached, she gave me a shove that was almost hard enough to topple me backward.

"How dare you! First you get fired for trying to help a freakish murderer. Now you want to get me fired, too?"

Her shoulders tightened as if she was about to push me again, but I stepped back. "Krystal, you've heard my side of the story more than once." The Tuesday edition of the paper, like all our papers, would be printed and delivered for distribution early in the morning. I didn't have much time. I needed this. "How else am I to get word out in time for the trial? Besides, you know that Biahn is just manipulating this whole thing to his own personal advantage."

"Biahn still has his job. So do I and I don't need you to ruin that for me."

"Is your job more important to you than the life of a

good man and the future of so many children?"

"Don't play on my sympathies, Iddo. I'm not getting involved."

"Just read the article before you throw it out altogether."

"No, Iddo, I won't. I have a good thing going here."

"Well, then just sneak it into the public commentary. I know you can find a place to put it that won't get you fired."

"Iddo, you're nice but naive. Understand, I don't owe you any favors. If anything, I've overextended my goodwill to you already."

I wanted to accuse her of being selfish, just like her father. Was she really keeping score? I knew that line of thinking wouldn't be very productive. Apparently, though, my stare was accusation enough.

"Since when did you grow such a spine?" Krystal suddenly accused.

My mouth dropped open. The affront surprised me. I didn't know how to respond.

"That's right, you've always been the timid one, afraid of your own shadow. Now you want to guilt me into this cause of yours. I'm not a philanthropist, Iddo. I'm struggling to make my own way in this world, just like everyone else. You've seen my dad. I'm not going to get any help from him. What I don't need is for you, of all people, to get pushy with me. I've got to do what's best for me. And what's best for me is what's best for the company I work for right now."

"I know I'm asking a lot—"

"No! You're asking too much! We're done here."

She took one step. I raised a hand in protest, but she caught it with one of hers. Her grip was manly-strong. The finger on her other hand threatened to skewer my chest like a dagger. I closed my mouth, my teeth clicking shut as if to signal my resigned silence.

Without a word she let go of my hand and marched back to her office. I was left alone next to the street holding my article. It would not get published by her. And if not by her, then not by anyone. I recalled the cliché about how people see their whole life passing before their eyes when they're about to die. My life wasn't in any danger, but my chances of publishing this petition were. Regret suddenly flashed its ugly montage across my mind.

I remembered every instance since the day I'd met Krystal that I could have been a better friend. Even if only once I'd made the simplest effort, or at least not shied away from her, maybe then things would've turned out differently. Some people burn bridges that they may someday need. Usually this happens in sudden disagreements. I'd allowed mine to slowly be eaten away by termites and rot over the course of several years, this despite the many chances Krystal had afforded me to fix it.

I was back at square one. Maybe square two, if there is such a thing. I wasn't hopeless. Quite the opposite, in fact. One door had closed, but maybe I could open another. I had to hurry, though. I had a lot to do and time wasn't on my side.

I jogged back to campus. Using my school credit, I planned to run a bunch of copies off in the student copy center. I would then post them everywhere that people might pass and read them. I was just about to place my article on the scanner when a hand grabbed my shoulder.

"No shirt, no service," an attendant with a prickly little mustache declared.

"Please, I just need to run a few copies, then I'll be out. I don't have time to get a shirt. Please just let me—"

The man grabbed my article, crumpled it, then threw it out the door. I chased after it, terrified that it would get trampled or worse. "Everyone, including you, big guy, needs to respect the rules. Come back when you decide to be responsible." He shut the door behind me.

I wasn't angry with the man. I just felt like a fool. Everything wrong up to this point had been a result of my poor judgment. This fit in line with my growing list of consequences. I had a feeling that when this whole thing was over, I was going to look back on the experience as a positive life-altering lesson in dealing with people. It didn't make sense, but something was happening to me. Despite the fact that nothing was going right, deep inside my confidence was growing. Weird, I know, but that's how I felt.

As my confidence increased, so did my boldness. I might not be able to get anything out of the copy center, but there were alternatives. I hurried back to the office of one of my professors. The door was locked. I ran to the next one. The professor wasn't in, but his door was open. I looked at the clock and realized that he was teaching a class that I was supposed to be in. I had twenty-five more minutes before he'd be back. With nobody watching, I slipped into the room and surveyed his desk.

On top of the monitor read "Dr. Dac Kien." Folders and files littered the office, but no printer. I knew he had to have some way of printing. I opened his word processor, typed a character, and clicked on the print icon. There was indeed a printer networked and I confirmed the print. Nothing in the room made a sound. If the printer wasn't in the office, then it must be a shared printer. If I could find the printer, I could type my article, then just run a bunch of prints.

I printed three more copies of the letter T and ran out of the office, my ears straining to hear the familiar mechanics. Hear them I did. I followed the noise. The machine finished before I found it, but by then I knew where to look. A common area, exclusive to professors and staff, contained not just a printer but a large copy machine. I smiled. I wouldn't have to type this thing after all.

There was one other person moving about, but her attention was elsewhere. I strolled up to the machine, as normal as could be. Easy to say, really. But when you're as big as me and shirtless in a place like this, attention has a way of gravitating toward you. I felt like a large beacon of muscle.

Luckily the other person, probably a student teacher or some other type of clerk, was busy enough that she didn't look in my direction.

I placed my crinkled papers on the copy machine's feeder, then tried to decipher the control panel. I'd never used anything like this, so it was completely foreign to me. I took a guess and typed in "99," then pressed the biggest round button.

Each of my lined drafts were suddenly sucked into the machine with a crumpling sound. I held my breath. The papers were ejected from a different slot. The machine hadn't jammed with my imperfectly flat notepaper. The copier fired to life and spit out one copy after another. I risked a look over my bare shoulder at the other person in the room. She hadn't looked my way yet. Copying would take at least a full minute, maybe more. I knew I couldn't hold my luck for that long.

I faded back around a corner, just out of sight. With my back to the copier, I released my breath through pursed lips. My heart was thumping, but I was grinning. I felt amazing. Iddo of yesterday would never have been so bold. Today I was bold. I was going to make my own luck.

Normally I would've jumped through the ceiling when I felt the cold thin fingers tap my side, but instead I just froze.

"Excuse me, I couldn't help but notice—you," the young woman said with a pause, and maybe a hint of disdain. She seemed unsure just what to think of me. With the copy machine running, she must've taken a break from her work to see who was here. "Is there something I can help you with?"

No need. I'm just here running a copying errand for Professor Dac Kien. That was a lie. And it was a lie that I wanted to say, but even my newfound confidence couldn't bring it to my lips. Why did I feel so compelled to be honest? "I'm staging a protest on behalf of the hangman, and the copy center wouldn't let me in," I said reluctantly.

I was so sure that this time I'd found a way to spread my letter, but the confused eyes of this young lady looking up at me said I wasn't welcome here, either. Finally, her face tightened and she turned her back to me. She left me standing while she walked back to the copier just as it finished printing its last page.

Grabbing the stack, she read through the first few pages that now made up a stack of almost three hundred papers. Returning, she examined me closely. "You do this again, and I'll report you." She shoved the heavy stack of paper into my arms.

"You're going to let me take these?" I asked with some surprise.

"What good is the paper to me? You've already printed it. Take it, get out of here, and good luck."

I cradled the bundle and exhaled a breathy laugh. "Thank you."

"Yeah, yeah. I've got work to do," she said in dismissal.

For once something had gone right. I was just about to go down the stairs to the main floor when I realized that I'd left my original handwritten copies on the printer. I turned on my heels to look back, then promptly tripped. I caught myself before I tumbled down the stairs, but in doing so, I let the whole stack of papers fly out of my arms. Some pages stayed close, but most of them fluttered down the entire staircase. I stood and watched until each piece landed. "Figures," I whispered to myself.

Five minutes later I had everything back in my arms,

but it took another fifteen minutes to organize them. I looked at a hall clock. Four forty-five. My heart sank. The last classes were just about to finish for the day. Voices down the halls were getting louder, signaling that some of these last classes were already ending a few minutes early. I could run around the whole campus and post these all. But even if I miraculously accomplished that in the next fifteen minutes, very few people, if any would read it in time to be useful.

Only one option remained that I could think of. I ran as fast as I could to the main student center. Students were lining up at the copy office that had kicked me out less than an hour ago. But that's not where I was going. Next door to the copy center was the school's computer lab. Soon that place would be packed with people trying to get their homework ready for the next day. It was also conveniently located right next to the main doors of the building. A huge flow of students would be exiting through those doors to go home for the night.

I posted myself right outside the computer lab door. From there I could give a handout to anybody going into the computer lab and also catch those on their way home. I had to hope that people would read my petition and share it with their friends and family. If not in person, then maybe on the computer.

Without any more time to think about it, I was busy shoving papers into distracted hands. Thirty minutes later, I was out. I leaned against the cinder-block wall. Sharp pangs of discomfort reached deeper than the wounds should have permitted. The cool masonry was a balm for my aches. I let myself rest for a minute until my body heated the wall to the point where it no longer soothed.

Pulling away from the wall hurt worse than leaning against it. My back wanted to stick to the roughly painted blocks. I looked where my back had just been. Yellowy milky-pink stripes patterned the off-white walls. Maybe I should have taken my professor's advice and gotten an ointment for my back. I couldn't afford to let it become infected.

Exhausted, I pushed the doors open. A small shred of guilt tugged at me for leaving those marks on the school's wall, but I ignored it and left the building. My lips parted in disbelief as I saw a few pages of my petition blowing across the road. I briefly considered chasing down the loose papers. I'd have to dodge foot traffic and cars at the same time. But as I considered this, I felt a drop of water on my back. It was followed by more until I was standing in a short burst of rain. It was the kind that would only last a few minutes, but it was enough to ruin every page that was exposed.

I looked in the nearest waste bin where any copies might still be dry. As expected, several copies had been tossed in there. They were ruined, not by rainwater, but by discarded food and drink that had been dropped on top. Would anyone care to read my article?

I didn't wait for the rain to let up. I walked home. After a few minutes, the rain cleared up. It was followed by the balmy shirt plastering humidity that generally follows the rain on a hot day like today. Luckily, I wasn't wearing my shirt. Unluckily, my back itched with intolerable zeal. I couldn't scratch it, or I'd risk reopening some of the deeper gashes.

Once home I filled a tub with water. The soap was

gone. For lack of any better idea, I sprinkled half a box of baking soda into the tub. With pants still on, I tested the water. My tub wasn't like American tubs. I couldn't fully soak my whole body. Shoot, even if it was like American tubs, I probably couldn't fit in either. But leaning at an awkward angle, I was able to get most of my back into the basin. There I stayed for a while. I let the water work on my back until the strain on my backbone hurt worse than the pain in my wounds.

After carefully drying off, I cooked some rice and dumped a cold can of spiced tuna on it. I nearly inhaled it, then went to my room and collapsed on my stomach. Unlike the nightmares of the night before, I was blissfully unaware of any dreams this night. I'd done all I could today.

All that effort; all wasted.

Chapter 28

Early that next morning, I woke with a start and jumped out of bed. Today was important; I couldn't sleep in. I checked the time. My heart settled down as I realized that I hadn't overslept.

For the next hour I got ready as quietly as possible. Jhon and Charles were still asleep; I tip-toed, mostly trying to be considerate to them. Duy and Thing Two were also asleep and not waking Thing Two had nothing to do with consideration. I just didn't want him blowing up in one of his temper rants by rousing him too early. Thing One was already gone. I didn't know if he'd even come back last night. Either he had his own projects keeping him busy, or his job was forcing some unbelievable overtime as they tried to manage all their new prisoners, guests, or whatever they chose to call the children of the woods.

I didn't feel like going shirtless again today, since that hadn't really helped me yesterday. So I dressed normally and was about to ease the door open when Duy appeared in the hallway.

"You're not leaving without me, are you?" He yawned, rubbing crusted sleep from his eyes. His breath still smelled like whatever he'd been drinking last night, mixed with morning mouth rot.

"Duy? You're coming with me?"

"Sure. Isn't that what friends do? Support each other. After some of the things I've put you through, it's the least I can do."

"Thanks, but I do need to leave right now."

Duy entered the kitchen, fumbled around with one of the cupboards and produced a few stale rolls. "I won't hold you up. I'll eat on the way. I would've gotten up earlier, but it's so hard to wake up this early anymore."

"At least I won't be the only person there." I smiled, hoping his breath would improve with his pathetic breakfast.

"Hey buddy, don't be so gloomy. You're not the only good fellow out there. You might be surprised by how many people have a heart and show up today."

"If you'd seen how well my little campaign went yesterday, you might think otherwise."

"Ha!" Duy laughed. "I did see how it went. I was a little preoccupied, or I would've helped. I'm sure that at least a few people read your novel of a flier. You probably should have kept it more short and simple."

"Gee, thanks. Next time I need an editor, I'll come to you."

"Seriously, do! You wrote your petition for a newspaper, then distributed it like a flier. In ten minutes you could've rewritten it onto a single page. It would've been more effective. Unless they're committed to reading the newspaper, people have short attention spans."

"Too late for that now."

"Seriously, Iddo, don't worry about it. I'm sure everything will turn out fine."

The front doors were just being opened as we arrived at the courthouse. A few other people were trickling in. They seemed as annoyed to be here as I was determined. We went in and waited as one of the clerks turned on the lights and organized her desk. I recalled the scent of peppermint, made stronger now that the lady was actually here. She wasn't as old or as friendly as I'd imagined. Her face seemed kind enough, but there was something in that smile of hers that made me feel like she was just here to collect a paycheck. At last she came to the counter where I was waiting.

"Can I help you with something?" she asked in a bittersweet tone.

"I was just wondering what the schedule would be for the hangman's trial today."

Her eyes opened wide. She grinned and looked at me like I was some novelty. "Hey, aren't you that kid—er, young man—who wants to save the hangman?" Her grin grew into a pouty twist. "Listen, save yourself the trouble and run along. You're probably the only person willing to side with that—thing. If you really do care, then go home so you don't have to witness his sentencing. You can't save him. Not even divine intervention could prevent his fate. Plus, there's plenty of men who might not look too kindly on a sympathizer. You seem like a nice boy. I'd hate to see you get hurt."

"I've already been beaten. I'm not afraid of that." Actually I was afraid, but that was beside the point. "I won't give up. He's not the monster everyone thinks he is. I need to convince the court of that. I just need a chance. Please."

"My boy, the court has already appointed him an attorney. There will be someone arguing on his behalf."

"Let me guess," I ventured. "This attorney is the freshest greenie that passed his licensing exam, right?"

"No, actually. He's a seasoned lawyer, and a really good friend of the judge."

"A good friend of the judge! The judge has already conspired with the mob that captured the hangman! How can any friend of his persuade him away from what he's already decided? They probably planned the whole thing!"

"Watch what you say about the honorable Fu Gang. I assure you, he'll judge this hangman with the highest degree of professionalism."

Duy slammed his open palm down on her countertop. A metal ring that I hadn't seen on Duy since we'd first met clanked hard enough to draw our attention. The ring was silver in color, with a small green coat of arms containing a few letters in it. I don't know what the letters meant, but both the clerk and I knew that only Believers wore such rings. As I'd come to learn, Believers were avid in pursuing causes if they felt the cause was just. The last thing this court would want would be to find a whole swarm of Believers outside their courthouse.

"Tell my friend when the trial is," Duy threatened, "All I have to do is make one call. Before noon the faith of my people will combine and cause the walls of this courthouse to crumble to the ground."

The clerk studied Duy for a hard minute. I studied him, too. I half guessed that Duy was bluffing. But like the clerk, I wasn't sure. "Ten o'clock," she finally relented. "Not like it's any secret. Excuse me now, I have work to do this morning." She turned her back and went to a corner desk, half hidden by a cubicle wall.

We stepped out of the courthouse. Duy was the first to stop. "I hate the smell of peppermint and will you stop staring at me like that?"

"Sorry, I was just trying to figure out if what you said back there was even possible. If so, then what I should have done was appeal to the Believers and not the local community. Do you guys really have that kind of power?"

"Yeah, sort of, maybe. I've heard of things like that happening, but I've never actually seen it done. Mostly I was just playing on the myths or rumors that everyone seems to associate with us. You wouldn't believe some of the pranks I've pulled in the last year. Everyone thinks we're just as spooky as witches. It's made for some pretty funny jokes with my friends."

"Are they jokes I'd want to hear about?"

This time it was Duy's turn to study me. "No," he finally concluded. "I get the feeling that you'd actually make a good Believer. You'd probably find my pranks a little offensive. Oh, but there was this one time when—"

"Duy—look." I pointed down a side street. At first, I was worried that it was a large group the mob had formed to make sure their fake trial went off as planned, but these people looked different. They were mostly younger, like college students. College students and a few professors. At the front of the procession was the young strict-looking lady from the school. The same woman who'd caught me using her copy machine.

As she and the crowd of nearly one hundred people neared, I noticed a few sheets of lined notepaper in her hand. The unmistakable crumples marked it as that original article I'd accidentally left on the copy machine yesterday.

She smiled at the surprise on my face. "Hello Iddo. I read your little petition. I hope you don't mind, but I decided to e-mail it to as many people as I know. Hopefully they'll keep forwarding it. Your words were compelling. I want—we want to help you make a difference."

I could have cried. Her group was strengthening in force as other small groups trickled in from all directions. By nine thirty, the entire square in front of the courthouse was packed with bodies. The noise was incredible. I could hardly believe the turnout. It was all because of one lady who happened to read the article that I'd carelessly left behind.

As I was admiring the crowd, Duy nudged me. "You know, you probably ought to give a speech now."

My eyeballs nearly popped out of their sockets. "A speech?"

"Yeah, a speech. All these people are here because of you. You have to organize them. You have to energize them."

These words upset me more than his still toxic breath. They practically melted the bones from my legs. I visibly wobbled. Duy laughed. "Don't worry. You'll be fine."

I knew he was right. Not about being fine, but that I had to do something. I might be able to write to the masses, but actually standing and speaking to them? I wasn't sure if I could do it. I looked at the three steps ascending toward the courthouse. They were so tall. Hesitantly, I placed one foot on the first step. What would I say? How did you rally over two hundred people that you didn't know?

My body shook as I raised my second foot to climb higher. I almost collapsed. No, I couldn't do this. I was just about to turn around when I heard Duy shout, "Speech! Speech! Speech!" Despite my wobbly legs, when I heard that, my spine stiffened. Maybe nobody noticed his shouts.

I could still turn around and come back down. I wasn't committed yet.

I wasn't sure, but I guessed that the clerk who'd sent the e-mail was the next voice to join Duy's chant. "Speech! Speech! Speech!"

Within five seconds the whole crowd was chanting. My breath came in ragged gasps. I didn't dare go forward and I couldn't back down. I could feel their eyes landing on my back. Like red-hot pokers, each person's eye seemed to pull at least five drops of moisture per second from my skin. Finally, my feet pressed on. By the time I was all the way to the top of the stairs, my sweaty palms threatened to drip in a continuous stream at my sides.

Slowly I turned to face my supporters. I wanted to wipe the sweat from around my eyes, but thought better of it. I'd probably just force the salty stuff into my eyes and cause more of a problem.

I surveyed the crowd. They hushed until silence filled the air. The stillness seemed to stretch that short five seconds into five minutes. I took in a deep breath. The jackhammer in my throat didn't calm me one bit. "Good morning," I managed to say.

"Louder," someone shouted. Probably Duy. It could have been a girl's voice, too; I wasn't in the right frame of mind to distinguish voices. The drumming of my heart was too loud for me to spare that much attention.

"Thank you for coming," I said as loud as my half-deflated lungs would allow.

"That's better," the shout came again. It was Duy.

"Thanks." I smiled. Somehow that made it easier. Finding my voice, I gestured toward the courthouse. "Most of you don't know who I am. My name is Iddo. Almost two years ago, I discovered the man known as the hangman of the woods."

As I spoke, my voice steadied. I was still terrified, but at least I didn't completely freeze up. "The hangman, or Daddy Smiling as his adopted children call him . . ."

In about ten minutes I unfolded my story. By the time I was finished, I was shaking. Not from stage fright, but from a furious passion that I didn't know I could tap. I don't think I ever spoke so eloquently in my life. I finished with a plea.

"In twenty minutes, a trial will begin, wherein a corrupt lawyer is going to be unable to defend Daddy Smiling from an even more corrupt judge. They have the power to end the life of this man. He may be deformed, he may be mentally disabled, but he saved and raised over a hundred and fifty children from these fathers, the ones who now wish to condemn him to death. He is a hero, held by a mob of murderers.

"Is Daddy Smiling a vigilante? Yes. But if not for him, many more innocent children would have been slaughtered by their own fathers. Do you trust these men to deliver a just verdict for the hangman of the woods?"

With one voice, the whole crowd shouted, "No!"

"Would you trust these murderers with your children?"

Again, a resounding, "No!"

"Then how can we trust them to care for the children of the woods?"

This time the answer was just a garbled mass of shouting. I guess I could have rephrased the question better.

"I stood alone against these men once," I continued, "and this is what they gave me!" I pulled my shirt off with a jerk. It hurt, but it also felt oddly empowering. I stood erect with my mutilated back to the crowd.

Now the shouts neared hysterics. Shirtless I turned around to face my supporters. "In just a few minutes, when they open the doors to that courthouse, I say we fill the building. We let them know that we will not stand for injustice! We will stand for truth! We will stand, not for some hangman of the woods, but for the hero of the woods!"

That did it. The crowd pushed the decibel level of the whole square higher and higher as they swelled closer to the building. I was just pulling my shirt back on, getting ready to join them on a march to the doors, when dozens of police and hired mercenaries, all decked out in riot gear, charged from around the corner. Before we had moved twenty feet, they'd set up a barricade.

A voice came across on a megaphone. "You are all engaged in unlawful protest. Stand down."

I may not have journalism in my blood, but I'd seen enough pictures and read enough to know that this little protest of mine could get badly out of hand. Whenever that happened, people got hurt, even killed. They were all here because of me. I couldn't let this cross the line between protest and riot.

With arms outstretched in a cross, I backed away from the protesters, facing them as I put myself between them and the barricade. "Please, listen to me!" I shouted.

Not everyone quieted, but enough did. "We are not

the bad guys. We will protest peacefully. Let us not display our anger by causing violence today!" Then, so as to be heard by all, I asked the police, "If you won't open the courtroom to all of us, will you at least allow me in, so that I may testify on behalf of the hangman?"

Shouts of "Let him in!" repeatedly crossed the square.

The policeman in charge brought the megaphone back to his lips. "I will speak with the judge. But if any of you move any closer, I will permit my men to open fire on you."

As if to accentuate his statement, his men aimed several tear-gas launchers and shotguns at the crowd. I wondered if they'd use rubber bullets. I hoped I didn't have to find out.

Several minutes later the police officer emerged. He looked nervous upon bringing the megaphone up again. But lift it he did. "The defense has consulted with the judge. The defense does not believe that he needs your testimony. Likewise, the judge has decided that you will be in contempt of court if he allows you in. You may continue to protest, but only if you remain peaceful, in the square, keeping behind the steps leading up to the building."

Angry shouts filled the crowd, my voice among them. I yelled out my objection. I tried to make a plea for my case. But nothing I said could be distinguished from the mass of noise that blanketed over mine. It was like a bad dream where you had to run as fast as possible but made little or no progress.

The next five minutes were just a blur. Luckily Duy

found his way to me. With some effort we calmed the crowd. Then, five minutes later, we were able to start a more organized chant. The first one started out as "Judge him fair!" We changed the chant every five or ten minutes to keep it fresh. There was no way the people inside the courtroom could avoid hearing us.

The morning passed dreadfully slow. I took refuge under a tree with long stretching branches that helped shade the middle of the square. I was afraid that by noon, people would start leaving. On the contrary; more arrived. They strengthened our numbers and our resolve. From there, the hours rolled by. Three o'clock. Four o'clock. By seven o'clock, I couldn't take it anymore. With outstretched arms, I approached the police line.

"What do you want?" the bedraggled police chief asked.

"Can you go inside and inquire for me as to the progress of the trial?"

He slumped his shoulders. "No, I can't."

I tilted my head. "Why not?"

He sighed heavily. "We're just here till you guys disperse. The trial ended three hours ago. The courthouse is all locked up. Nobody's in there anymore."

I just stared at him. Nobody had used the main doors all day. Nobody that is, except for me and Duy in the morning. They'd all sneaked in and out by some other way and now it was over. I shook my head, trying to understand. I wanted to ask, but was afraid to form the words. I was afraid of what I knew I'd hear.

As if reading my mind, the chief shook his head again. "Guilty."

This time I really did fall to my knees. Before I knew it, Duy was at my side again, helping me back down the stairs. The news spread through the crowd like ink on a paper towel. The weary crowd of protesters seemed to dissolve until only Duy, the lady from the school office, and I were left. She placed a hand on my shoulder. Then, without saying another word, turned and walked away.

Duy and I walked back home. I don't think we spoke a single word to each other the whole way.

Chapter 29

Morning came. I rolled out of bed. My back ached and I should've felt more depressed, but the fire of hope or determination hadn't left me. I knew the trial had been rigged. I'd known that the verdict would be guilty, even before I'd staged my protest. Still I was crushed to actually hear it.

The first thing I did after leaving the apartment was to pick up the day's newspaper. My protest yesterday had made the front page. I wasn't surprised to find Biahn's name under the headline, "Protesters Rally Behind Liar." I read on. The whole article was just the usual propaganda. It debunked me and anything I'd said. It painted the hangman as a terror who was finally caught and tried.

If I didn't know better, I could easily see myself being swayed by Biahn's argument. Worst of all was the last paragraph. The judge decreed that the children be sent away to a foster agency in China, and that the hangman be executed in the same manner that he murdered so many others. He was scheduled to swing at noon tomorrow.

"Barbarians," I screamed beneath my breath.

Those prison tents with all those children looked foreboding. Even from several blocks away, their faded tan canvas rippled like a stale nightmare. Careful not to raise any alarm, I approached the camp. The tents smelled worse today than I remembered. Nothing much had been done to improve the sanitation of those living spaces. In front of each tent were two armed guards. Two other guards were positioned at the rear corners of the tent, in case anybody felt inclined to dig or cut their way to freedom. I wondered if they'd heard the bad news yet.

The guards around the boys' tent seemed tougher and more vigilant. There must've been some escape attempts from there. Those guards were actually some of the guerilla fighters, more mean and vicious than the ordinary guards watching the girls' tent.

I couldn't see Thing One anywhere near the girls' tent, so I figured that he was off duty. That made me wonder where he might be, since he wasn't at our apartment. I still couldn't believe that he'd throw his lot in with these men. With little chance of a sneak meeting with Chirp-chirp, I meandered closer to the girls' tent. I waited until one of the guards had his back to me, then I scurried with as much stealth as I could.

Leaning up against the tent, I searched for a hole or rip or anything. The tents were old, but in surprisingly good condition. At last I found a small burn hole. Maybe it was from some ash of a campfire or cigarette, I couldn't tell. The hole was smaller than my pupil, but I pressed my eye to it, anyway. Inside I could just make out the profile of a little girl, maybe six years old. "Pssst."

She was alert. Her head swiveled around to find the source of the sound.

"Over here," I whispered as I tapped the canvas.

She glanced from side to side before easing over to me.

"Find Midnight," I whispered. "Tell her it's Iddo."

"Midnight? Iddo?"

"Yes. Hurry."

She stood, didn't move for a minute, then ran off. Great. She wasn't going to be much help. I pressed my face up to the canvas to search through the pinprick again. Maybe someone older would wander by. It better be soon. I wasn't sure how much longer I could go unnoticed by the guards.

A figure passed by the hole. I couldn't see who it was, but I knew that she was much taller than the six-year-old I'd just talked to.

"Pssst."

The figure backed up past my hole again. "Iddo?"

It was Midnight. The little girl had found her after all. "Midnight, it's me. Are you okay?"

"I'm scared, Iddo, yes I am. Children scared, too. You help? Please you help."

"I'm here, don't worry, it'll be okay," I tried to calm

her.

"Daddy Smiling—you see Daddy Smiling?"

"No. They want to execute him, though." I winced. Maybe that wasn't the best way to calm her.

"Ex-y-coot?"

"I'm sorry, they're going to kill him." I didn't know how to break it any easier to her. I shouldn't have told her. "They want to kill him, then send you all far away."

"Why?" she whimpered.

"They don't like Daddy Smiling and they want you all far away so you don't tell anybody the truth. At least they don't want anybody around here to know."

She went quiet, but I heard a sniffle. Then she spoke again, her voice trembling. "I want be with you. You help?"

She sounded so sad. My heart ached just listening to her. "Yes, Midnight. I will help. I don't know how yet, but I'll find a way. I'll be back here soon. Can you stay by this spot, so I'll know where to find you?"

"I wait for you, Iddo. You be Daddy Iddo with me soon. I wait for you."

"I love you, Midnight. I promise I'll find a way to get you out of there."

"Hey!" one of the guards shouted.

I looked up. The guard who had his back to me was now running toward me. I jumped up and sprinted away.

I easily outran the guard, something my former fatty self could never have done. He quickly lost the mood for chasing and I was left alone, not more than a block away. I leaned against a tailor shop and caught my breath. The sewing machine in the windowless shop raced against my own thoughts.

I tried to calm myself and think about how long I'd been by that tent before getting noticed. It had to be under five minutes. The guards might be a little more vigilant now that they'd seen me. I wouldn't have much time. Even if I did manage to stage a breakout, I doubted I could free anyone but Midnight.

Midnight was my biggest priority, but I knew I'd still feel bad about leaving the others behind. She probably wouldn't let me, either. I tried to think of alternatives but there weren't many. Even if I could free all the others, there was no way I could get them all back to the woods safely. I almost felt guilty for wondering if they'd be better off in China.

The Americans and Europeans wouldn't likely be too interested in taking the children. So far, their interest seemed to stretch only as far as planting their language into our culture, or like Krystal's father, taking advantage of certain local hospitalities. The Chinese were increasingly fractured, but were still the closest major country where it made any sense to send the orphans.

I'm sure that enough families could be found locally to take them all in, but that would risk exposing the corruption for what it was.

I wasn't sure when the children would be sent away, but I knew they couldn't stay much longer in the tents.

Not only was sanitation a problem, but the city was too small to afford feeding and guarding them much longer. I had no time to wait.

I didn't have a plan as I hurried back to my apartment. All I knew was that I needed a knife.

I returned less than an hour later. The same two guards were on watch. Luckily my encounter with them earlier hadn't affected their level of vigilance. Perhaps they supposed me to be long gone. All the better for me.

Still, I didn't want to rush. From behind a row of dense shrubs surrounding a neighboring building, I watched for about fifteen minutes. Aside from the guards, who rarely checked around where I wanted to free Midnight, there was no other people around. I could do this.

With one last look at the sharp reflective metal waiting in my hand, I stepped out from hiding. I crept closer, only to shimmy back as the guard decided to walk around the tent, right to where I was wanting to go. With lazy ease, the guard lit a cigarette and puffed away directly in front of me. Even if he casually turned around, he'd see me crouched down. I didn't have enough time to fully retreat and thus was in the open.

I gripped the wooden handle tighter. With a quick lunge forward, I could bury my blade in the man's back. It would be easy, but no, I couldn't do that. Never could I do that. He hadn't done anything wrong. He was just doing his job. Instead, I stood frozen in place, not daring to move lest my slightest motion or noise draw his attention to me.

I waited for him to finish his smoke. Once done he

dropped it on the ground and stepped on it. Then, as if he'd just finished a bowel movement, he left his designated waste area to return to his former position.

Keeping him in the corner of my eye, I sneaked over to the tent. The guard was stretching, not paying attention as I carefully slipped the knife into the canvas. I had to be careful. I didn't want to accidentally stab my future bride.

As the knife penetrated the canvas, it made a parting rip that I was sure could be heard clear up on campus, nearly two kilometers away. I paused long enough to look over. The guard was still unaware of my actions. I hoped that the cut couldn't be seen from the cameras inside the tent. I proceeded to saw-cut a vertical slit up the fabric. My teeth ground together after each centimeter of canvas voiced its approval at being divided.

So close to freeing the woman I loved, I couldn't help but wonder again, how would I support her. With no job I'd have to either get a paid internship or find another job. Not only did the internship pay better than any job I'd likely find, but it would also be a good step at a real career. My only problem, I was still short two years of schooling to qualify for it.

I could take her back to the woods, and we could live off the land, like she had done most of her life. But then, what would I do? Could I give up my dreams of helping people?

Daddy Smiling had found a way to help, even if it involved a measure of punishment for the guilty.

One more pass of the blade was all I'd need. I glided

the knife out, finishing the cut. But the tearing threads of the canvas had other plans. I stared in horror as the cut turned into a rip. The tightly stretched tent, old as it was, made up its own mind to continue my new door higher and higher. The higher the rip climbed, the louder and faster it parted.

Now my intrusion was receiving notice. The guard responsible for watching this portion of the tent was running and yelling at me. Another guard from the other corner of the tent stepped around to join him. All I had to do was stick my head in, grab Midnight, and run. So why did I just stand there, looking from one guard to the other, back to the climbing rip, then back to the guards again?

After a sufficiently stupid amount of time, my body decided to respond to my will. I shouted, "Midnight!"

Her face appeared in the opening. I reached for her, but she moved so slowly, like she was unsure of what to do. The whole world had slowed down. When at last I could grab her hand, I pulled her through the tent and started to run with her in tow. I lost my grip on her as the first guard slammed into me, flattening me on the ground.

He was just about to get to his knees when the other guard caught up, bent down, and slammed a steely fist into my head. I felt the blow, and surprisingly it didn't hurt as much as I had expected. I felt my muscles tighten. I started to lift the man off of my, my own strength surprising me. I could fight back!

I saw the fear in the first guard's eyes as mine met his with defiance. Then the other guard swung something large and metallic at my head. My world went black.

When my vision returned, I could see that the tent had fallen down. The out-of-control rip had stretched all the way up and over the tent, eventually causing the tent to split in half. The two guards had left me unconscious on the ground. A plastic zip-tie held my hands together. Another zip-tie fastened my feet together. The girls must have stampeded out of the collapsing tent. Why else would the guards have been too distracted or overwhelmed to finish dragging me off?

Luckily, I'd gained consciousness before they finished wrangling the horde of confused girls and placing them in the boys' tent. No doubt they'd return to arrest me, or worse. Midnight was back under their guard. I'd lost my opportunity. Before the guards noticed me, I flexed my arms and legs. The plastic bit into my skin, but it was no match. Both broke with a quick snap and Igot up to leave. I'd taken only a few steps when one of them shouted "Stop!"

I paused. My luck exactly. I'd come around just long enough to gain a degree of hope, only to be captured again.

"Hey, I said stop!" He shouted again.

But I was stopped. Suddenly thoughts of brutal beatings entered my thoughts. He was going to over-react and give me a royal beating when he caught up to me. I slowly turned, raising my hands above my head.

One of the guards from the boy's tent only spared me half a glance as he sprinted past and took the arm of one of the orphaned girls that I hadn't seen just ahead of me. My head must have been hit harder than I thought. I didn't recognize the girl, but her simple primitive woven clothing marked her as one of the girls from the tent.

I took a quick look around, just in case I'd been mistaken and Midnight hadn't been taken. None of the girls that were still being gathered were her.

Quietly, I slipped away before any guards could recognize me.

Oh, my head hurt. The pain kept pounding at my temples. The pain of failing Midnight squeezed the rest of my head.

I returned an hour later, my wrists were now ringed with purple bruises from the zip-tie that I'd removed. By this time, the commotion I caused had settled, not to mention the throbbing in my skull. My hopes sank when I beheld the new arrangement. All the children were in a single tent. The guards from the damaged girls' tent had joined the guards for the combined tent now. In addition, they'd been strengthened by about four more guards, including Thing One.

Anger boiled inside me upon seeing Thing One. It wasn't fair of me. He was just doing his job. Besides, he truly believed that the children would be taken somewhere better. What irked me was that he wouldn't help me free Midnight. Maybe he might, but there was no way of getting to him to talk about it. He was in the company of far too many other guards. If he'd at least come back to the apartment I could've talked to him about it, but given his recent behavior, that was unlikely.

No matter how hard I thought, my mind refused to

cooperate. There was no way to free Midnight and the children. Maybe if I went for a walk, I could clear my head. I had to make a plan.

Once out of sight of the guards, I couldn't help but think, maybe Midnight would be better off without me. No, that was still muddled thinking. I had to free her. But there was still the problem of not qualifying for the paid internship for another two years. That didn't matter. "Focus," I scolded myself. "How do I free her?"

After all, if worse came to worst, we could get by without an apartment. It's not like she wasn't used to living in the woods. For me it would be a longer commute to school, but cheaper. Dropping to my knees, I wanted to shout. I couldn't concentrate for the life of me, or for her!

Still with no clear idea of how to rescue her, I found myself back at the makeshift concentration camp. In the ten minutes I'd been walking, several buses had arrived and the children of the woods were being ushered onboard. There would be no camp left here tonight. I watched as Thing One, once my role model, ushered Midnight onto one of the overcrowded buses before following her in and shutting the door.

I imagined myself chasing after the bus, but it would do no good. There was nothing I could do. I sank to my knees. I'd lost, again. This was the last time I'd ever see Midnight, Chirp-chirp, Grub, or any of the others.

I sat on my knees long after everyone else was gone. There was only one thing left for me to do. It would be just as defeating, just as hard. Just as well; I knew I couldn't avoid it.

Chapter 30

Not a cloud in sight. I squinted as my eyes adjusted to the morning light. I'd slept in, and by the time I left my apartment, the sun was blazing away with all its might. Funny how such a bright sunny morning could feel so gloomy.

"Are you sure you want to go through with this?" Duy asked. "Maybe it'd be better if—"

"I'm going."

"Okay, okay. Let me just grab a drink. I don't think I want to be sober for this." Duy jogged back into the house. I shouldn't have been surprised that he kept alcohol in our apartment, but I was annoyed. The last thing I needed was a drunken sympathizer, but I doubted that I could talk him out of coming.

By eleven o'clock the town square was packed. In the center there was an old massive tree with a canopy that covered much of the square. It was the same tree that I'd occasionally found shade under during my protest two days ago.

This morning, with a throng of onlookers to rub shoulders with, we surrounded that tree. At its base, there now stood a mobile podium with a park bench at its side. As the sun moved higher and the shade grew smaller, all spectators were forced into the sun while this stage hogged the coveted shade. Above the bench, hanging from one of those thick outstretched branches, was a rope. The noose at the end of the rope made the once serene tree now appear ancient and evil, as if it were the very heart of the woods themselves.

The crowd of people continued to grow denser as the hour crawled slowly toward noon. At first, I thought they were a bunch of morbid townspeople, here to witness an old-fashioned execution. I wanted to yell at each one of them, tell them how wrong they were to allow this. Turns out, that wasn't necessary. Several of them noticed me. Taking turns, they placed hands on my shoulder, or gave me a hug. These were the protesters who'd stood with me. I wanted to cry. Biahn's article, scathing as it was for my reputation, hadn't disheartened my supporters. At least not all of them.

I had one last fleeting hope that I could use these people to my advantage, maybe storm the lynching and save Daddy Smiling when he was brought out. Maybe the execution could be postponed until an appeal to a just court could be arranged. That was a wild fantasy. I knew it couldn't work. A large clock on the courthouse donged in the noon hour. Riot police and riot gear were marched around the tree. They weren't going to take any chances. The cops all knew me by now. More than once I saw them carefully studying me behind their face masks. They knew that if I found some opportunity to stop the execution, I might take advantage of it.

Oh, if only I could have gone back in time! I wondered what, if anything I could've changed. Could I have saved Daddy Smiling, or had his fate been sealed from the beginning? Could I have acted faster? Maybe I could have done something more to help Midnight and the other children.

I looked into the sky, not because I expected God to look back. Faith is funny. If I was to have faith, it couldn't just be unto power for changing everything to my will. I had to accept his will also. I doubted he wanted Daddy Smiling killed, any more than he wanted his own Son tortured and murdered. But in his infinite wisdom, if nonintervention was wiser, who was I to argue otherwise?

All I could do now was what I knew would happen as I walked here this morning. I would pay my last respects to Daddy Smiling. He deserved so much better than this. I had no idea what he'd be thinking. I couldn't hold his hand, or even speak to him, but I wouldn't let him die alone. Even if it killed a part of me to watch, I was here for him. Most of us in the crowd were.

Aside from the gruesome picture of the hangman that was printed in the paper yesterday, few if any of these people had ever seen him. In his picture they twisted his enormous smile to look menacing and dangerous. I wondered how these people could support and love him on my word alone.

My heart calmed as the minutes ticked slowly away. What was taking so long? Half an hour passed.

I couldn't claim to be eager for the ceremony. Postpone it forever!

I knew that wouldn't happen. I don't know why I cared about the punctuality of the execution. Maybe I was ready to have the whole disgraceful event over with. Even that thought made me feel guilty. With all this extra time to think, another morbid thought entered my mind. Without the him, who would protect the children? Not the children taken to foster homes, but the unborn children that would inevitably be taken to the woods by irresponsible fathers.

How could a man and woman willingly spend an hour of careless pleasure for a lifetime of guilt? Yeah, they could abort the child early, but wasn't that the same? Kill it early or kill it once it became a financial burden. The thought made me angry. That's what this was all about. People didn't like the idea of some mentally challenged saint having a stronger moral compass than them.

The clock now read twelve forty-five. I heard him before I saw him. That signature song of his, bellowed in a deep bass voice that resonated with everyone around me. "Swing low, sweet chariot . . ." Even when Daddy Smiling was marched to the tree, few shrank back at his appearance. Those who did were the few morbid fellows who'd come just to see a hanging. When Daddy Smiling finished all the verses of his song, he started back over again. Even in his last hour of life, that head-splitting smile refused to shrink.

He was placed just behind the bench that he'd soon be standing on. The executioner fingered a megaphone, handed him by the chief of police, and surveyed the crowd. He looked surprised that anybody had shown up at all. I don't think he had much of a speech planned. At least not one that was meant for a crowd this size. He looked over at Biahn, who gave him a discreet thumbs-up. Ooh—that man really was despicable.

With finger on the megaphone trigger, the executioner cleared his throat for all to hear. It wasn't like he didn't already have their attention. But the crowd was still a bustle of mixed voices mingling into a distracting hum. Now they hushed as he spoke to the crowd. "On this bright sunny day, we—will you stop singing that ridiculous song!"

Daddy Smiling didn't even acknowledge the demand.

"Someone help me out here," said the executioner. One of the men who'd led Daddy Smiling out pulled a dirty handkerchief from his pocket. It wasn't nearly big enough to fit around the man's mouth. A second handkerchief was then tied to it, then a third. Together they tightened it around the giant smiling mouth. Even then it was useless. The man's abnormally large mouth just dwarfed the pieces of cloth. The handkerchiefs rolled into a relatively small cord that rested between his teeth. He almost looked like he could use the cloth to floss those enormous pale-white ivories.

The executioner gave up. The singing wasn't even muffled. It bellowed just as loud as the executioner's megaphone.

"On this day," he shouted, clearly annoyed, "we execute judgment on a convicted murderer."

Some cheers, but more overwhelming boos echoed

across the square. Those who'd started out cheering shied back. Either they were surprised that the majority opposed the hanging, or they were afraid of causing a fight that might end badly for themselves. Either way, all voices now criticized the speaker.

He might've been able to ignore the crowd, but he clearly couldn't ignore Daddy Smiling's singing. He continued. "Known to us all as the hangman of the woods, this ruthless serial killer," he pointed with rigid disdain, "was tried and judged in a court of law. He has not only been found guilty, but has been condemned to die by the same implement he used to strangle his own victims. There will be no long ceremony. He doesn't even deserve the sympathy that you all give him today."

More angry shouting arose from the crowd. I was silent.

"It is time. Help the felon onto the bench."

A man on each side of Daddy Smiling prodded the singing giant. He stepped onto the wooden picnic table bench. One of the men backed down as the executioner stepped up. The bench swayed under the high center of gravity imposed by the three men standing on it. The executioner moved slowly, not wanting to ruin his dignity by having them all fall to the ground.

Then, with some trepidation, he strained to place the noose around Daddy Smiling's watermelon-sized head. The executioner was very careful and tried not to lean on, or even touch, what he considered a large monstrosity. As if Daddy Smiling had a contagious disease, the executioner seemed afraid of catching whatever handicap had so affected the appearance of this giant.

Once the noose was secured, the executioner gave a nasty sneer as Daddy Smiling sang, "A band of angels coming after me / Coming for to carry me home . . ."

Both the guard and the executioner carefully stepped down from the wobbly bench. Grabbing the megaphone, the executioner again tried to be heard over the deep reverberating bass that was Daddy Smiling. I'd heard Daddy Smiling sing this song every time I'd seen him. I wasn't sure that his vocabulary extended very far beyond the lyrics of this song. Paying attention to the executioner was difficult. Daddy Smiling's low melodic voice drummed peace into my heart. "Tell all my friends I'm coming there too / Coming for to carry me home . . ."

"We'd ask this murderer if he had any last words," the executioner shouted, "but I think we all know what he'd say! Ha ha! So without further delay, we finish this."

"Sometimes I'm up, and sometimes I'm down / Coming for to carry me h—"

The executioner kicked the bench. It wobbled, but the steady weight of the hangman kept it in place. He kicked again and it wobbled some more. He motioned for the two closest guards to help him with the next kick. They came over.

I wanted to turn my eyes, but they were helplessly glued to the man who'd saved me and so many other children. I willed the bench to find solid footing on the earth so that no force of man could tip the giant from his perch. If ever my newfound faith could help someone, this was the man who deserved that otherworldly power of protection. Little puffs of dust splashed at my toes as salty rain dropped from my dark cloudy eyes.

Then Daddy Smiling did something I hadn't expected. He locked eyes with me!

I gasped. I don't know why, but I felt a clarity passing between us that I'd never expected. He was no longer mentally deficient or monstrously deformed. He was incredibly and unmistakably seeing into my very soul, and my soul was seeing HIM!

Words alone can never describe what passed between us. But somehow I knew things I'd never known before. Everything that had happened to me in the past couple years had been preparing me for this moment. It was the epiphany of epiphanies.

Daddy Smiling was the mythical Hangman of the Woods, but he was getting old. I saw that just now, for the first time, in his eyes. He couldn't go on forever. But he was a myth, a legend, an immortal force, weather he understood the full weight of that concept was impossible to know, but somewhere deep inside him, was an emotional intelligence that let him know that he couldn't keep saving the innocent forever, perhaps not even for more than a few years. He had to of had some health problems too, issues I hadn't been aware of. Nobody with his condition could be all that healthy this late into their lives.

I understood him. And in those brief seconds of seeing him, he too, saw my commitment. I would still be able to help people. I would still be able to save people. And the legend of the Hangman of the Woods would survive.

His eyes, those impossibly deep eyes, broke contact with mine and looked up to the sky, his voice resounding with even deeper power than before. "But still my soul feels heavenly bound / Coming in his chariot of gold!"

With the force of the added kickers, the bench went crashing down, and the world went silent.

A long unending minute passed until finally the thick branch that held the swinging man, a branch that could have held a car off the ground, snapped, the remaining attached fibers of the beam, gently lowered Daddy Smiling to the ground, as if the tree was alive, and giving the dead man his final respects.

He looked so peaceful in death. He'd lived for the children, and he died knowing that his work would live on, not only in the kids who found new families, which I now knew would turn out fine, but also in me.

Epilogue

Two weeks later, I stepped down from the same courthouse that had condemned Daddy Smiling. It had taken that long for the courthouse to open back up. A different judge presided over our marriage. Only a few people attended. Seven, to be exact. Two were court-appointed witnesses. One was Thing One, and one was Duy. The other three weren't exactly visible, but I felt their presence. They were my own two parents and Daddy Smiling.

Funny thing about Thing One, he'd always been a good friend. He knew about me and Midnight, and after helping load all the kids on the bus, he'd had the bus driver stop a few blocks away, claiming that one of the girls had been put on the wrong bus. He was able to escort Midnight off, and keep her hidden until the whole matter had blown over.

After the ceremony, the judge and two witnesses left for their lunch break.

As I escorted Midnight out of the courthouse, I saw

Krystal. Her attention was on another recently married couple. Finishing her interview with them, she turned to face me. A wingless sparrow couldn't have been more surprised if it had just found a cat standing right behind it.

"Iddo! I was just writing an article on all these marriages. I—what? Is this—"

"Midnight," I half replied, half introduced, "I'd like you to meet Krystal. We grew up together."

"You're so pritty, yes you are," Midnight cooed, as she reached up and fingered a strand of Krystal's thick blond hair before running her palm across that Caucasian face. "Like sun, you're so bright, like angel. Pritty angel."

Krystal blushed. Not something she was used to doing, at least I don't think she was used to it.

"How are you, Krystal?" I inquired.

"I'm good. It looks like you're not doing too bad, either," she laughed with a hint of anxiety. "Listen, Iddo, about what happened last time we met, I was wrong, please—"

"Please, Krystal," I interjected, "It's all right."

She let a small smile show. "Listen, if you want, I can help you get your job back at the newspaper."

I laughed. Not rudely of course, just a friendly chuckle. "Don't worry about me, Krystal. I appreciate all you've done for me. I know I haven't always treated you the best, and I'm sorry for that, but I'm good now. I hope you are, too."

"You already have another job?"

"Yeah, sort of. They let me intern early, and it's a paid internship."

We talked for a minute or two more, then Krystal raced off to weasel out an interview with the new judge who was in the middle of his lunch break.

I shook Thing One's hand, and Duy gave me a big hug. "I'm going to miss you buddy," he said.

"I'm sure you'll be just fine without me," I said, giving him a light punch on the shoulder.

He cradled it in mock pain. "Who am I going to play party jokes on without you, big guy?"

I gave him a withering look.

To his credit, he just smiled wider. "By the way, I haven't touched the bottle in two weeks you know."

"Way to go," I complemented him, sincerely. Watching the hanging had done something to Duy. I don't know what it was, but something had flipped inside him. He had a way to go still, but I felt that he'd never truly abandoned his beliefs, and I guess, deep down, he hadn't.

"You'll still visit us, won't you?" Duy asked.

"I'll be around, making a name for myself," I teased.

My mother had sacrificed too much for me to abandon my schooling. I would become a doctor. I would learn the healer's art, a skill that I knew would be all too valuable, but I would not be living in town. Classes could be arranged so that I only had to attend a few days a week.

My internship was only part time. In the meantime, Midnight and I would have plenty of time to build a new life together back in her neck of the woods, literally.

Not only would I save money that way, but I could also take the torch of my new calling. But first, I did have one expense of my new life's mission.

We stopped in at the local hardware shop, and I took my time, as if in ritual, feeling and handling the different diameters and fibers of the manila and hempen ropes with my strong hands, humming a certain shared song we knew by heart. At last, having made my selection and paying the clerk, I coiled the cut rope around my broad muscled shoulders, and together, my wife and I began our journey out of the city, and into the next chapter of The Hangman Of The Woods.

The End

Dear reader,

Please visit my website at LightMindedArts.com. There you can follow my storytelling journey. I love to write books. I also love all forms of storytelling, from visual to personal. As such, I have started an independent film studio, where I can turn my written words into movies.

While I plan to continue writing, I also plan to express my art in multiple forms. It's not easy being self published and running an independent film studio these days. Artists have struggled for as long as I can remember, and I don't plan on creating for the masses, I plan on creating what I feel is good. This may not always fit mainstream media.

So... If you enjoyed any of my content, I urge you to share it with your friends and family. You and people like you, are what makes my job possible, and who help ensure that my style of content can continue. Without your support, I'm just another lonely struggling artist.

Thanks you for reading.

I wish you the very best.

Sincerely,

Brent Lindstrom

P.S. Please remember to leave a review where ever you bought this book!